# MIST ON THE MOUNTAIN

# MIST ON THE MOUNTAIN
## by
## *KATHLEEN DAY*

Copyright©1999 by Kathleen Day

Published by DAYBREAK ON THE LAKE PRESS,
P. O. Box 931, Guntersville, AL, 35976-0931  (256) 582-8495

ISBN 0-9675071-0-3

Library of Congress Card Number: 99-067467

Published in the United States of America.

1 2 3 4 5 6 7 8 9 10

First Edition

*To my husband, Jack, for his patience, encouragement, love and affection when I deprived him of my company and good housekeeping while writing this book. He's a sweet and sensitive mountain man.*

## ACKNOWLEDGMENTS
My special thanks go to Julie Applegate, Rodney Deal, Fred W. Meyer, and Joyce Moultis for their support, input and efforts in making this an entertaining and accurate (though fictional) book. The hours that they spent with the manuscript will be forever appreciated.

Cover Design by Lynette Howard/LY designs

**ALSO BY KATHLEEN DAY**

*REDHEADS, A Murder Mystery*

*GEORGIA WOMEN, A CELEBRATION*,
Contributing Author for the
American Association of University Women

*THE FACE OF MATURITY*, National Library of Poetry

# *1*

Daddy Bug was a big, mean man who loved no one but his family, at least most of what was left of it. He had lived his entire life for his family. Now one of them had turned on him. Sadly, it was his own nephew, Junior, who was elected Sheriff of Dixon County. During his campaign, Junior foolishly promised to eliminate all the home distilleries. Because of a sorry murderer and Junior's wife, the government wanted to help the Sheriff. Suddenly, those agents were all over North Alabama.

Daddy Bug knew they were after him. He had just gotten the phone call that warned him.

Even after several pulls from his jug, he couldn't rest on this night. They were after him for what he did for a living. What he did wasn't the worst thing in the world. True, he made a few mistakes. Had a few bad batches. So what. It wasn't the end of the world. Nobody ever died from it. The worst thing that happened was a few people got pretty sick.

On the whole, he had been careful. He had never put his family in jeopardy. He lived his life to reflect the values his daddy had given him.

The worst time of his life was when his Pa died and he had to take over the family business at sixteen. It was a good thing his Pa taught him the recipe. The money that he got when he made his runs came in handy. He remembered how he had struggled to bring in enough money to feed the family. Even though they grew most of their own vegetables and he hunted and fished, they sometimes went hungry.

Back then, they didn't have a refrigerator. All they had was the cold water of the cistern to keep the food from spoiling. In the winter they lived on pancakes and powdered milk and whatever game or fish he managed to bring home. He thought it was a wonder his sister grew into such a beautiful, healthy-looking woman. Her son, the Sheriff, turned out to be a traitorous bastard though.

He knew his Momma was never going to be the same after his Pa died and he watched her turn into a silent, pale, wisp of a woman who sat on the porch and looked into some secret world of her own. She died only two years after his Pa. Everyone said she died the same day; it was just that her body kept breathing.

Daddy Bug thought how things had turned from bad to worse after his daddy died. The day of the funeral old man Thurmon came over to the house and wanted to take over the family business. He said no snot-nosed kid could run it and he wanted to be the only one on Cather mountain with a still. The biggest insult was that Thurmon offered him a mere two hundred dollars for it, and said he'd move it himself over to his place. He gave Daddy Bug three days for an answer and then "sparks would be flyin'." Daddy Bug knew what he was saying. Old man Thurmon was as good as saying he was going blow up Daddy Bug's still and Archie, Thurmon's son, would help him. Old Thurmon got the message though, when

Archie Thurmon somehow fell off of a cliff and his head broke open on a rock.

At that time, he wasn't known as Daddy Bug. He was simply called Bug. Christened at birth as Billy Unger Garland, he was nicknamed Bug around the age of ten. They called him Bug, not only because the letters of his initials spelled the word bug, but because he had developed a thyroid problem and his eyes started to protrude. He was tall and skinny with blond hair and dark-blue, steely eyes. When he was angry, his eyes resembled those of some evil insect, piercing and menacing as if they could see into the very depths of one's soul.

He did not mind that they called him Bug. He thought it sounded tough and that's what he was. He would fight with anyone for any real or imagined threat or insult.

Blessed with the common sense of his Pa, Bug was sly and secretive, even with his own family. He learned at an early age to seek revenge in the truest sense of the word. His enemies didn't stand a chance, but his friends had a staunch and loyal ally. On rare occasions, he misjudged a person, but usually his intuition rang true.

He thought about Vanessa. At age eighteen, he married an enchanting girl with black hair and one-eighth Cherokee blood. Through the years they had two children who called him Daddy Bug and the name stuck. Since then, he was known to everyone in the mountains as Daddy Bug.

Daddy Bug knew that what he did tonight would decide his fate. He had fought for his whole life to keep what he had and now they were trying to take it away from him. He had to be smarter than them. He knew he was smarter than them.

He also knew that tonight they would be creeping to his still. He sat watching the mist rise slowly from the valleys and the lake, to settle eerily on the hills surrounding him. It was not too late to make a decision.

It wasn't theirs. They hadn't helped his daddy build it with their bare hands. He helped his daddy cut the trees to build the framework for the still. That still had stood gleaming in the moonlight for thirty-some years. His daddy and he had been doing a service for the population for nearly that long and they loved him for it. Especially when the "sin" taxes got so high. The Government tried to take away the pleasure of the common man by taxing everything they enjoyed, until the prices went through the ceiling.

He was the savior of the mountains. What did they want from him, that nephew-Sheriff and those government men?

He sat back on the lounge chair that he had placed on the back deck of his mountain cabin. His gaze measured the enormity of the red blaze of sun sinking slowly behind Cather Mountain. It glared into his eyes as it lowered itself, as a virgin covering herself before finally surrendering to a long lamented lover. The mountain side looked as if it were on fire, so vibrant were the crimson rays.

How terrible life really is, he mused, as he lifted the jug to his withered lips. I tried to do the best for those that I loved. It just does not work for all of us. Some of us seem to have to suffer more.

He sat and watched as the moon climbed slowly over the crest of the hill, the light reflecting softly in the lake below. Now he knew he had to act quick. "I'd rather blow it up myself than let them destroy it," he said aloud.

Groaning from the pain of his arthritis, he eased himself from the chair and went into his cabin. Opening a cabinet in his storage room, he extracted two sticks of dynamite. He grabbed some wooden matches from the box on the mantle, some twine from the cabinet, picked up his twelve-gauge shotgun and headed for the still.

In the quiet darkness, he walked through the woods down the slant of Cather Mountain. The mist was thick, even in the trees, and he crept through it quietly. So stealthily did he move, it appeared that an apparition was advancing down the mountain side.

Several critters scattered away into the dense undergrowth as he approached. An owl screeched its indignation at the human intruder.

When he neared the clearing, he slowed and crouched in the brush. He parted the bushes with his twelve-gauge and looked into the clearing. The mist had lifted slightly and he could see a portion of the still shining in the moonlight. It was partially covered with bushes the way he had left it.

Apparently, they were going to try one of the midnight raids they were so famous for, he thought. No one seemed to be around just yet.

He crept forward, stepping into the clearing. He knew he would have to be quick in his retreat once he lit the dynamite. He scanned the clearing with his bulging eyes, now long adjusted to the darkness. There was nothing around that could delay his escape.

He laid his shotgun on the ground. Next, he took the twine he had put in his pocket and tied the sticks of the dynamite to the framework. He struck one of the matches on the wood and held it to the wick.

"I wouldn't do that, Daddy Bug. Put out that match, step away from the still." Sheriff Junior Haywood and two ABC agents rushed into the clearing with guns drawn.

# 2

Bug sighed with despair on that sunny Friday afternoon in June of 1958. There wasn't a cloud in the sky, but gloom hung heavily over the cemetery.

He watched the pallbearers lower the rough wooden casket into the ground. His mother leaned against him in a swoon. He put his arm about her shoulders and assisted her to the grave side. He let her go when she stepped forward silently and threw the red rose into the grave. She turned to go back to the car parked on the dirt road that ran through the center of the small cemetery. Her shoulders were slumped, and he watched for a moment her slow, halting steps.Bug motioned for his smaller brother and sister to follow him. He guided his mother forward, grasping her by the elbow. "Come on, Ma, let's go home."

He opened the passenger door, urged his younger brother and sister onto the small back seat, and gently nudged his mother onto the front seat. Benjamin James "Benji" started shoving Lydia Anne as soon as Bug started the car. "You kids stop that or I'll have to hurt you," he shouted over the rattle of the engine. "Don't you have any respect for Ma, or for that matter, Pa?"

"Leave them alone, Bug. They just have a different way of getting the grief out of their heads," his mother said.

"Well, I've got a different way too, Ma. I'm gonna find out who set that trap by the still. Whoever it was, had to know that Pa would step in it. He lost so much blood so fast, and the trap was all rusty, to boot. Somebody planned for him to die. Everybody know it takes at least an hour to run and get Doc Champs over here. Somebody planned it for when Doc Parsons was out of town. We've just got to get a telephone on this mountain, Ma."

Mabel Garland stared straight ahead without replying to her angry son.

"I wonder if a phone would have made any difference, anyway," Bug continued. "He lost so much blood when that trap cut off his foot, he was too weak to keep on going."

There was still no word from his mother.

"I've got to find the money to get a phone in the house, Ma. The phone company said they'd run the lines to the mountain if we could get three other families to get a phone in. I figure we've got twenty families up here and I know I can talk three more into getting a phone. Then I'll make a few extra runs to pay for the twenty dollar charge to get it put in."

"Bug, that's like closing the chicken coop door after the fox already got the chickens," Mabel Garland sighed.

"But, Ma, there's you and the kids to worry about," he said.

"Bug, go ahead and do what you want to. I'm just too tired to argue. Just take me home so I can go to bed. I'm plum tuckered out."

Bug gunned the old Dodge as it labored to reach the higher elevation of their cabin. The house stood on the highest part of the mountain overlooking the beautiful Lake Chastain. Bug always marveled at the breathtaking scenery.

He imagined no one would ever believe that poverty was rampant for the people who lived here. The evergreens and hardwoods covered the sloping landscape to form a panorama of different shades of green. Bald eagles soared through the sky over the lake and wild flowers of every color filled the few cleared areas with an exotic splash of color.

He parked the car by the sagging front porch and all of them sat silently for a moment. Finally, Bug ran around and opened his mother's door and helped her out. He took her arm and she shuffled slowly through the front door. She turned toward the room she had shared with her husband for seventeen years.

Bug knew Mabel Garland was not an old woman, having just turned thirty-two years old, but her hair was partially gray. She had the worn look of a woman who had struggled and toiled, and was now ready to give up the worries of this life for the pleasantness of the next.

He helped her into the bedroom and stood there while she took off her black straw hat with the white plastic lily. She reached for the quilt that she kept folded across the rocking chair. She lay under the quilt on the bed and hugged her husband's pillow to her chest. She was asleep immediately. Seeing her eyes closed, Bug left the room.

He hustled Benji and Lydia Anne into the house and told them to be quiet. They went inside and sat around the kitchen table.

"But, Bug, who is going to feed us supper?" Lydia Anne cried.

"Yeah, Bug, we're hungry," Benji whined.

"I'll feed you, and then I've got to go check on something. I want you both to keep quiet and when Ma wakes up, tell her I left her a plate on the stove."

Bug hurried around the kitchen and gathered together some salt pork, eggs and bread. Within minutes, he had fried the pork and the eggs. He laid the small wooden table with plates and flatware, dished up the pork and eggs, and cut some slabs from a loaf of bread. The children ate hungrily under his watchful eye.

Then, he filled a plate for his mother, put it in the warming oven of the old wood stove and went out the door. It occurred to him that he was now the man of the family.

He grabbed his father's twelve-gauge shotgun from the corner of the porch and made his way through the woods to a clearing five hundred feet from the house. There stood the new still he had built with his father only three months ago, when the weather broke and Spring arrived in Dixon County.

He carefully drew back the branched camouflage on the still and inspected it. Everything seemed to be as he had left it. Bug was relieved because he heard from some of the guys that old man Thurmon might try to come and get it while he was at his Pa's funeral.

Bug thought of the history of the business on the mountain. It kept his mind off of the funeral and the enormity of his new responsibilities.

He was aware the feud between the Thurmons and the Garlands was long running. His Pa had told him old man Thurmon had the first still on the mountain. He became enraged when Jake Garland built his still many years later. The way Bug heard it, the Thurmon family had held a monopoly on the moonshine business in North Alabama for at least thirty years and they weren't eager to let anyone else in on it.

It didn't surprise Bug that Thurmon had every Dixon County Sheriff in his pocket for at least that long. Everybody knew it. The succession of Sheriffs had left his operation alone, and in return, they got their share of white lightning and five percent of net.

Bug had heard the story many times. It seems it worked out to be a good partnership for Thurmon, especially during prohibition. Then, when Jake Garland built his still, the Sheriff started cornering Thurmon in town and asking for a higher percent if Thurmon wanted him to make it tough on Jake Garland. Thurmon refused, so the Sheriff paid a visit to Jake Garland. Jake was anxious to make the Sheriff happy. He cut him the same deal that Thurmon gave him..

His Pa told him that since then, the Garland and the Thurmon families had, at best, coexisted in the business. They were the only two families on the mountain making moonshine. Their business expanded far and wide, and they both formed their individual network of distributors. Each of these distributors made payoffs to the local and county law enforcement agencies, guaranteeing that no one would cooperate if the Feds came snooping around.

Bug was proud of the way his Daddy set it up and, in fact, Jake Garland and Thurmon worked it out together. Each distributor in the two networks carried the additional responsibility of making sure there were no competitors. As a result, there were no less than thirty murders and fifty still bombings through the years. His Pa told him that was a necessary evil in the business. The distributors always called the local paper and gave the Feds credit for these honorable acts of cleaning up the crime of bootlegging in the South. No one ever tried to correct the information.

The two families of that so-called Southern Connection hated each other from the beginning. There had been many fights between different members of the two families, with not a few near-death experiences. Yet, the two families had managed to survive and remain prosperous in their individual businesses of selling corn liquor for many years. His Pa had lived with the situation and Bug hoped that he could continue. It all depended on Thurmon.

The economy for the business at the time was not too good and Bug knew it was because of the Feds. A few years before Jake Garland died, the Feds had launched an all out war on the distributors and had pulled plenty of them out of the network. The Feds weren't choosy whose distributors they busted, and both families suffered the reduced revenue. Old man Thurmon had been after Jake Garland to sell his still and his network and Jake Garland told him he wouldn't sell him the sweat off his brow if he was dying of thirst; said he'd die first.

Bug knew as sure as he pulled the jars from a storage shed nearby, that with his Daddy dead, Thurmon would be chompin' at the bit for his still. He began to fill the containers from the barrels stacked along the wall of the shed. He'd make a run tonight and unload a few dollars worth. Then, he'd get that phone hooked up in case anything happened to his mother.

He finished filling the jars and reached down and picked up the rusty trap that was covered with blood. It brought back the scene of three days ago. His father's screams had pierced the night air when he stepped on it. Hearing the high pitched wail from her rocker on the front porch, Mabel Garland had run into the house to find Bug. Bug had already heard the doleful sound through the opened windows and ran to the still. He found his father gasping in pain and trying to stem the geyser of blood spitting from the stump of his leg. The foot, still in the shoe, was laying separate from the trap.

Bug tried to pull his father up the steep incline to the house, but he was progressing slowly and his father was losing blood fast. Bug ran back to the house as fast as he could and told his mother what had happened.

He got in the old car and sped off to find Doc Champs who lived twenty-five miles away. By the time he returned with the Doc, his Pa was dead.

Looking at the blood, which was slightly darker than the color of the rust on the trap, Bug vowed revenge to the person who had deliberately hidden it, camouflaged near the still. I'll find out who owns this and whoever owns it will answer personally to Pa, wherever he is now, he thought.

He put the trap and the jars he had filled in the big wagon he kept in the shed and started back up to the house, wagon in tow. The path was narrow and uneven and it was difficult to maneuver up the hill with the added weight. Bug tugged and labored and finally reached the clearing around the house. He dropped the handle to the wagon when a car pulled into the yard.

"Hey, little Bug. Where you going with that wagon full of juice?" Henry Thurmon yelled out the open window of his car. Seated beside him was his son, Archie, a guy that Bug hated more than anybody else near his age.

"I don't see as how that's any of your business, Henry," Bug said as sarcastically as he could manage.

"Hold on, little Bug. I came to pay my respects to your mama and talk a little business." Henry showed a big gape-toothed smile.

"Ma's asleep and we won't do any business with you."

Henry Thurmon and his son got out of the car and stood directly in front of Bug. "Now, son, let's see if we can make a deal on that still. You know you can't run the business alone and your Ma sure can't help you. I'll give you two hundred dollars for it and move it myself. I got cash money on me right now and it's yours if you'll sign the still over to me."

"You got about as much chance of buying our still as I have giving birth to triplets. Now get off my property," Bug said.

"No snot-nosed kid like you can run a business. I intend to have the only stills on this mountain and if you don't sell, sparks will be flyin'. You can bet on it. Now, I'm giving you till Monday to come around. After that, I can't guarantee that there won't be another accident."

"Are you telling me you set this trap down by our still, old man?"

Bug reached down and grabbed the trap from the wagon and shook it in Henry Thurmon's face. Archie Thurmon stepped forward as if to grab the trap from Bug's hand. Henry stepped back with a shocked look on his face.

"Don't be messing with my Pa, Bug," Archie said..

"If I find out this trap belonged to him, I'll do more than mess with him. Now get off my property and take that killer father of yours with you."

Bug raised his shot gun and pointed it directly at Henry Thurmon's heart. Without a word, Henry and Archie retreated to the car, started it and spun down the steep dirt driveway. Bug stood and aimed at the car until it disappeared. He knew he would take care of Archie this weekend. That would show old man Thurmon what he could do. Both those Thurmons were cowards unless they had all their stooges with them.

Bug wasn't afraid of any of them. He'd run the business, control the last of the distributors, and outwit Thurmon.

Just now, though, he had to start his run. He had a lot of miles to drive and he wanted to be back before midnight. He loaded the liquor in the back of the car and trunk and drove slowly down the road to S.R. 66. He had stops to make in Charity and North Bluff, Alabama, and Sweet Place, Georgia, just over the line.

That would make the whole run about a 100 mile round trip. He pulled out his pocket watch and saw that it was almost six o'clock. With any luck, he could cut his visit at each place to about fifteen minutes and he could be home around eleven o'clock.

Bug had been going on the runs with his daddy long enough to know that the people of the hills didn't like it if you just came, delivered the jars, got your money and left. You had to sit a spell with them and tell them the latest gossip from your side of the mountain. It was also considered impolite to refuse to sample the new batch with them. That's why his daddy was usually a little tipsy by the time he delivered all the juice. At that point, Bug would put a Sears Catalog on the driver's seat and drive the car home. He had been doing that since he was ten years old.

He would have to take it easy tonight and drink just enough to be polite, but not enough to fog his brain. With moonshine, that wasn't an easy task.

# 3

Henry Thurmon was boiling with rage. His fat, pig-like face was normally red, but as he drove away from the Garland place, it was a bluish crimson.

"I'll make that kid pay for what he did back there," he shouted at the top of his voice. "Ain't no one on this earth that can point a gun at Henry Thurmon and get away with it."

"What you gonna do to him, Pa?" Archie said.

"I'm gonna find a way to get that still, or at the very least, I'll put him out of business. There's no way he can stop me. One way or another, I'll own it."

"Well, we could always report him to the Feds, Pa."

"Now, that's a dumb idea, Sonny. If we did that, he'd know it was us that turned him in and he'd just turn around and tell them about ours."

"What about if something happened to him? I don't mean something fatal. I mean, what if Bug had a bad accident so he couldn't work his operation? His mother and sister and brother sure couldn't take over. Then he'd need the money for them to live on and then you really could get it for a couple hundred dollars."

"Son, you're a man after my own heart. Let's get our heads together after supper and figure the whole thing out. I don't want him to be able to blame it on us. It was just pure luck that his daddy died or Bug might have been able to find out that we put that trap there. The way it is now, Bug can only suspect. He don't have no proof."

Archie grinned at his father and looked around. The car was approaching the access road that led to the Thurmon house. Henry had built the house before things got bad in the business and in comparison to all the other houses on the mountain, it stood as stately as a mansion.

It was a two-story, white colonial, with columns across the front porch. Because of the decline in his business, Henry Thurmon had not spent the money to have it painted recently and the hot sun had blistered the West side, leaving it looking neglected.

They pulled into the circular driveway and a beautiful girl, about seven years old, opened the door and came out. She was followed by a German Shepherd dog.

"Hi, Daddy. Supper's ready. Ma said to hurry up and wash up because she's got to go into town after we eat."

"Hi, Precious. You just tell your Ma that I'll be in when I get good and ready. Archie and I have to go check on the business before supper."

They tried to avoid saying "still" around Precious so she wouldn't inadvertently say the word in school or Sunday School. Whenever anyone asked her what her Daddy did, she would say, "He does the business." They referred to the business product as the "mist" when they talked in front of her.

As Precious turned to go back into the house, Archie and Henry Thurmon strode to the back and down a path leading though a heavily wooded area. It was so overgrown that no one would ever see the path unless it was pointed out. They reached a small clearing and noticed their still stood as they left it, intact. Nothing, or no one had touched it since they left. Everything was O.K. for tonight, but tomorrow was another day.

Henry Thurmon was aware that you had to take everything one day at a time when you played the game. The game was dangerous. The game was moonshine. The game was whether you lived and survived on the mountain. You couldn't trust anyone when it came to keeping your business alive - least of all, Bug Garland. He was just like his daddy, the one who stepped on the trap and was now dead.

Henry and Archie Thurman smiled at each other as they looked at the still. Then, as if in unison, they turned and made their way back toward the house. Sue Thurmon was waiting at the edge of the back lot. She stood with her hands on her hips. It was a stance that made Henry nervous. She was up to something.

"Henry, get in here and eat your supper. It's on the table and I need to leave. I ain't gonna take your macho crap tonight. I have to go to town. Now get yourself and that no-good son of yours in here and eat. I'm taking the Lincoln."

Henry Thurmon smiled once again at his eldest. He had married Sue eight years ago, only a few months after his first wife died. Sue was a feisty redhead, just the kind he needed after he had suffered through three years of his first wife's illness.

She turned him on with her sauciness and her pertness. He let her have her way in a lot of things because she rewarded him later with her warmness and her submission in bed. In bed, he was the boss and she did his bidding, whatever it was. Even though she was fifteen years younger than he was, he tried to keep up with her. Sometimes she had to help him, and she did everything she could to make him feel superior to her, but everything was relative. She did for him beyond his wildest dreams.

She knew just what to do when he couldn't perform unless he was stimulated, and he let her have her way in everyday life. She had the mansion. He gave her a daughter - Precious. A mirror of Sue. It was an unspoken agreement.

"See you later, Stud," she said as she started to pull out of the driveway in the Lincoln.

"Sue, be careful, I haven't paid for your life insurance yet, you know," he grinned.

"I'm due in town, Stud. What else haven't you done? Don't you know how to do anything?"

She gunned the motor and careened out of the circular drive. The sun was setting as she drove the steep winding road down the mountainside. The Lincoln was six years old but was still impressive enough for the likes of the people of Lake Chastain. In fact, Sue Thurmon was the only person in the whole area who had such a luxury car.

She loved to speed through the streets of the small sleepy community and laugh and wave at the people, pretending that she liked them. They would smile and wave back as if indulging a precocious child, when in reality she was thirty-five years old.

Sue Thurmon hated the people of Lake Chastain. She thought she was too sophisticated for the sorry bunch of yokels. She only tolerated them because she was married to Henry Thurmon and had to keep up face for him.

Henry Thurmon was her second husband. She had divorced her first husband after he went to jail for manslaughter, and vowed she would marry rich the next time. She had also promised herself she would make these towns people sorry for treating her like so much poor, white trash.

And she did. When Thurmon's wife died, she went in for the kill, making sure she was plainly visible each time he came to town. Since she had an apartment over the feed store, she could watch his comings and goings while sitting on her sofa, looking out the window.

She knew he came to town on certain days, and as soon as she saw his car pull up to the restaurant down the street, she would throw on her sexiest low-cut dress and make an appearance at the same restaurant. She would walk slow and sway suggestively past his booth, knowing he had stopped talking to his cronies in sheer amazement at her radiance and her perfect figure.

Before long, he had her phone number and she had a new, rich husband. They got married a short two months after they met.

Henry was clearly the wealthiest man in the area. He was ugly, but he had a beautiful house and some money. Every one knew he ran moonshine and nobody seemed to care - not even the Sheriff.

Now, after eight years, she was bored with his pig face, his big belly, and his dirty ways. She was basically bored with life as she knew it. If it wasn't for Precious, she knew she would go stark-raving mad.

Henry was losing business fast because the Feds were trying to break up his network. Money was getting short and that was a sin in Sue Thurmon's mind. Why, he couldn't even get her a new car and the Lincoln was getting old. He had bought it in Gadsden two years after their marriage and parked it in the driveway with a big blue ribbon on the hood.

When he came in the house, he picked her up and carried her outside to look at it. She whooped and laughed and kissed him. Then, without a word, she ran and drove it down the mountain to City of Lake Chastain. Every head turned as she honked the horn and sped through the town as if to say, "White trash wouldn't be driving a car like this, so there!" From that day forward, she acted like a queen in Lake Chastain and was treated like visiting royalty.

The street lights were already on when she parked the car in front of the cafe. The place was crowded with farmers and locals, since most people went out to eat on Friday night. She sauntered to the counter and took the last available stool, glancing around the room as she sat.

The Sheriff and his deputy sat at the back booth. She had noticed him many times since he had been elected two years ago. She knew Henry had already talked to him and explained the way things were in this County. The Sheriff had no complaints when he heard what his cut would be.

Sue gave him one of her best smiles and a half wave, knowing that he had noticed her, also. He was a tall man with brown hair and an athletic body, possibly twenty-seven or twenty-eight years old, she thought. She paid particular attention to the way his uniform fit his taut, masculine form. Now, he was getting up and coming her way.

"Evening, Ma'am. I'd be honored if you'd join my deputy and me? I can't stand to see a pretty lady like you sit here on a stool by yourself. You need some protection from all the bad men in this town and that just happens to be my line of work."

"It sounds more like just your line," she said, smiling into his gray eyes.

He smiled back at her, showing gleaming, white teeth - a refreshing change from Henry's. "I only ask once, Ma'am."

"Well, I guess it can't hurt none if I sit with the County Sheriff, now can it?"

She picked up her purse and followed him back to his booth. Every eye in the place was locked on her body and she knew it.

They joined the deputy, but the Sheriff turned his whole attention to Sue Thurmon. "Ma'am, I know who you are, and my name is Mark Halbert. This is my deputy, Cy Davis. Cy, you'd better get back and monitor the radio. You know how rowdy Lake Chastain can get on a Friday night. I'll just sit here with the lady for awhile and I'll be over later."

Sue grinned as the deputy tipped his hat at her and slid out of the booth. "Better be careful of him, Ma'am. I've seen woman plumb faint before him because they get so overcome by his handsomeness."

"I think I can handle him all right, Cy. It does a girl good to see a handsome face sometime in her life."

The deputy left the restaurant and she turned to Mark Halbert, "Sue's bored, and Sue's hungry. Why don't we go someplace and get unbored and unhungry?"

# 4

Bug cooked breakfast for his brother and sister while he pondered his dilemma with old man Thurmon. He watched the bacon sizzle in the pan and he thought about two main things. How to get back at Thurmon for setting the trap that killed his daddy and how to keep Thurmon from causing another accident.

He was absolutely sure either Thurmon or that stupid Archie had crept in under cover of darkness and set the trap. He also knew that either one of them would be capable of trying to hurt him.

His run the previous night had netted him about $50.00. Not too bad at $2.00 a jar. He had unloaded all twenty-five of them easily. Since the Feds were cracking down on the moonshiners, everybody wanted to stock up and he had to stop at only three distributors to get rid of it. Now he would be able to pay the phone company to get the phone put in the house.

He filled four plates with the bacon and pancakes, put three on the table and took the fourth, along with a fork, back to his mother's bedroom. She was sitting on the side of the bed staring into space. She was in her cotton night gown and her salt and pepper hair hung limply down her back.

Turning her head toward Bug as he came in the room, she said, "Son, it was nice of you to bring that to me, but I won't be able to eat it. I'm just not hungry."

"Ma, you gotta eat this. You didn't eat no supper last night, either. The food was on the stove when I got back from the run. Now I've got to go round up some more people to get phones so the phone company will run those wires up the mountain. Then I've got to go make a new batch of shine. I sold everything we had last night and now we can afford to get the phone in."

"Don't forget, we've got to pay something on Pa's casket, too. I promised Mr. Martin we'd pay him five dollars a month until it was all paid," she said.

Bug grimaced. It would take him a year to pay it off. "Sure, Ma. I'll find a way to do it. Now, when I get back I want this plate empty. Pa wouldn't like you starving yourself over him."

"I'll try," she whispered before he went back to the kitchen.

Benji and Lydia Anne were eagerly devouring their breakfast by the time he sat down at the table to start eating. How strange, he thought. They're not fighting today.

"I want you two kids to behave today and be quiet. Ma ain't feeling so good, so don't bother her. Stay in the house and play Go Fish or some kind of card game, and don't let anybody come in. If someone comes to the door, tell them to come back this afternoon if they want. I'll be home by four o'clock."

"O.K. Bug," they said in unison.

Bug finished his breakfast and glanced at his pocket watch. It was almost ten o'clock. He was usually up by six o'clock, but this morning he had slept until nearly eight-thirty. He'd have to hurry, if he was going to get everything done. He got up from the table and put his dirty dishes in the old cracked enamel sink.

"You kids do the dishes as soon as you're finished," he said and went out the door.

He got in the Dodge and started down the mountain. His first stop would be at the Martin's, then on to the Collins', and finally the Thompson's. If he couldn't talk them into getting a phone, he would just have to keep going until he persuaded three families. Bug knew he would probably be successful, since he prided himself on his charm in any given situation; especially if he wanted something.

He slowed down near the approach to the Martin's house. There was someone walking in the road ahead of him. It was Archie Thurmon carrying a sack. Bug drove past the Martin's entrance and stopped the car just ahead of Archie. He got out of the car and walked in back of it. Then he stood and waited for Archie to approach.

Archie came face to face with Bug and said, "Get back in that car and get out of here before you get hurt."

Glowering into his face, Bug said, "Just try to make me Archibald. I just want to warn you if you or your old man try anything at my place, I'll kill you both and your sister and step-mother, too. Get my drift?"

Archie Thurmon was a big, muscular man and two years older than Bug. Bug was tall, skinny, and only sixteen years old, but he had tremendous strength.

Archie grabbed Bug by the shoulders and yelled directly in his face so that spit from his mouth hit Bug in the eyes. "You won't do anything bug eyes. How can a pip-squeak like you do anything?"

Quickly, Bug twisted and grabbed Archie's right arm. He turned until Archie was behind him, then did a back kick straight into Archie's groin. Archie screamed in agony and folded over. Bug jumped in back of him and directed another kick, this time forward, into Archie's back. Archie fell perilously close to the edge of the road which ran along the top of a cliff. Taking advantage of Archie's momentary incapacity, Bug grabbed him by the legs and threw him over.

The grade was steep and Archie fell like a rag doll, unable to grab the skimpy underbrush to stop his descent. His body gathered speed as it fell and he came to rest against a giant boulder.

Bug looked down and saw the red blood gushing from a hole in Archie's head. The impact of his head slapping the rock when he stopped rolling had crushed it in. He wasn't moving.

A stupid man might go down and help him, Bug thought. He turned and got in his car to go back to the Martin's turnoff.

He pulled into the Martin's gravel driveway and saw Mr. Martin working in his open workshop. Wooden coffins stood around the side walls. Bug knew as everyone knew that Mr. Martin took great pride in carving ornate designs on most of them, so that each one was different. Mrs. Garland could afford only a plain one for Bug's Pa.

"Hi, Mr. Martin," Bug yelled as he approached the work shop.

"Well, hello, young man. How's your momma doing today? I imagine she's not doing too well." It was a statement rather than a question.

Mr. Martin dealt with death and dying on a daily basis and Bug thought he would know, if anybody would, how long it took to get over the death of a loved one. It would take Mrs. Garland a long time.

"She's not doing too well. That's one of the reasons I came over. First, I want to tell you, I'll be making that five dollar payment on Pa's coffin and I brought you the first five dollars today. Then, I want to ask you if you would consider getting a telephone. The phone company said if I can get three others beside myself, they'll bring the lines up the mountain and then it only costs each family twenty dollars installation charge and the monthly bill. I figured that Pa would still be alive if we could have called the doctor instead of going to get him."

"Son, I can't tell you how sorry I am about your Pa. You're probably right about the telephone. Let me talk to my wife. It may help my business to have a phone, too. Then I could put an ad in the paper and maybe get some more business from town."

"I sure would appreciate it, Mr. Martin and so would Ma," Bug said, handing him the first five dollar payment.

"I'll let you know right quick. Stop back Monday morning."

Bug waved and walked back to his car. While driving away, he thought, hope he's got a coffin big enough for Archie.

# 5

"Sue, come out here quick, girl. Something's happened to Archie!" Henry Thurmon yelled from the front porch.

Sue Thurmon stepped outside and saw Henry, and Sam Collins (who lived across the hollow), unloading Archie's enormous bulk from his pickup truck. Sam's son, Marlin, stood in the bed of the pickup and pushed Archie's shoulders toward the two older men. It had been all the Collins men could do to drag Archie's body up the steep cliff, using a tarp as a make-shift stretcher. Nothing is harder to carry than dead weight, and Archie certainly qualified as dead weight now, Sue thought.

She watched then carry him into the parlor and lay him on the sofa. Dried blood coated his face and matted his hair. She covered her mouth and gasped when she actually saw him. A piece of gray matter hung out of the gaping wound in his temple area. His eyes were open and had a look of terror in them. Archie Thurmon was decidedly, as dead as the proverbial door knob, she was certain.

"My God, how could this have happened?" Henry moaned and cradled his son in his arms.

"Henry, I really can't tell you, but Marlin and I were riding along the Stop Gap Road down there and Marlin just happened to be looking down the slope at all the wild flowers just out. He saw Archie laying way on down, against a big rock. We stopped the truck and ran down there real quick. We had to be careful that we didn't start goin' ass over tin cups ourselves; it was just that steep. You know the place, Henry."

"Yeah, I know it. Was he alive when you got to him?"

"No, didn't appear to be breathing. I listened to his chest and put my finger on his neck where his pulse should have been. His eyes were open just like they are now."

Sue and Precious were standing behind the men who were hovering over the body. "Precious, go on to your room. I don't like you standing here staring at poor old Archie. I'll be in later and try to tell you what happened."

"Is Archie going to heaven, Momma?" Precious asked.

"Honey, I think he's already there. Now go to your room like a good girl."

Precious cast one more curious look at Archie and left the room. There was silence while Henry closed Archie's eyes. Then he said, "Sue, go get a sheet and cover him up. I got to go into town and get the doctor to come out here and write a death certificate and get the undertaker to come and get him. Then I've got to go and see Matling Martin about making a casket. I guess I know the dimensions."

"Henry, I'm so sorry, it happened," Sue said. "How do you suppose he fell over the cliff?"

"He didn't fall, honey. Somebody shoved him over and I'm going to find whoever did it and make him pay. I've got a pretty good idea who it was and somehow I'll get back at him."

Henry gave Archie's limp arm a squeeze, turned and wiped the tears from his own eyes with his shirt sleeve. Sue had never seen her husband cry before and she felt a momentary sadness for his loss of his only son. She put her arm around him and walked him to the door.

"Try not to think about revenge, Henry. We got to think about planning a nice funeral for Archie now. You'll have time for revenge later."

"Woman, don't try to tell me what to do," he said, shrugging her away and going out the door. With Sam and Marlin Collins following him, he yelled, "And get that sheet like I told you. Do it now!"

Sue watched the men climbing into their respective trucks and thought. Men are all alike. The only time they treat you right is in bed. That is, until after you marry them.

Well, Henry, I got somebody else that will treat me right all the time. Sheriff Mark Halbert had the manners and the right equipment to satisfy a hungry woman like her, and Henry Thurmon had the money - or at least enough for now - to keep her in fancy clothes and a nice house. She could work with that setup, she thought, turning to go and get the sheet.

She would get her best sheet to use for Archie's death shroud. The black satin one would do quite nicely.

Henry sped out the circular driveway and got to Stop Gap Road within minutes. He turned left and started for Matling Martin's turn-off which was only about a mile down the road. He drove faster than was safe for the winding, narrow road, but he didn't care.

He felt that he was suffocating. His grief produced a rage so intense that, for a single moment, he felt like driving over the cliff. He hadn't even been able to say good-bye to his son. Archie's life was gone in a minute and Henry would never again go hunting or fishing with him. Henry would never again have "man" talks with him about women, and after the funeral, he would never see him again. Life just wasn't fair.

Suddenly, he spotted Bug Garland driving his old Dodge just ahead of him. He stepped on the gas peddle and went even faster. He got just behind the Dodge and bumped it with his pickup.

"Bug, I'm gonna get you. I know you did it," he shouted out the open window.

Bug pulled the car to the narrow shoulder and rolled down the window. Henry had a crazed look in his eyes.

"What's the matter with you old man. Are you crazy? You could have caused an accident."

Henry parked his pickup side by side. "You mean like the accident when you tossed my son over the cliff?" he screamed. "He's dead and I know you did it."

"No, I mean like the trap that accidently got set for my Pa to step on. Now, you sure don't know anything about that do you, but I bet Archie did. Don't push it old man, or other accidents can happen. Got that?"

"Is that a threat, Bug?" Henry gunned his motor impatiently.

"No, that's just a statement of fact, old man. Now are you going ahead, or am I?"

Henry spun ahead of Bug leaving him in the dusty aftermath and turned left on the Martin turn off. That means he did it, he thought, and now he's threatening more. I'll have to lay low for a while, but someday my turn will come.

He saw Matling Martin sanding a casket by the front of his work shop when he drove in. Martin looked up from his work and waved at him while he opened the car door and got out.

"Hi Henry, what brings you here on a Saturday afternoon?"

"I came to see if you had a casket for my son, or, if you don't have one big enough, if you could make one special. Archie fell or was pushed over a cliff some time this morning and he didn't survive it. His head got cracked open on a rock. Sam Collins and his boy found him. He's dead."

Matling Martin looked shocked. "Why, I'm sorry to hear that, Henry. When did it happen exactly?"

"We don't know, but it had to have happened between ten and twelve, because he left at ten to carry some radishes and carrots to old Mrs. Sweet and they brought his body home at twelve. The Doctor will be able to tell by the blood and things, I think."

"That's a damn shame, Henry. I really mean it."

"Well, I guess we'll have the funeral on Monday. Let's see what you have."Henry selected a lavishly carved coffin and told Matling Martin to make sure it got to the funeral home in Lake Chastain. He said he would tell the undertaker that he was not going to use one of theirs and that Martin would be bringing the one they should use. After all, Matling made caskets for everyone on the mountain and this would be no exception.

After completing his business with Matling Martin, he drove to Lake Chastain and finished his instructions to the doctor and the undertaker. He then went to the Sheriff's office and told Mark Halbert that Bug Garland murdered his son.

Upon returning home, he parked the truck in the circular drive and went in the front door of his house. Archie lay shrouded in a black satin sheet on the sofa and the house was quiet. "Where is everyone?" He shouted.

"Get back here to Precious' room, right now!" His wife screamed.

Henry walked through the long hall and went through the door of Precious' room. Sue and Precious Thurmon sat on the bed with Precious protectively cradled in Sue's arms. The mascara on Sue's eyelashes had smeared to form a black vee under each eye. She looked at him tearfully and angrily. Precious just looked at him fearfully.

"Why, honey, what's going on here?" Henry asked.

"That son of a bitch was screwing Precious," she shouted.

"Whatever do you mean, honeypot?" He looked at her

incomprehensibly. Did she say someone was screwing Precious, his little girl?

"I said that no-good Archie was screwing our Precious. I'd kill him if he wasn't already dead," she screamed even louder.

"Now wait just a minute. How do you know this to be a fact?"

Henry was beside himself with grief for Archie and astonished at this accusation against his son. He sat beside Precious and put his arm around her. "Did you tell Momma that Archie did something to you?"

"I told Momma I was sorry Archie was going to heaven, but I'm glad he can't hurt me anymore. When she asked what did I mean, I told her how he carried me upstairs and made me lay down. Then he put his thing right there." She pointed to the spot between her delicate legs. "It hurt me most of the time but Archie said if I told, he'd have to hurt me more. So, I decided since Archie's going to heaven, I could tell Momma." Her angelic face was alive with concentration on what she was saying.

"I want that bastard's body out of this house, right now. If you don't get it out right away, I'll call the Sheriff to come and get it and dump it on the nearest rubbish pile," Sue said.

Henry stared at her before taking his arms from around Precious and said, "Sue, pretty soon Doc Parsons is going to be here to examine Archie and write a death certificate for him. The undertaker will also be here soon to take Archie to the funeral home. The Sheriff's coming right away to make a report. Until then, I want you to calm down and stay away from Archie's body. I've had just about enough for one day. A person can only take so much."

"I'll stay away from your precious Archie, but when the doctor gets here, I want him to examine Precious, first thing. I wouldn't put it past that dirty bastard to give her some disease."

Henry walked slowly from the bedroom with his head hung forward and his shoulders drooping. The last thing on his mind was taking over Bug Garland's operation.

# 6

Mabel Garland was cooking supper when Bug walked in the front door. At least she was out of bed, he thought. She stood silently at the sink peeling potatoes. He walked over to her and gave her a kiss on the cheek.

"How are you feeling, Ma?" he asked.

"I'm pretty good. I can't get the sight out of my mind of Pa laying in that casket. I keep expecting him to walk through that door, like you did just now."

"Ma, get that notion out of your head. Pa ain't coming back. He's gone. Now, we have to figure out how we're gonna make do and get the kids raised. I'll have to take over and make the recipe. Pa showed me how to do that, but it means I'll have to quit school. We've got just enough vegetables in the root cellar to last until our garden gets all grown, but I'll have to go out and get some meat and game for us. Do you feel up to canning and stuff like that?"

"Bug, you can't quit school. That's your only hope for getting ahead and getting out of this God-forsaken place. Give me a few days of mourning and I'll be back on my feet. I can help make the recipe if you'll show me how, and Benji and Lydia Anne are getting big enough to help. Why, you were Benji's age when you started helping your Pa."

"I don't want to get out of this place. I love the mountain and don't ever intend to leave it."

"Promise me you won't quit school, Bug. Pa and I never got through it. We had to quit just to help out. Pa started the business so you wouldn't have to quit. He always said, "Bug will be the first one in our families to graduate high school, so don't make a liar out of him.""

"All I can promise is I'll try my best, Ma. If bad comes to worse, I might have to, but I'll hang in there as long as you and the kids don't suffer."

Mabel fried the potatoes and pork chops and boiled the greens. Bug set the table and called his sister and brother from their card game in the back bedroom.

As they all sat down to eat, he bowed his head and said grace aloud. "Dear Lord, we thank you for this food we are about to eat. We ask that you bless Pa and take him into heaven with you. Thank you for giving me the opportunity to make his murderer sorry for what he did. Amen."

"What are you talking about, Bug? Pa wasn't murdered. He stepped on a trap and bled to death. What do you mean, make his murderer sorry?" Mabel appeared stunned.

"Ma, somebody had to put that trap there on purpose. I know who did it and I took care of one of them. There's still plenty of time to take care of the other one. The less you know, the better, so don't ask questions."

Benji and Lydia Anne stared at Bug in astonishment. Benji, age 12, had a natural curiosity about anything his older brother did. Bug was his hero and could do no wrong.

"Did you kill someone, Bug?" he said.

"Let's just say he won't go near the edge of a cliff again," Bug said, smiling at his little brother.

"Don't go getting yourself in trouble," Mabel Garland said. "Who are you talking about?"

"Those wonderful Thurmons. While we're talking about them, if old man Thurmon comes over here trying to buy our still, don't talk to him. Tell him I'm handlin' the operation now and to stay out of our face. I don't even want him on the property."

"I won't talk to him if you think he put the trap there. Then it was Archie you settled with today, wasn't it?"

"Yup. Now don't ask no more questions. Let's eat up and I'll carry you in the car to Pa's grave. I want to make sure you-know-who didn't disturb it out of spite."

After they finished supper and cleared away the dishes, the four went to get in the Dodge. Just as Bug started the engine, he looked up and saw the Sheriff's car pull into the front yard. Bug looked around at his family and said, "Y'all stay put. I'll see what he wants."

Approaching the Sheriff's car, he waved and said, "What can I do for you, Sheriff Halbert?"

The Sheriff looked at Bug walking slowly toward him and waited until he leaned on the car. "Bug, I've got to ask you if you know anything about Archie Thurmon falling down a cliff. He's dead - or am I telling you something you already know?"

"Why, Sheriff, I'm sorry to hear that," Bug said solemnly. "There's no love lost between Archie Thurmon and me, but I hate to hear about something like that."

"Old man Thurmon thinks you had something to do with it - like maybe you pushed him. His skull got crushed on a rock, and that's what killed him. But his testicles were all swollen like somebody kicked him in the groin, and his arm had dark bruises on it. I was there when the Doc Parsons was examining him. Looks like he was in a fight before he went over."

"Sorry, Sheriff. The last time I saw Archie was yesterday after Pa's funeral. He and his Pa came over to offer their condolences."

"Well, I don't have any affection for old man Thurmon, or for that matter, didn't have any for Archie. It's my job to check out any accusations, though. I'll be going. Keep your nose clean, Bug."

"Wait a minute, Sheriff. I made a run last night. Did pretty good."

Bug reached in his pocket and brought out some dollar bills. He slipped them to the Sheriff and winked.

The Sheriff winked back, took the bills without acknowledgment, and said, "Now Sue Thurmon is another story entirely."

Bug threw back his head and laughed out loud as the Sheriff drove away. The Sheriff was not in a minority in his admiration of the beautiful Sue Thurmon.

# 7

Bug watched the telephone company technician run the telephone lines from the road to the house. It had taken almost a year for them to run the lines to Stop Gap Road. He had finally succeeded in getting the Martin, Collins and Thompson families to agree to get telephones. Matling Martin was the first to agree, and then Sam Collins and Frank Thompson followed.

Bug had not bothered asking Henry Thurmon if he would consider getting a telephone. Upon hearing that Matling Martin was getting one, Henry was not to be outdone. He demanded that his be the first installed on the mountain and since he supplied the local telephone company manager with shine at half price, he got his way.

Now at last the telephone company had installed the lines to the Garland turnoff on Stop Gap Road. Finally, the Garland family was connected by wire to the outside world.

Bug could see that Mabel Garland, who was becoming a mere wisp of her former self, was grateful that the time had finally come. He was glad that she could call someone to help in case of an emergency - especially since Bug was running the business and old man Thurmon was bad-mouthing him in town. Bug told her Thurmon was capable of doing anything.

She had told Bug there was something wrong with her and now she would be able to call the doctor in an emergency. She told him not to worry, but on occasion, she would experience a sharp pain in her abdomen. She explained that at those times, she would double over with it. Then, as quick as it came, the pain would disappear. Listening to her, he got a feeling of doom. Was he going to lose her too?

He begged her to go and get a checkup, but she was afraid of what the doctor would find and said they could not afford an operation.

Bug had managed to keep her condition from the children until now, but he knew her intervals of pain were getting closer and closer. He knew he would make her go for a checkup if he actually saw her double over.

He only had one more year to go in high school and then he would graduate. If she had to have an operation, he would have to quit school to make more money to pay for it. He was in a total fix. His mother refused to go to the doctor and refused to let him quit school.

He worked hard enough now, trying to run the business and go to school. He spent his entire summer on the business, and growing food and hunting. He would just pray she could hold out one more year.

When the telephone man finished installing the phone on the kitchen wall, he turned to Bug and Mabel. The technician lifted the receiver of the wall phone and started to explain the service.

"Bug, you are on what's called a party line. What that means is that there are people at four other houses that can hear what you say to anyone on this phone, and they can hear what anyone says to you if they happen to pick up the receiver when your using it. By the same token, y'all can hear what they're saying, too," the man said.

"Who else is on this line?" Bug asked.

"You've got the Martins, the Collins, the Thompsons and the Thurmons. Now, I'll tell you like I told them already, it's just a matter of common courtesy to hang up and wait if you pick up the receiver and hear someone talking. Of course, if there is an emergency, you can excuse yourself and ask for the line. I've told everybody that an emergency takes top priority and they must hang up immediately if someone says it's an emergency."

"I understand. Ma, make sure Benji and Lydia Anne know about this, too."

"Yes, son, I will. Do you know where they are?"

"I saw them go running toward the woods about thirty minutes ago. I'll go see if I can find them."

Bug went to the front of the cabin and started toward the woods. He had noticed the kids had used the obscure path to the still. He walked quickly through the underbrush and approached the clearing. One of Benji's shoe lay by the still

He yelled loudly, "Benji, Lydia Anne!"

"Bug, I'm over here. I'm scared," came the small delicate voice of Lydia Anne.

Bug walked over and looked behind the bushes surrounding the still. Lydia Anne was crouching behind them with a terrified look on her face.

"What's going on here? Where's Benji?" Bug stooped to grab hold of his little sister.

"That man took him away. We were playing hide and seek and Benji was it. He was standing out there with his eyes closed counting to one hundred. All of a sudden, that man came and grabbed him. Benji tried to kick free, but the man was too strong."

"Lydia Anne, what man took Benji?" he asked.

"That man you don't like. That Thurmon," she whispered. "That man that came over to the house after Pa's funeral. I saw him out the window that day. I hid because I was scared and afraid he would come back and get me. He just carried Benji off."

"Which way did he go, Lydia Anne? How long ago did this happen?" Bug asked.

"It happened when we first got here, but I've been so scared, I didn't want to move. He came on the path, just like you did."

That's funny, Bug thought. I would have seen him if he came up the road to the house. He must have cut into the woods before he made the turn to the house.

Bug grabbed Lydia Anne's hand and said, "Come on, I'll take you back to the house. Stay there with Ma, and I'll go find brother. Don't worry, nothing's going to happen to him."

Bug hurried back to the house with Lydia Anne in tow. He was worried that Thurmon would do something to hurt Benji. It had been a year yesterday that Archie Thurmon fell down that cliff and old Thurmon had been getting crazier and crazier by the day, since he died. Most folks thought he should be put away, Bug included.

Bug had managed to avoid any further confrontations with him, but he knew now that Thurmon was carrying out his threat of revenge. To top it off, he was drinking his own stuff all the time and it seemed to be rotting his brain. Even his wife couldn't stand him anymore and she was openly carrying on with Sheriff Halbert. Old Thurmon just seemed to ignore the situation and stagger around in a crazy, drunken rage.

Bug brought Lydia Anne in the house and told his mother, "Ma, old man Thurmon's kidnaped Benji. I'm gonna go get him. You call Sheriff Halbert and tell him to meet me at Thurmon's house. Tell him what happened. I've got to get going, so call right away."

Mabel Garland lifted the receiver and started to dial as Bug raced for the door, stopping long enough to get his shotgun. He dashed to the Dodge and pushed the gas peddle to the floor.

If Thurmon hurt Benji, he's a dead man, he thought, careening along the winding, narrow roadway. He must have been checking out the still behind my back. Then, when he saw Benji, he thought he'd get revenge for Archie. His mind is so screwed up, he didn't have the presence of mind to realize that Benji is an innocent child. He just thinks that he's a Garland and fair game for revenge.

Bug made a quick turn at the Thurmon turnoff on Stop Gap road and sped up the narrow driveway, slamming on the brakes in front of the house. He jumped from the car and pounded on the door with his fists.

Suddenly, the door opened and Sue Thurmon came out, closing the door behind her. She had a fresh slap mark on her lovely face and was crying.

"He's gone completely crazy," she sobbed. "He's got your little brother in there and says he's going to get even with you for killing Archie. When I tried to stop him, he whooped me up side the head. We need to get to a phone and call the Sheriff. I'm afraid to go back in there and use ours. I'm afraid for all of us. I'm sure glad Precious is at her friend's house."

"Ma was calling him when I left to come over here. He should be here any minute."

Bug got his shotgun from the car and opened the front door. It was eerily quiet as he entered the large, two-story entry foyer. He took a few steps and looked to the dining room on the left and the living room on the right. No one was there. He moved slowly to the back of the house. As he neared the kitchen and den, he heard the snorting, drunken laugh of Henry Thurmon.

"I got you now, little Bug," he slurred.

Bug held the shotgun with both hands and dashed into the den. Thurmon stood holding Benji in front of him with his hand over his mouth and a pistol to his head. Benji's eyes were wide with fright and he shifted nervously in a tenuous effort to breathe.

"You better let that boy go, old man." Bug leveled the shotgun and pointed at Thurmon's forehead.

"I don't care if you shoot me, Bug, but I'm gonna get one of you before I go." Thurmon was visibly weaving back and forth and taking Benji with him as though they were partners in a strange ritualistic dance.

"Let him go, Thurmon. He's just a kid. Aren't you man enough to deal with me? Do you have to use a kid as a hostage, because you're too much of a coward to face me alone?" he taunted.

Bug looked at the window behind Thurmon and saw Sheriff Mark Halbert creep slowly past it, heading for the open sliding glass door. His gun was drawn and he glanced quickly through the window, putting a finger to his pursed lips in a shhh gesture. He stepped through the door and using both hands, fired one shot at the back of Henry Thurmon's head.

Henry fell forward like a giant oak, crashing on top of the horrified Benji. The back half of Thurmon's head was missing.

The Sheriff quickly pulled the body to the side and helped Benji to his feet. He ran to Bug and wrapped his arms around his waist and started sobbing loudly.

"That's O.K. Benji, he can't hurt anyone anymore," Bug said. "Thanks Sheriff, I thought one or both of us was a goner."

Before the Sheriff could answer, Sue Thurmon raced in the door and saw her husband. She screamed and ran to him. Then she looked at Bug and looked at the Sheriff.

"I don't know which one of you did this, but he had it coming."

The Sheriff held his gun, barrel up, and said, "Sue, honey, this little baby did its job. It was going to come to this between me and him sooner or later. I just lucked out that I had to save these Garland boys' lives for them. You might just say I set you free, too. That means there's still justice in this world."

# 8

He saw her blue-black hair before he saw her. He glimpsed its shine reflected in the window of the assembly room. The sheen caught his eye and he turned to look at the whole image.

She sat demurely, taking notes from her book. It was a class about Native Americans and was being taught to educate the teenagers of Lake Chastain about their beginnings and who was here before them.

Bug did manage to absorb some of the information and was even more interested because he suspected that she might be related to the people who were in Lake Chastain first. Part of the history taught in the class was about the Native American Indians and the white man's displacement of them. The teachers thought they should know that part of history, so the Native American class became part of the regular curriculum.

Bug learned about the Trail of Tears, when thousands of Cherokee Indians were forced to give up their land and relocate. He also learned that there was an Indian Chief called Chief Seattle who, in 1854, made a speech in response to the Great White Chief's offer to buy some Indian land, and to provide a safe reservation for the Indians. In the response, Chief Seattle indicated he would consider accepting the offer and give up the land, but the spirits of the dead of the tribes of the Puget Sound would always live there. The eloquence of the words rang true to Bug. He was moved by the statement of the great Chief.

He was not sure at the time what any of it was supposed to mean to him. He was sure that the girl with blue-black hair had tears in her eyes at the end of the class. And, he was sure she was the most beautiful woman he had ever had the honor to see.

He was speechless in front of her. She lowered her ebony eyes when he met her in the hall. Her long braid trailed down her back to her waist and he turned to watch in awe when they passed each other.

How could her introduce himself to her? What could he say? He wanted to meet her.

His opportunity came more swiftly than even he could imagine. One day, as he was drearily going from class to class, he noticed one of his classmates making a move on her and she was shyly rejecting him. It was Bobby Joe Baxter. "Come on squaw, you should be glad I'm even looking at you."

Grasping her books, she looked down and said, "I can't imagine why you would look at one so ugly as me."

Bug watched Bobby Joe Baxter grab her arm and hiss in her face, "I can turn you respectable if you play along. You're cleaner and better looking than most of your kind."

"I am of only one kind," she said. "I'm one-eighth Cherokee and I'm seven parts your race, but if I could say it before God, I'm one hundred percent Cherokee if you're the only choice of a white man I'd have."

Bug saw her dark eyes flashing and moved in to rescue her. He took her wrist in his hands, shoved Bobby Joe Baxter against the lockers and said, "Leave your lousy, dirty hands off her or you'll regret it and your family will regret it. I'm with her from now on."

"You can have that dirty squaw if you want her, Bug. I just feel sorry for your family if you're with her from now on, as you say."

"If you ever call her a dirty squaw, again, Bobby Joe, I'l kill you. The same thing holds true if you bother her in any way. Now, don't you forget it," he yelled.

Bug was sure that Bobby Joe knew he would carry out his threat. It was rumored that he'd killed Archie Thurmon, even though the Sheriff said there was no evidence to even arrest him.

He was also sure that everybody knew of his ruthlessness and strength whenever any of the guys had said something about one of his family or friends. There were plenty of guys around that didn't want to take him on.

He watched Bobby Joe start down the hallway to his next class. He would be glad when his Senior year was over.

"Thank you so much for helping me." She smiled her irresistible smile at his bashful grin. "My name is Vanessa Henderson."

She extended her right hand toward his as if to shake it. He took it in both of his hands. "It's nice to meet you Vanessa. I've seen you around before, but I just couldn't get up the nerve to talk to you. I guess I've got that stupid Bobby Joe to thank, even though I hate what he said to you. By the way, my name is Billy Unger Garland, but everybody calls me Bug."

She smiled again at him and said, "Nice to meet you too, Bug. I hear that kind of thing all the time. I think people think I'm full-blooded Indian because of the color of my hair. I'm not ashamed of being part Cherokee. In fact I'm proud of it. My great grandfather was the Chief of his tribe."

He was holding her hand while she told him of her heritage. He smiled into her eyes.

"If you're proud of it, then I'm proud of it," he said shyly. "If Bobby Joe Baxter ever so much as talks to you again, let me know."

"I will. Shall we get a soda or something?"

The words were music to Bug's ears. He clasped her hand even tighter, and they turned to go to the soda machine. It had just been installed in the gym and was full of ice cold sodas. She picked a grape drink and he picked an orange drink. By the time he had opened both sodas, Bug knew he was in love.

They became constant companions. Bug wore his heart on his sleeve and walked around with a grin on his face in school. He was even nice to some of his enemies. He knew he would marry her after graduation.

# 9

The wedding day was set for the second Saturday in December, but it was apparent by September 1st that it would have to take place much sooner. Vanessa told Bug she was pregnant with their first child and was due to deliver in February of the following year. She also told him that the Doctor told her that the labor could come earlier since the baby was growing more rapidly than normal.

Bug was elated that he was going to be married and become a father. Vanessa's parents informed him they were not as excited about it, knowing that their beautiful daughter would be wedded to a man barely eighteen. Not to mention, a man who already had a reputation as one of the meanest men on the mountain if anyone crossed him.

He had slowly taken over Henry Thurman's network and now had a few distributors. He had even recruited his future brother-in-law, Stan Henderson, to help him. Under Bug's general direction, Stan, who was two years older than Bug, learned quickly the art of intimidation and general ruthlessness.

Even though Bug assured Stan's parents that the partnership would work fine, his parents were not amused. They voiced their worry to him that Stan could get hurt or even killed when he helped Bug make the runs to the network.

Bug didn't worry too much because he knew that Mr. and Mrs. Henderson thought the one saving grace in the whole matter was that Bug was so gentle to their daughter. They had to know he literally worshiped her. Vanessa told him they were grateful for that since it was apparent to them that nothing, or no one, could break the couple apart. That's fine with me, he thought.

He had never exposed the mean side of himself to Vanessa. The only time she witnessed his temper was when he protected her from Bobby Joe Baxter, and he knew she thought he was the bravest, nicest boy she had ever met.

Mabel Garland was happy for her oldest son and the thought of her first grandchild. She had not been feeling well since Jake died two years earlier. Since then, she had lost weight and her appearance bespoke someone many years older that she was. She had no appetite and would sit on the rocker on the front porch in a trance, looking out over the mountain. Now, with the thought of a new baby on the way, she seemed to perk up and act interested in life again.

She happily helped plan the wedding, which was to be held in the Baptist Church on the last Saturday in September. She helped make Vanessa's wedding dress so that it would hide her "condition," not that everyone didn't already know about it.

Mabel Henderson knew very well that everyone in Lake Chastain was aware that Bug Garland had gotten that Indian girl in the family way and now had to marry her. That was the way news traveled. That's how they were. She had heard they thought it a shame that Bug, who had such a great future ahead of him in the business, had to take on the added responsibility of a new family.

She had been told they thought Bug was already working hard enough to support his mother, brother and sister. The mailman had filled her in on that. She was told that a lot of people conceded that Vanessa was a sweet, unassuming girl and really quite attractive for an Indian, and maybe she and the baby wouldn't be too much of a burden on Bug.

Mabel and Vanessa and Vanessa's parents had gone to a shower the decent ladies of the Baptist Church held for Vanessa. They brought proper gifts, such as dish towels, sheets, pots, pans and dishes.

Mabel saw that Vanessa was appropriately thankful and she overheard them say they might one day invite her to become a member of the Ladies Aid. Of course, they would observe her for a while and see if she came to church every Sunday. Then, if all went to their satisfaction, they would invite her to become a member of their stately organization. Mabel smiled to herself since they had never asked her to join.

As the day of the wedding approached, Bug began to get nervous. He started snapping at everyone whether they deserved it or not.

Stan Henderson was to be his best man and sat next to him the night of the wedding rehearsal. "Bug, you sure are nervous, man. You're hands are shaking," Stan said.

"Yeah, I'm nervous. Who wouldn't be, you stupid idiot?" Bug said.

"Hey, man, don't take it out on me. I didn't get her pregnant, you did."

Turning rapidly, Bug grabbed Stan by the shirt collar with one hand and pulled his fist back. His face was red and his eyes were bulging - a sure sign of his unabashed anger.

"Don't ever say that again. I never want to hear that from anybody. Do you hear me?" Bug said through clenched teeth.

He dropped his raised fist and grabbed Stan by the shirt collar. Vanessa, her maid of honor, and her parents, who were sitting together in the back of the church waiting for the Preacher, rushed forward to pull the him off of Stan.

"Bug, what's the matter?" Vanessa said.

"Your brother just said something that made me mad, Honey. Now don't go and worry your pretty head," Bug said in a pleasant voice. "I won't hurt him none."

Bug released Stan and took Vanessa's hand. She looked at him with concern.

"What did he say, Bug?"

"I told you not to worry your head. Now, I'll say this and hope I don't have to repeat it. When I say something, I want you to listen. I don't want you to ask me any questions. When I want you to know something, I'll tell you." Bug said it slowly and emphatically as if Vanessa were hard of hearing and had to read his lips.

Bug wanted to impress on Vanessa's parents that those words were going to set the tone of the marriage between them. And if they wanted to speak out, to cancel the wedding, let them get it out in the open right now.

But all they said to Bug was that there was the baby to consider - and Bug would be a good provider.

Just at that moment, Preacher Terry came in and said, "Folks, let's get this show on the road." The piano player, who observed the whole scene in silence, started playing the wedding processional. The Preacher positioned the wedding party in front of the alter.

"Dearly beloved," he began.

# 10

The morning of the wedding was filled with activity. Bug had checked to make sure that things were going right at the church. He found that the Ladies Aid had decorated the church with magnolia leaves and wild flowers. After everything was in order at the altar, they prepared the sandwiches, potato salad, cole slaw and sweetened ice tea for the reception in the church basement.

The president of the Ladies Aid made a wedding cake adorned with the small bride and groom figures which were used on every wedding cake she made. When Bug commented that Vanessa would really like to take it home, she told him that after the wedding, she would tuck the figures away for the next time.

Once home, Bug paced around the house and walked the path to make one last check on the still. It stood as he left it, the copper gleaming in the sun.

Sitting to the left of it was the still Bug had purchased from the estate of old man Thurmon. Sue Thurmon had eagerly taken the hundred dollars he offered. Stan Henderson and Bug had borrowed a truck and carted it to its present location. They now had it in full operation.

Bug ran his hand over the smooth copper and remembered with relish how Henry Thurmon had tried to take over his business. Now the tables were turned. He smiled to himself and started toward the cabin, his feeling of nervousness gone.

When he reached the house, he bathed in the tin tub and dressed quickly. Mabel had pressed his shirt and his one dark suit. Benji had polished his shoes.

He checked himself in the mirror. His image stared back and he thought himself quite handsome. He saw Mabel, Benji and Lydia Anne were already dressed in their Sunday clothes, sitting on the front porch ready to go. Although it was late September, it was over ninety degrees and humid. He watched as Mabel, who had been fanning herself suddenly bent over and hold her abdomen.

Bug came out on the porch with the car keys and said, "Ma, what's the matter. Is that pain back?"

"It's nothing, Bug. Just a little indigestion. It'll go away soon."

Her face appeared flushed and she was slightly perspiring. Bug was worried about her. Should he postpone the wedding?

"Ma, I'll go over and tell everybody the wedding is off for now. You look sick."

"You'll do no such thing, Bug. Kids, go get in the car. I couldn't be better, Bug. It's just hot."

"Well, if your sure, let's go get me hitched. When I come back in this house, I'll be a married man and we'll have a new member of this family."

Lydia Anne laughed and said, "Hooray for Bug."

Bug saw Benji smile and wink at his mother before they all got in the car and started for the Church. He joined in the singing voices of Mabel, Benji and Lydia as the car wound around the curves in Stop Gap Road. When they arrived at the Church, he was surprised to see the cars of every family on Cather Mountain.

Bug noticed that Vanessa's parents' car was already in place in front of the church. The newlyweds were going to drive it to Lake Chastain, where they would spend the night in the Dew Drop Inn. He grinned when Bug saw it. The car was decorated with old shoes and tin cans trailing off the back bumper and had "Just Married" written on the back window in Glass Wax. The Hendersons were to take his own family home in his car.

He led his family into the church which was packed to the rafters. Many people had to stand in the back area and the front pews were reserved for the families of the bridal couple. He nodded to them all in greeting.

Bug walked his family to the front and went through the preacher's office door at the right side of the front altar. Stan Henderson and Preacher Terry were waiting for him.

"Are you ready to walk that last mile, son?" Preacher Terry boomed in a corny imitation of a warden.

"I guess it's now or never Preacher Terry," Bug said solemnly.

Preacher Terry led the trio out the door and stationed himself in front of the altar. Bug and Stan stood to his immediate left. The piano player, who had been playing "The Old Rugged Cross" and other hymns before the service, now switched to Wagner's beautiful wedding march, which the people of Cather Mountain referred to as "Here Comes the Bride."

The haunting strains of the music echoed in the tiny church. Vanessa's only attendant marched slowly up to isle and stood on the preacher's right. Then, Vanessa, dressed in a short white lace dress, began the trip. She gripped the arm of her father with one hand and held a bouquet of flowers in the other. Her eyes were moist with tears, but she stepped carefully in time to the march.

Bug watched from his position next to Preacher Terry. He knew he was the luckiest man in the world to be marrying this beautiful woman who would soon bear his child. Vanessa approached the front of the church and he went forward to take her arm. He stood shoulder to shoulder with her in front of the preacher.

Preacher Terry began, "Dearly beloved, we are gathered here together to unite this couple in holy matrimony and make no mistake about it, we'll do that before we leave here today."

Then he continued the ceremony in his practiced, patriarchal voice. Within fifteen minutes, the couple said their "I dos" and the preacher pronounced Billy Unger Garland and Vanessa Louise Henderson husband and wife, ending with, "What God had joined together, nobody better mess with. Right, Bug?"

"Damn betcha," Bug said as he leaned to kiss Vanessa Garland squarely on the lips.

Bug took Vanessa's arm and turned her to face the clapping crowd. He felt her shiver and knew she was blushing. He was as proud as he could be.

The piano player promptly began Mendelssohn's wedding opus from "A Midsummer Night's Dream" and the couple dashed to the rear of the church to stand in the reception line.

Bug's mother and Vanessa's parents stood proudly by their side to shake hands with the good people of Cather Mountain who had come out to wish their children well. Bug looked down at his mother as she gently offered her hand to each person. He noticed that she was pale and trembly.

"Ma, what's wrong?" he whispered in her ear.

"Nothing, son. I guess all the excitement just got to me. I wish your Daddy could have been here today. He'd be so proud."

"Ma, I do too, but he ain't. Do you want me to take you home?"

"No, son, I'll be just fine after I get me some tea," she said.

Bug handed his camera (his one luxury) to Vanessa's father and Mr. Henderson took pictures of the wedding party. They joined the rest of the people in the church basement where the Ladies Aid had spread out the food on big folding tables.

Bug and Vanessa ate off of paper plates, along with everyone else. The sweetened tea was served in paper cups. When it was time for Bug and Vanessa to open the presents, Bug led Vanessa to the stack on a card table by the door.

He handed each gift to Vanessa to open and acknowledged the giver with an enthusiastic thank you. When he came to the last gift on the table, he looked at Vanessa in confusion. The gift was wrapped in the Sunday funnies and was tied with a shoe lace.

He was aware that people on the mountain were poor, but even these poor people took pride in the wrappings on the presents they gave. Many of them had hand-crafted their wrapping paper ornately and used their own hair ribbons to decorate the boxes..

He heard the people murmur their displeasure that anyone would show such bad taste at a wedding, but ignored it. Vanessa slowly untied the shoelace and peeled the funnies away from the box. It was a plain shoe box from J. C. Penney's. Bug took the box from her and lifted the lid. Vanessa peered in and screamed as she saw the dead, maggoty rat that lay inside.

Bug's face reddened in anger, and he spoke to the room, "Who was the charming person who gave this to us?" He held the box for all to see.

The women screamed and the men gasped. Who could have done such a thing? Bug knew he was feared and hated by many, but surely none of them had the courage to show it to his face.

To Bug, this was evidence that he had another enemy. One

day soon, he would find out who did this and even the score.

For now, he would have to make light of the situation, for everyone's sake. He had not seen Bobby Joe Baxter slip quietly down the basement steps just before the ceremony started.

"Well folks," he said, "seems somebody thought we couldn't afford to eat." He handed the box to one of the Elders who had rushed forward. "Let's forget about it and have us some of that good-looking wedding cake."

They walked over to the cake and with great ceremony, he put his hand over Vanessa's trembling one and together they sliced and ate the first piece. Then the president of the Ladies Aid sliced the rest and everyone got a piece of the "best cake they ever tasted."

After they had cake, the bridal couple went to the Preacher's office to sign the wedding certificate as witnessed by the best man and the maid of honor. The rest of the people went outside and waited to throw rice on the departing newlyweds.

Bug and Vanessa ran through the hail of rice and got into Vanessa's father's car. The engine roared to life and they left the church listening to the good wishes and congratulations tossed to them by the crowd. When Bug glanced back out the open window, he saw them waving and getting smaller and smaller.

Soon, Bug was driving fifty miles an hour. He didn't notice that Vanessa was holding on tight to the door handle.

"Wow, this baby really tears up the road. We'll have to get us a Buick one of these days," Bug said at the top of his voice.

"Bug, please slow down," Vanessa said in a frightened voice.

"Now, honey, don't tell me what to do. Just sit back and enjoy the ride. We'll be in Lake Chastain before you know it."

Vanessa seemed resigned and she leaned her head back against the seat and closed her eyes. She knew it would do no good to talk to Bug about the speed. She was trapped and she knew it. The baby would be born in a few months and there would be no getting out then.

Although she loved Bug, she had noticed that he had a terrible temper if anyone disagreed with him. She was quickly learning that he could fly off the handle with the least provocation. She, too, had heard that he had killed Archie Thurmon two years before.

She let out a long sigh as she sat with eyes closed and crossed her hands on her lap. The new wedding band reflected the highlights of the sun as it shone from the third finger of her left hand.

Grabbing that hand, Bug said, "What's the matter honey?"

She opened her eyes and looked at him with a forced smile, "I'm just tired, I guess. And it's so hot."

"The Dew Drop Inn's got air conditioning, Honey. We'll be there in one minute, and I'll get some ice and fix us a nice drink of the mist."

He stopped in the circular driveway of the Dew Drop Inn Motel and Restaurant and went in to register. Vanessa sat in the car and waited.

She could feel the stirring of the baby she carried within her. She put her hand to her abdomen. The little one had been moving around and kicking her for over a month and she delighted in the feeling of love she felt each time it moved.

Sure that it would be a boy, she tried to picture what the baby would look like. In her spare time, she had drawn many pictures of her image of him. In Biology class, she had learned that dark hair was predominate over light hair and subconsciously she had drawn pictures of a baby with all of her own features.

Bug returned and jarred her from her daydreaming. "Let's go, honey. We're in the honeymoon suite right next to the office." He drove the car to the assigned parking space, stopped the car and ran around and opened her door for her.

"We'll have to get the luggage from the trunk, Bug. I put your suitcase in with mine last night. That was good thinking to bring it with you to the rehearsal."

"I'll get them. You go on and open the door." He handed the key to her.

She opened the door of the room and looked around. She had never seen so much red velvet. The curtains and bedspread were made from it. The sofa was covered in it and although it wasn't velvet, the rug was red, black and green. There was a small kitchenette next to the bedroom. A bathroom with a toilet, tub and shower was separated by a half wall. The closet was an open rack on the bedroom wall with a luggage rack underneath.

Just as she had completed her inspection of the honeymoon suite, Bug burst through the door with two suitcases. "Ain't this the most luxurious thing you've ever seen?" he said. "It cost me almost twelve dollars, with tax."

"It's real nice, Bug," she gulped. "I guess we should be comfortable here for the night."

"Now you get on something pretty and I'll get us some ice from the office. Look, we've even got one of those televisions."

Vanessa bustled around hanging up their clothes and putting their toilet articles in the bathroom. She quickly showered and put on her negligee. It was pink and low cut with a pleated front that hid her slightly bulging abdomen. Her mother bought the gown and matching peignoir for her at Penny's Pretty Peignoirs and Things in Lake Chastain. She had never had anything like it, and she knew it was a once in a lifetime extravagance.

Bug came through the door with the full ice bucket in his hands and a big grin on his face. "Oooeee! Honey, you sure look good. You sit right down there and I'll whip us up something to take the parch out of your mouth. I got some soda to mix it, since you don't like it straight."

They sat on the sofa with their drinks and looked into each other's eyes while they toasted their marriage. Bug, who Vanessa had never seen scared, much less cry, had tears in his eyes.

He said, "This is the happiest day of my life. No, I'm lying. The happiest day of my life was the day I met you at school. Here's to us, Honey."

They tapped their glasses together and took a sip of their drinks. Bug put his glass on the side table and took Vanessa's hand. He pulled her to him and lifted her in his arms. He kissed her and carried her tenderly to the velvet bedspread.

She sat and waited while he went into the bathroom and showered. She sipped her drink, wrinkling her nose at the bitterness which permeated through the sweet soda.

Soon, a freshly showered Bug came to her and started to caress her with great gentleness. And she responded with an urgency she had never known.

The phone ringing by the bedside pulled her from her passion. Bug groaned and reached for it.

"Speak to me and this better be good," he said into the receiver.

She watched him as his face took on a look of agony. Something was wrong.

"I'll be right home, Stan. Thanks."

"Bug, what's wrong?"

"It's Ma. She passed away. We have to go home right away."

"Oh no. I'm so sorry."

She hated that the beginning of their marriage started in sadness. What irony to marry a woman and lose the woman who had borne him and nurtured him on the same day. She finally realized what her momma was talking about when she read from the Bible, "The Lord giveth and the Lord taketh away." The Lord had certainly done that to Bug on this day of days.

# 11

After the death of his mother, Bug grew strangely silent and thoughtful. He kept to himself when he was home, speaking only when necessary. Bug had never been much of a talker, and he was aware that this silence worried Vanessa and the children. He just couldn't change himself. Not that he was unkind to them, he just acted like he was in another dimension, as if in a trance.

Bug grieved for his mother with his whole being. Even though he had to provide for the family for the two years since his Pa died, at least his mother was there and he didn't feel he was alone. It had been a tough two years and last winter, they had lived on pancakes and salt pork for days at a time. Most of the vegetables had been ruined by the drought and very little had been canned and put away.

When he made his runs, he brought home enough money to pay the electric and telephone bills and buy a few staples and an occasional pound of hamburger and some vegetables. He had to make sure he saved enough for gasoline for his car or he couldn't get to his distributors.

Now, Bug knew it was all up to him and he thought constantly about the new responsibility coming soon in the form of a new mouth to feed. The business had been pretty good lately, but sharing it with Stan had cut the profits in half.

If only his mother were still alive, he could talk to her about things. He didn't want to burden Vanessa with his worries. She had not grown up rich, but she had not experienced anything near poverty. He would have to work hard to make sure she lived as good as she had with her parents. If he couldn't provide at least that standard of living, she might think he wasn't a man.

All in all, he felt it was a lot of responsibility for a man who had just turned nineteen years old. He tried to put it out of his mind, but he couldn't.

Vanessa tried her best to remain cheerful and take care of Benji and Lydia Anne in spite of her rapidly expanding waistline. She cleaned and scrubbed the drab old cabin and cooked nourishing meals for the family with the meager food supply. Trying her best to brighten the home, she made new curtains for the window and a new spread over the shabby sofa in the parlor. She got the material from some sheets that they received as a wedding present.

She was glad that the weather was getting cooler as she grew larger and larger. The baby was kicking day and night and she got very little sleep during the last two months.

Two weeks before the baby was due, she rolled over in bed for the twentieth time in two hours. All of a sudden, she felt she must stand up. She experienced a sharp pain in her lower back that radiated around to the front. Then, without warning, her water erupted onto the floor, soaking her feet and the rug beneath them.

"Bug," she whispered. "Wake up. The baby's coming." She shook him as she spoke.

'What'd you say, honey? Speak up." He rolled over to face her.

"My water broke. Can you call Doc Parsons?"

"I'll call him now. You lay back down on the bed." Bug jumped out of bed and ran to the kitchen. The phone was hanging on the wall by the door. He lifted the receiver and put it to his ear, only to hear voices.

"Whoever this is, please hang up. This is Bug Garland and this is an emergency. I have to call Doc Parsons. Vanessa just went into labor."

"Bug, this is Sheriff Mark Halbert. I'm talking to someone on your line. Hang up and I'll call the Doc. Do you want me to bring someone to help?"

"Yes, but hurry. Vanessa's mother said she was only in labor about an hour with Vanessa." He hung up the receiver.

Listening, Vanessa thought that this exchange was the most anyone had heard Bug say at one time for over three months. Maybe having the baby would snap him out of it, she thought.

Suddenly, a labor pain hit her and she stifled a moan. It was time to start timing the pains. Looking at the clock on the bedside table, she saw that it was twelve o'clock. They had gone to bed about ten o'clock that evening with a cold rain hitting the outside of the cabin. The radio was forecasting an ice storm.

She looked up as Bug came back into the room carrying a glass of water. Another pain wracked her body.

"The Sheriff is calling the Doc and bringing someone to help out. How are you feeling," he said.

"I'm just fine, Bug," she smiled up at him. "Did you check the weather? Remember, they're forecasting an ice storm."

Bug went to the window and looked out. Vanessa was right. He saw that the rain had turned to sleet and was beating against the cabin. Bug went out the front door and stood on the front porch.

Blowing sleet was starting to stick on the driveway. Since the road wasn't paved, a car should be able to get through if it came pretty soon. Bug knew that by morning nobody would be moving if the storm kept up all night. The bad ones took out all the electricity and isolated them for days.

He went back in the house and back to his parents' old bedroom, now occupied by Bug and Vanessa. He looked out the window again.

"It's sleeting pretty good out there. I hope the Doc gets here soon."

"I do too. I just had another labor pain and it hasn't even been fifteen minutes since the last one. Maybe we'd better get prepared, just in case."

"I'll go wake up Benji and Lydia Anne to help. Then you can tell us what to do to get ready."

Bug rushed from the room and woke his sister and brother. They went back to see Vanessa, who was taking a sip of water from the glass Bug brought to the bedside table.

"Honey, tell us what to do," Bug said.

"Will you call my mother and father and see if they can come over right away. Lydia Anne, you can put some water on the stove to boil. Benji, you get a bunch of clean towels." Bug was surprised that she ordered them quietly and efficiently as if they had all the time in the world.

Bug dialed the phone and spoke to Mrs. Henderson, finishing with, "Why don't you just calm down and get over here."

Vanessa heard the exchange and thought, he's really just a boy. He's just as nervous as my mother, but he doesn't want to show it.

Just as another pain started, Vanessa heard the sound of the Sheriff's car in front of the house. She looked at the clock. Ten minutes apart. Where's that Doctor, she wondered.

She heard the voices of Sheriff Halbert, Bug and a woman. She lay drenched in sweat and writhing in pain. She had expected pain during labor but not to this extent. Her mother told her it got worse once the pains started coming closer together. She could not imagine them being any worse, but something told her they would be. Could she stand it? She knew she didn't have any choice. This baby was coming and nothing was going to stop it.

Bug and the Sheriff came into the room followed by Sue Thurmon. Sue came over and sat down on the bed, taking Vanessa's hands in hers.

"You poor little thing," she sympathized. "Let Sue help you. I've been through it before."

Vanessa looked at Bug who was standing helplessly by the Sheriff. "When will my parents be here?" she asked.

"They'll be here shortly, Honey. They were leaving right away."

Sue Thurmon knelt by the bed just as Vanessa was beginning another labor pain. She took Vanessa's hand in hers.

"Now pant like a dog during the pain. Do it just like I am."

She panted and Vanessa tried to imitate her, but it still hurt. It hurt worse than when she had broken her arm as a child.

"It's only been five minutes since the last one," Vanessa gasped when the pain subsided.

Benji came in with the towels and Lydia Anne announced the water was almost ready to boil. They sat wide-eyed against the bedroom wall under the window sill.

"Bring those towels over here and get me some clean string and a scissors and put them on the table here," Sue ordered. "Let's get things ready, in case the Doc don't make it in time."

Sheriff Mark Halbert stepped forward and said, "I had to take medical emergency training and I think I could handle it, Sue. But from the looks of Bug, I think he's going to faint. Bug, why don't you take the kids and go out and wait in the parlor?"

Vanessa saw Bug's frightened face watching her as another pain ripped through her abdomen. Sue panted with her and held her hand. A scream escaped Vanessa's mouth and the Benji and Lydia stared in horror when they saw her twisted face and heard the piercing sound.

Turning to Benji and Lydia Anne, Bug said, "Come on kids. Vanessa needs her privacy."

Vanessa was too busy with her labor to notice him leaving with the two children. She felt Sue holding her shoulders and was thankful for the support. Sue spoke up. "Mark, you better go scrub your hands. I think you're going to have to deliver this baby soon. Lydia Anne said the water is hot. Scrub them good and get back here, pronto."

Mark hurried out as another pain assaulted Vanessa - only one and a half minutes since the last one subsided. In two minutes, he rushed back in the room, shutting the door behind him. He instructed Vanessa in getting into the proper position and draped her legs with a blanket. He then placed the clean towels beneath and below her buttocks and moved the lamp closer.

"She's fully dilated. I can see the head," he said. "Don't push until I tell you, Vanessa. I know you want to but don't do it until I tell you to."

Sue Thurmon bathed Vanessa's head with the handkerchief she had in her pocket. "There, there, honey, it'll be over soon. How does it look, Mark?"

As soon as she said it, another pain started. Vanessa panted and screamed. Mark said, "The head's partially out, Vanessa. Push hard on the next pain."

The next pain came almost immediately and Vanessa let out a final bloodcurdling scream, pushing with all her might. Mark gently pulled the head and the body of baby boy

Garland from her. A loud cry permeated the room. "It's a boy, Vanessa," Mark said. "A beautiful baby boy."

Her eyes were closed in relief while Mark delivered the afterbirth, and tied and cut the cord. She wrapped the baby in one of the towels and handed him to Vanessa.

Vanessa looked with wonder at the miniature hands and feet, each one of them perfect. Then she ran her hands over the great shock of blue-black hair that covered the head of her son. Baby boy Garland looked up at his mother with his dark-blue eyes; exactly like the eyes that had driven fear into the hearts of so many people.

As Sheriff Mark Halbert cleaned the blood from Vanessa and tidied the blankets around her, the door to the bedroom opened. Bug, Doc Parsons, Mr. and Mrs. Henderson came into the room followed by Benji and Lydia Anne .

"I'm sorry, the roads are starting to get bad. They say we'll all be ice-stormed in by morning," Doc Parsons said.

"He's here, Bug," Vanessa said softly.

She handed the baby to Bug so he could look at their first born. Ever so gently, he took him from Vanessa and examined his features. "He's got your hair, but he's got my eyes," he said proudly.

Vanessa watched proudly as everyone crowded around to get a glimpse of the little miracle. Doc Parson checked the baby carefully, looking in his eyes, ears, nose and mouth.

"Sheriff, you did a right fine job. This little guy is in great shape. Now let's weigh him." The Doctor took out his hand scale and put the baby on it. "Nine pounds, eight ounces and he looks to be about twenty-one inches long. Good size."

Vanessa smiled as he winked at her and proceeded to fill in and sign the birth certificate. He showed her the document and she noticed the name line was not filled in.

"Bug, you name him. He's your son," she said.

"I'm gonna name him Jake Unger Garland, after my dad, the greatest man I ever knew," he said.

"Folks, let's all get out of here and let this little lady get some rest. She's been through a lot," Doc Parsons said as he tried to bustle everyone except Bug through the door.

Mr. and Mrs. Henderson, who had said nothing during the interlude, and had only caught a glimpse of the baby hesitated. "I'd like to get a chance to talk to my daughter and see the baby. After all I am the girl's mother and the baby's grandmother," Mrs. Henderson said.

"You heard the Doc, Mrs. Henderson, and I heard the Doc, so do what he says," Bug said soberly. "And don't ever forget that I am the baby's father and the girl's husband. She don't belong to you no more. Now you better go on before you get stuck here during the ice storm. I can take care of my family."

Vanessa hated the ordeal of labor, but hearing Bug take charge made her proud that she had given him such a wonderful baby. Maybe now he would be happier. She was positive she would be happier.

# *12*

Vanessa was happy that Bug was so enchanted with Jake Unger Garland. She had watched him became a doting father. From the day the baby was born, he held him at every opportunity. He spent any extra money on toys and clothes for him.

After Jake learned to walk, She would often find that both Bug and Juggie, as they now called the baby, had disappeared. She knew just where to look. She discovered that the proud dad took him to the stills with him. She found Juggie sitting in a stroller under the big elm tree nearby. Bug proudly explained to her that he could work and watch Jake at the same time.

She spent her days cleaning and cooking, and watching her brother-in-law and sister-in-law grow like the weeds in the garden.

Now at ages fifteen and thirteen, respectively, they were company for her when Bug was gone on his runs at night and they helped take care of Juggie. On just such a Friday night in June, when the moon was full, Vanessa heard a knock on the front door.

She peeked out the window and saw Sheriff Mark Halbert standing on the front porch. He had his hat in his hand and stood impatiently, first leaning on one foot and then the other.

She opened the door and stood wiping her hands on her apron. She looked with alarm at the Sheriff. Something happened to Bug, she thought.

"Sheriff, what seems to be the matter?" she asked.

"Vanessa, now don't get thinking anything's wrong with Bug. I know he's on a run. I just came up here to tell you and him that I hear by the grapevine that there's going to be a big sweep on the mountain by the State boys. Could be soon. Better tell Bug and Stan to take those two stills apart and hide the pieces somewhere. And, by the way, you don't know who told you about this."

"I'll have to tell Bug how I know. I can't keep anything from him. He won't allow it. He should be home pretty soon, Sheriff. Do you want to come in for some iced tea? Bug got us a new refrigerator and we've got ice."

"Don't mind if I do, Ma'am. Do you mind if Sue and Precious come in too? They're out in the patrol car."

"Why no, tell them to come on in right now," she smiled toward the car idling in the drive.

Vanessa welcomed the three in. While she made the ice tea, she mused about their friendship with the Halberts. Sheriff Halbert and Sue Thurmon had gotten married shortly after helping deliver Juggie. Bug and Vanessa stood as best man and matron of honor at their wedding. Since then, the couples were close friends, as well as neighbors.

Vanessa was glad they lived so close since she was alone with the children at night frequently. The Sheriff had moved into the big house and was making some needed repairs. He had become a respectable husband to Sue and a loving father to Precious.

At the Ladies Aid meeting, Vanessa heard the ladies gossip about Sue and the Sheriff. It seems the people of Lake Chastain thought the whole situation was just fine with them. The ladies noted Sue wasn't quite as wild and seemed content to be the Sheriff's wife. Since she had not made any secret about Archie's abuse of Precious, they were happy that Precious finally would have a chance to grow into the beautiful young lady she was fast becoming.

Sheriff Halbert motioned for "his two girls" to come in and they got out of the car and came toward the house. "Now, we don't have to spend the evening talking about business, do we?" Sue Halbert said.

"We'll wait until Bug gets home, which should be pretty soon. I know he only had a few stops to make before the weekend," Mark said.

Vanessa hugged Sue in greeting. "Come on in. I've got some iced tea and Precious can play with Benji and Lydia Anne. They're playing Monopoly."

"We can't stay but just a little while, honey," Sue said. "Precious ain't got all her homework finished. She's going for the honor roll and they've got finals next week. Ain't that right, Precious?"

"Momma, you shouldn't use ain't. The teacher said you should say isn't or hasn't or aren't," Precious responded.

"Don't that beat all?" Sue said. "Here she is - so smart already, she's correcting her Momma."

"I'm almost eleven, I should be smart." Precious smiled at Vanessa so radiantly that Vanessa could only wonder how many hearts she would break in the future.

Just as they settled down with their iced tea, she heard Bug's Ford pickup in the driveway. He had discussed it with her and they decided to keep the old Dodge for family outings. He had managed to save enough for a used pickup for the business. He could carry more of the recipe that way, so it proved to be a savings for him. She agreed but made him promise to make sure the tarp covering the liquor was tied down tight.

She went and opened the door for him. He kissed her and came in. He shook hands with Mark and nodded a smile at Sue.

"What brings you here on this hot night, Mark?"

"Well, I need to talk a little business with you, Bug." He looked at Sue who took his signal to leave.

"Come on Vanessa, let's take the kids and go out on the porch. We ain't, I mean aren't, interested in that boring old talk, are we?"

"Bug, will you listen for Juggie while we're out here? I just put him down about an hour ago," Vanessa said.

"Sure thing, honey. Be my pleasure."

When the women and children went outside, he said, "Lets have some of the mist, Mark. I got some right here in my new refrigerator. It's a lot better cold."

Bug poured a small glass for each of them and listened while Mark told about the possibility of a raid on the mountain within the next week. They discussed the solution of dismantling the two stills and burying the pieces on different parts of the mountain.

"That would be too time-consuming and cumbersome. I've got a better idea," Mark said. "We'll store both of them in my basement. It's as big as a barn, and we can take them in through the boat door."

No one was sure why Henry Thurmon had built a boat door to his basement because he didn't have a boat. Now Bug was glad he had thought to do it.

"That's a great idea, Mark. Those State guys would never think to look for a still at the County Sheriff's house. And you know, where the State men are, the Feds won't be far behind.

They work in conjunction with each other, I heard."

"You're right about that. I've got a friend in the office in Montgomery. Don't tell nobody, but he lets me know pretty much what's going on."

"When can we get started with the moving? I've got my pickup and Stan's got his. Shouldn't take more that two trips each to get everything. Have you got room for the inventory? We've got to empty this last batch. It's ripe by now, so the State timed it just right for me."

"I've got room for everything. Let's get moving at dawn. My friend said he wasn't sure exactly when, but we better get started, pronto."

"I'll call Stan right away and tell him. Hope he's not out with his girlfriend."

He went to the phone on the kitchen wall and dialed Stan Henderson's number. After two rings, Stan answered the phone and Bug told him what was going on. He hung up the phone, saying, "Everything's set. We're going to start emptying and taking the stills apart around eleven tonight. That should take up about five or six hours. We should be over to your house with the first loads around dawn."

Bug bid the Sheriff and his family goodby just as Vanessa's brother, Stan Henderson, drove up the driveway in his pickup truck. Bug went out to meet him and then got in his own truck. He advised Stanley they would take the back road to the still site.

The moon lit the clearing with an eerie brightness. Bug was thankful for the light. They worked swiftly to fill the barrels from the shed and load them on Stan's truck. Then as quietly and efficiently as experts, they dismantled first one of the stills, then the other. It was a painstakingly slow operation, since they had to be careful not to damage the soft copper pipes as they took them apart.

The main vat of each one was also made of copper and domed at the top. Each vat had a fifty gallon capacity. Bug and Stan decided it would be most important to get those hidden safely at the Sheriff's house since they were the most difficult parts of the stills to replace.

They were also the most important parts. Later they could come back for the piping and cooling vats.

The moon began to set and the first light of dawn appeared by the time they had their first loads ready to go. The tarps they brought with them were tied securely over the truck beds. If anyone was curious, it would look like they were hauling straw or anything.

They put the piping and cooling vats into the shed and padlocked the door. Then, they spread the fire ash around and took some old branches and swept the ground where the stills had been. Finally, they gathered shrubs and underbrush to scatter around the site.

"Guess that ought to do it," Bug said, grinning at his partner. "The revenuers won't be able to see a thing if they come blasting in here before we get back for the rest."

Bug had been nervous when Mark told him about a possible bust and he knew Stan was also. Now, he felt a sense of security that they were ready to get out of there.

His Daddy told him those agents called it a bust because they busted up the stills when they found them. He sure didn't want to be around to watch them do it and he was anxious to get going.

They each got in their pickup trucks and slowly eased down the back road to Stop Gap Road. The sun was just starting to rise up the hollow on the other side of the mountain. Once on Stop Gap Road, it was only a short distance to the former Thurmon house.

Bug looked at his watch when he pulled into the circular drive followed by Stan. It was 5:45. The Sheriff's car was parked in front of the house and a Chevrolet sedan was parked in back of it.

Bug and Stan got out of their trucks and started to walk

to the front door just as Sheriff Halbert and a man in a suit came out.

"Well, hi there boys. This here is Agent Walker with the State of Alabama. He wants me to take him around the mountain a little bit and see if we can find any illegal distilleries. You boys happen to know where any are hidden?"

Bug stepped forward and put out his hand in greeting. "Right nice to meet you Agent Walker. My name is Bug Garland. It's a little early to be riding around isn't it?"

Agent Walker smiled. "We like to bring an element of surprise to our visits, Bug. We find that many of the folks we're looking for are out kind of late at night and don't get moving in the morning until around seven o'clock."

Mark Halbert winked at Bug. "Now you go on in and get some coffee, fellas. Sue will make you some breakfast when she gets up. You can start unloading those straw bales anytime you want."

"What are you doing with all that straw, Sheriff?" Agent Walker said.

"Well, the yard is looking kind of poorly, so I decided to get Bug and Stan here to help me with some landscaping."

"How come the bales are all covered up?" the Agent asked suspiciously.

"Why, Mr. Walker, you know what it's like in the spring here on Cather Mountain. It can be clear one minute and start to rain the next. Shall we get going before the word gets out you're in town?"

The Sheriff and Agent Walker walked together toward the Sheriff's patrol car. Agent Walker stopped and looked back toward the two pickup trucks. Bug and Stan stood watching him and waved goodbye before going into the house.

"Let's have that coffee and get started," Bug said. " We want to be unloaded and out of here before they get back."

The two men gulped their coffee loaded with cream and sugar, and rushed to pull the pickup trucks to the side boat door.

Working at full sweat, the got first the stills inside and then lined the basement walls with the extra barrels of moonshine.

"How's the Sheriff going to explain to that agent the fact that there're no straw bails sitting in the yard," Stan said.

"Well, I guess somebody up there likes us. Listen to that thunderhead that just came up. We sure couldn't unload it with such a gully-washer coming up, could we?"

They left the basement and shut the boat door. Bug locked it with the key that the Sheriff had left in the handle. By the time they drove their pickup trucks to the front driveway, the rain was coming down in torrents.

"I've got a better idea. Lets go get some bails of straw right quick and we'll be here waiting with it covered when the Sheriff and that nosey agent get back," Bug yelled to Stan through the open window.

"Besides, I want to find out where the Sheriff and him went. We can go get the piping after we're sure the Sheriff has escorted the good Agent Walker out of Lake Chastain."

Bug and Stan drove to Herman's garden center in Lake Chastain, quickly paid for and loaded the bales of straw onto the pickup beds. They covered the bales with tarp and made every effort to make the loads appear to be the same as the covered equipment they took to the Sheriff's house.

They pulled in the driveway of the Sheriff's house and had turned off their car motors only five minutes before the Sheriff eased his patrol car into the driveway behind them.

Bug watched Agent Walker walk to the front of the pickups and lift the corner of one of the tarps. He saw the Sheriff had his hand resting on the handle of his pistol.

"Guess it got too rainy to unload the straw, Sheriff," Agent Walker said while pulling the corner further back.

"Ain't it great that the boys waited? It's like I told you, never know when it's going to come a flood in these parts." Bug noticed that the Sheriff breathed a sigh of relief when he saw the straw bails sticking out.

Bug and Stan both got out of their pickups and stood in the rain with Agent Walker. Their clothes were wet from head to toe.

"We started unloading it, Sheriff," Bug said, "then all of a sudden there was this cloudburst and we had to put back what we unloaded. You know, Mr. Walker, straw will mildew if it gets wet," he lectured.

"Boys, go in the house and get something to eat. I'll escort Agent Walker out of town. He's got to get back to his headquarters and report that the mountain is clean. We didn't find a thing.

Bug grinned at Stan. "Sure thing, Sheriff. Some food would taste real good."

"When I get back, I'll help you unload if the rain's stopped," he called. Then to Agent Walker, "Those boys are the salt of the earth and real good friends."

Agent Walker smiled at the Sheriff of Dixon County, "Too bad everybody can't be as nice as the folks on Cather Mountain, but there will always be those bootleggers who give the mountain folks a bad name."

Bug had to smile at the comment. A bad name to Agent Walker was nothing more than a way to make a living to Bug.

# *13*

Bug was right. It was only a week after the first one that the Federal men made another sweep of Cather Mountain. He left the two stills in the Sheriff's basement along with the barrels, cooling vats and piping. He had moved the cooling vats and piping to the Sheriff's basement right after Agent Walker left town, and after returning the straw to the garden center.

One week after the Feds left town, Bug and Stan brought the equipment back to the site and set it up. They were in business again. The two-week delay hurt them but by selling the moonshine in the extra barrels, they managed to get enough money to survive.

They knew that they wouldn't have to worry about another bust attempt for a long time and they worked long hours each day to make up for the lost time. Soon, they were again running at peak capacity.

Despite the long hours he put in at the stills and on his runs, Bug spent every spare minute with his son, Juggie.

Juggie, who could talk in sentences by the time he was two years old, called his father Daddy Bug. The name stuck and soon Vanessa, Benji and Lydia Anne were calling him Daddy Bug.

He was proud of the name. He thought it gave him stature and respect. By the time of the birth of his second child, a girl they named Tessa, everyone who knew him called him Daddy Bug. He was twenty-one years old and life was good for him.

His sister, Lydia Anne, had grown into a beautiful girl. The boys her age and older had been prowling around the house since she was thirteen and now, at age fifteen, she had finally settled on her "one and only" boyfriend, Jimmie Haywood.

She begged Daddy Bug to let her get married, but he refused, saying that she would have to finish high school first. She cried and begged, but he would have none of it. She would finish high school and make Pa and Ma proud of her, even if they were in heaven.

Since Lydia Anne and Benji were both put in accelerated classes, Benji graduated a year early. Through scrimping and saving, Daddy Bug was able to supplement a State Grant and send him to the Junior College in Lake Chastain. During the summer, Benji worked with his brother in the business, but he wanted to be an accountant eventually.

One evening, as Daddy Bug sat and read to Juggie and Tessa, Lydia Anne and Vanessa came into the parlor to see him.

"Daddy Bug, can we talk to you?" Vanessa said.

"Vanessa, you know I don't get to spend much time with the kids. Is it important?"

"It's real important," Lydia Anne said with tears in her eyes.

"Juggie and Tessa, run and play now. Daddy Bug has to talk to Momma and Lydia Anne ."

Daddy Bug looked at the two women and indicated they should sit down beside him on the Couch. After they were seated, he spoke.

"Now, tell me what's so important that you should interrupt the precious little time I get with the kids."

"Daddy Bug, I'm going to have a baby," Lydia Anne said, crying into her hands.

Vanessa hugged her sister-in-law as she seemed to crumble under Daddy Bug's glare. He got up and left the room and immediately came back in. His face was red with fury and his eyes were bulging with a hideous gleam. He knew he was scaring the girls, but he didn't care. He wanted to make a point.

"Whose is it?" he demanded.

"It's Jimmie Haywood's," Vanessa said.

"When is it due?"

"I'm not sure, but I'm guessing it's due around November. I've missed two periods and I've started being sick in the morning, so all things considered, I should have the baby about November 15th."

Bug's face turned redder still as he listened to the intimate details described by Lydia Anne. He didn't want to hear any more and turned gruffly to Vanessa.

"Call Jimmie Haywood and tell him to get over here, and his parents too," Daddy Bug yelled, storming from the room.

Vanessa left Lydia Anne sobbing on the couch and went to the kitchen to phone the Haywoods.

Daddy Bug stood on the front porch and listened to Vanessa dial the Haywood's number. He knew he would have to come to grips with his anger before they got to his house or he would most certainly tear Jimmie Haywood's head off.

Vanessa spoke quietly into the phone, but Daddy Bug could hear her anyway. "Mrs. Haywood, Daddy Bug wants you and Mr. Haywood and Jimmie to come over to the house right now. It seems Lydia Anne is in the family way and she says it's Jimmie's baby."

Bug came back in the house and sat at the kitchen table. He watched Vanessa hang up the telephone and start making some iced tea. Evidently, that meant that the Haywoods were coming right over.

Vanessa got six glasses from the cupboard and laid some homemade cookies on a plate. She set the kitchen table with the glasses and napkins.

When he first came in the house, he was visibly calmer, but when he saw that Vanessa intended to serve tea and cookies to the Haywoods, he flew into a rage.

"Put that stuff away and go get the kids in bed. This won't be no picnic tonight."

Without a word she cleared the table and went to put Juggie and Tessa to bed. Even though he seldom yelled at her, it unnerved her each time. She would stay in the bedroom with the children while the Haywoods were here, she thought, and out of Daddy Bug's way.

Soon after the children were in bed, Vanessa heard the sound of the front door opening and the voices of the three Haywoods. Finding it strange that she had not heard Daddy Bug's greeting to them, she went into the parlor and sat quietly on the chair near the kitchen door. From this vantage point she could hear the chairs scraping the floor as the four sat up to the table. She would also be able to hear the conversation.

She could now hear Lydia Anne sobbing softly in her bedroom. Daddy Bug would probably call his sister when it was time for her to come out and listen to his plans for the couple. Vanessa knew that he had already formulated his thoughts on what action would be taken. She could not guess his mood or what turn the conversation would take.

Vanessa came into the kitchen to greet the Haywoods, but Daddy Bug ordered everyone to be seated at the kitchen table. Everyone looked at him. Finally he spoke, "I ain't exactly proud of having to have this meeting, but I've got a sister who's in the family way. She says it's yours, Jimmie. What do you have to say for yourself?"

"I love Lydia Anne, Daddy Bug, and I want to marry her," Jimmie Haywood said.

"What about her high school education? She's supposed to graduate in a year. I don't want her married until she gets her diploma."

Mr. and Mrs. Haywood had remained silent up to that point. Mrs. Haywood finally spoke.

"After graduation, she and Jimmie could get married and come and live with us."

Daddy Bug yelled for Lydia Anne . She came slowly into the kitchen with her head hung almost to her chest. Her eyes were red and puffy from sobbing. She sat beside Daddy Bug and continued to look at the floor.

"Now, here's what's going to happen with this situation," Daddy Bug said. "Lydia Anne , you're to stay here with us so we make sure you graduate high school. You, Jimmie, Vanessa and I will go to Lake Chastain to the Justice of the Peace to get you two married as quietly as possible. You'll finish out this year at school. Then, when you start your Senior year, I'll get the school to arrange for you to take your lessons here at home so you can get your diploma. The principal is a good customer of mine and I'll work it out. Maybe he'll let you come in after school hours to take your tests. Let me worry about that.

"We won't tell anyone about this until after you two are hitched. Then, Jimmie, you'll come over here and live. I want Lydia Anne to be around Vanessa while she's pregnant. Vanessa knows what to do and what to watch for during that time, in case there's any trouble.

"Mr. and Mrs. Haywood, you'll contribute ten dollars a week to their support and Jimmie will work for me here. After the baby is born, we'll all help build them a house here on my land. We'll split the expenses fifty-fifty."

Daddy Bug, having laid out the plans, got to his feet and left the room. Vanessa was a little ashamed that he had said neither hello nor good-by to any of the Haywoods.

She looked at each of them. They looked at each other and then at Daddy Bug's back leaving the kitchen. She sighed, helpless, when Lydia Anne put her hands to her face and cried uncontrollably. Jimmie leaned across the table to comfort Lydia Anne, but she pulled away and ran from the room. Vanessa rose to follow her and comfort her.

The Haywoods got up from the table and left by the kitchen door without saying goodby to Vanessa. She was left with an incredible feeling of sadness.

# 14

Daddy Bug was not sure how he felt. So many things had happened to make him happy and sad. On November 22, 1963, President John F. Kennedy was assassinated and James Michael Haywood, Jr. came kicking and screaming into the world. It had been an easy birth for Lydia Anne who delivered one week late.

Bug got the impression that every person on the mountain and in Lake Chastain was saddened by the death of the President of the United States, so there was no celebration of the new birth. He didn't feel it would be proper to celebrate even though it was his own nephew.

Even as Jimmie Haywood held Lydia Anne's hand during her labor, Bug noticed that his eyes were filled with tears. He wasn't sure if they were tears of joy or mourning and he didn't ask Jimmy to explain..

Because of his birth on that fateful day, Jimmie Michael Haywood, Jr. (soon called just Junior) never had a birthday party on the day of his birthday. His party was usually held on Thanksgiving day unless the holiday fell on November 22, at which time the party was held the day before or after.

Lydia Anne, Jimmie, and little Junior soon settled into the new two bedroom house that Daddy Bug, Jimmie and the Heywoods built for them and life had started to go smoothly for all concerned.

The Principal cooperated fully at Daddy Bug's urging, and Lydia Anne took her classes at home. She graduated second in her class and hung her framed high school diploma on her bedroom wall.

Daddy Bug made sure that even though Jimmie was only seventeen when Junior was born, he took his father and husband roles seriously. He was soon was adept at changing diapers and spoiling Lydia Anne and the baby.

Daddy Bug taught him the business and sent him on runs. Stan Henderson was drafted into the army and sent to Vietnam leaving Daddy Bug without help. He was glad now that Jimmie had married into the family, since Benji and Stan weren't around to help him. He had a lot of mouths to feed.

His brother, Benji, was given a student deferment from the draft and was finishing his Senior year at the University of Alabama. He had already told Daddy Bug that after graduation he was enrolling in Divinity school and not to count on him coming back too soon. His love of accounting fell by the wayside when he heard the call to the Baptist Ministry, plus he would qualify for deferment until he was 24 years old.

Daddy Bug wanted to go to Vietnam and fight for his country as every red-blooded Southern man did, but with a wife, two children, a sister, brother-in-law and a nephew to take care of, he resisted the urge.

Besides, as everyone said, America wasn't in the war to win it. The bigwigs were just letting it escalate and kill a lot of soldiers.

Daddy Bug thought they should go in there and nuke those North Vietnamese and get it over with. He said this to everyone he knew, but since he had a marriage and dependant deferment, people didn't take him seriously.

With the war on everyone's mind, the business took a turn for the better. It seemed that more and more people were deciding that life was too short and certainly too stressful to abstain from every vice. White whiskey was first on the list to help alleviate that stress, much to Daddy Bug's satisfaction.

He set up more distributors until they had the entire area of North Alabama and Northwest Georgia covered. The stills were working at break-neck speed to keep up with the demand.

Soon, Daddy Bug and Jimmie were cutting corners and delivering some batches before they were ready. An epidemic of alcohol poisoning broke out in the North Alabama sector. People were rushed to hospitals. Fortunately, nobody died, but the headlines did get the attention of the Agents in Washington, D.C. and the State boys in Montgomery.

Daddy Bug quickly called a meeting of his distributors, James Wallace, Pinky Gleason, Alan Cotter, Bill Edwards, and John Doyle. In order to avert attention from a gathering of five distributors at his house, he called each of them and asked them to meet him at a lodge in Cedar Falls, Tennessee, which was a few miles over the border of Alabama. They all agreed at once and the meeting was set for the next day.

He told them it was imperative that they get rid of any of the recipe they had before they came to the meeting as their houses might be raided. If the Feds talked to the sick people they might tell them where they got the liquor. He further urged them not to tell anyone where they were going and to call all their customers to warn them not to talk.

Bug arrived before the distributors and was struck by the beauty of the area. The lodge stood on the banks of the Ooga river, a fast-flowing, treacherous body of water that sported steep falls before it made its way into North Georgia and emptied into the Chattahoochee River. It was a popular river for white water rafting.

Sitting at the head of a table in a conference room of the lodge, Daddy Bug waited until all of his distributors were seated. He began the meeting without fanfare.

"I called all of you here because you know dang well that the Feds will be hot on all our trails after they get done talking to those sick folks down yonder. Now, if the folks don't talk, we'll be fine. If any of them do, we've got to have our defense in line and our stories straight. Any ideas?"

Bill Edwards, who covered extreme Northwest Alabama, said, "Daddy Bug, I don't know about everybody else here, but I'm right scared. Some of those people who got sick were on the phone to me and they were mad."

"How'd you handle them, Bill?" Daddy Bug said.

"I didn't back down. I told them if they wanted any more stuff from me, they'd better keep their mouths shut. I also told them that just buying it was against the law, too. I don't think they'll tell the Feds anything, but some of them want me to pay their hospital bills, and they were pretty mad when I told them where to go."

"I think you handled it just right, Bill. If they give you any trouble, just call me," Daddy Bug said. "What about the rest of you? Have you warned all your customers to keep quiet?"

They all nodded yes and Daddy Bug was satisfied that they had done as he had told them. He worried about Bill Edwards, however; a scared man was always a danger in this game. A scared man could lead the Feds to you.

Fixing each of them with a stern look, he said, "The Feds don't know anything about my operation and they won't find any stills at your houses. If they do come snooping around, just deny any involvement. It's your word against theirs. If by some piece of bad luck, any of you get arrested, don't tie yourself to me. Is that understood?" They all shook their head yes.

Daddy Bug said, "Well, that's all the work we need to do, now let's go get some lunch. After that I'd like to try some of that rafting. I hear it's a true test of a man."

He led the men into the big dining room and ordered lunch. It was served family style in big bowls and platters which were passed around the table. The fare was fried chicken, creamed potatoes, and field peas, with apple cobbler for desert.

Daddy Bug seemed in an almost jovial mood and he joked and laughed with his distributors. All seemed to join in the fun except Bill Edwards who was strangely quiet. Daddy Bug watched him toy with his food and sit looking out the window as if concentrating on something outside the lodge.

I wonder if he told me everything, thought Daddy Bug. He's hiding something, and it's starting to worry me.

"Something on your mind, Bill," he said.

"Nothing much, Daddy Bug. Do you happen to know someone named Bobby Joe Baxter?" Bill answered.

"I know him. I don't like him much. Why do you ask?"

"Well, I ran in to him at the cafe in Lake Chastain the other day when I came to pick up my supply from you. He told me he was gonna get you some day. He's carrying a real grudge about something. He said he gave you a real nice wedding present though, which seemed kind of strange?"

The rat, thought Daddy Bug. A rat from a rat. "He's gonna have to go some to get me," he said aloud. "Did he say how he's intending to carry out that threat?"

"No, but he said that everyone associated with you would go down with you. I'm getting worried, and I don't mind telling you, I'm thinking of getting out of the business. It's getting too damn risky and I don't fancy no stretch in the Federal pen."

All of the men gathered around the table watched Daddy Bug's face to see his reaction to Bill's comments. His face showed he was clearly surprised to hear anyone say they were quitting to his face, let alone in front of everyone.

His face started to get red, his eyes started to bulge and he turned to stare into Bill's frightened eyes. "Bill, we'll talk about that later," he said harshly. "Let me say this just once. I'll take care of Bobby Joe Baxter. Y'all are not to worry. And Bill, you're starting to whine too much, so put a lid on it for now. Now, let's go rent us one of those rafts and have a little fun for once."

His words seemed to dissolve the tension in the room and the men got up and milled around. The waitress brought the bill.

"I'll take care of this men. Meet me down by the raft launch in ten minutes."

Daddy Bug took the check and started out to the cash register outside the dining room door. He paused outside the door and heard Bill Edwards speaking to the other men.

"You guys better think about protecting yourself. That Bobby Joe Baxter is a mean critter according to Sheriff Halbert. I wouldn't put it past him to try to take us all out."

Daddy Bug didn't hear anything for a second. He imagined the other four men knew better than to say anything. This was clearly treason on Bill Edwards' part.

John Doyle, the distributor for Hanks County, broke the silence. "Come on boys, I don't know about you, but I, for one, am tired of talking about this. Let's have a smoke and then go down to the launch."

Daddy Bug peeked in the door of the dining room. The men were now all visibly relaxed. The sat back down at the table and lit cigarettes.

Daddy Bug waited patiently at the launch, hands on hips, chewing a toothpick and grimacing into the bright sunshine. Soon the men came out of the lodge and walked toward him.

"Get a move on, boys. We can only use this thing for three hours. I've got to start back then. There's a paddle for each of us. I told them we didn't need no life jackets. They're just for sissies."

The six men got in the raft and shoved off. Daddy Bug had a map provided by the lodge and he assumed the natural position of leader of the group. Looking at the map, he directed them toward an ominous looking section of the river, abounding with rapidly flowing water and large boulders.

"Lets head over there boys. We don't want to take the chicken way. If we're going to do this thing, let's do it all the way," he said.

Pinky Gleason, the distributor from Northeast Alabama, usually said very little. Suddenly he spoke up.

"Daddy Bug, you'll get us all killed. That looks right dangerous."

Sitting next to Daddy Bug on the back seat of the raft, Bill Edwards agreed. Daddy Bug was not to be daunted, however.

"I'd expect that out of you Bill, but I thought Pinky had some guts?"

"Daddy Bug is right. We're men ain't we? No river can get the best of us, can it?" Alan Cotten said.

"That's right," James Wallace and John Doyle chorused.

"Lookee here, if you two guys are so afraid, jump out and swim back. That is, if you're not afraid to swim," Daddy Bug jeered.

Bill and Pinky looked shamefaced and started to paddle with the rest of them. Soon, they were moving in the swift water, working mightily to control the craft. They deftly dodged around the boulders and held their course.

Soon, they all noticed the rush of water was moving faster. James Wallace yelled over the increasing roar of the water, "I think we might be coming to some falls. What does it say on the map."

"How right you are. Just around that next bend, there's a three foot drop. We can make it, I'm sure. You all keep one hand on your partner and one hand on the raft when we go over. I'll hang on to you Bill, and you hang on to me,"

Daddy Bug shouted. "All of you tuck your feet under the seat in front of you."

Just as the raft was going over the falls, Daddy Bug grabbed Bill Edwards hand. The water splashed upon the small craft soaking the occupants and blinding them temporarily. Finally, the raft jetted even with the water and the soaked bunch prepared to take control from the river.

"Where's Bill?" Daddy Bug said. "I had hold of his hand and all of a sudden, he wasn't there."

"My God, he must have fallen overboard. He can't swim. We've got to try and find him," John Doyle said.

They managed to get to a fallen tree in the river and tie the raft. Standing on the tree trunk, they stretched their necks and peered anxiously at the falls. They called Bill's name over and over for fifteen minutes. There wasn't a sign of him anywhere.

Then, Pinky Gleason shouted, "Look over there. Isn't that Bill floating down stream? He may still be alive."

The five men got back in the raft and paddled swiftly to reach the bobbing figure in the water. Within a few minutes, they had pulled the lifeless figure of Bill Edwards into the raft.

Rolling him onto his stomach across one of the wooden seats, John Doyle began to push on his back as the others looked on. Water came out of his mouth, nose and ears, but he had been in the water too long. Daddy Bug pronounced to the others that Bill was dead and could not be revived.

"We'd better get him back. We'll leave the raft and walk back. We can take turns carrying him. I reckon we're only about a mile away from the lodge if we cut through the woods," Daddy Bug said.

"We should have put on those life jackets they offered us. Poor old Bill," Alan Cotter said as they hoisted the body by the arms and legs.

Poor old Bill is right, thought Daddy Bug. At least he's one less worry that I have to put up with. The Lord works in mysterious ways, but sometimes he needs a hand.

# 15

Bobby Joe Baxter sat in the Lake Chastain Cafe drinking a cup of coffee and reading the newspaper. Sue Halbert, the former Sue Thurmon, sat next to him drinking a diet coke. Sheriff Halbert came in and looked around.

"What's the latest gossip in the newspaper, Bobby Joe?" He said.

"Well, Sheriff, the whole front page is about all those people that got sick on white lightning. I happen to know where that stuff came from, too."

"Now Bobby Joe, you better be careful when you go around accusing people of illegal activities."

"How would you know such a thing, Bobbie Joe?" Sue interrupted.

"I'm telling you, I can prove where it came from, but the time ain't right. I want to wait and see if any of those people die and then I'm calling the Feds."

"The Feds are already investigating and they can't get anybody to cooperate - even the sick ones. They haven't got a lead yet, so if you know anything you can tell me and I'll make sure it gets to them, Bobby Joe."

"You just check out Bug Garland's place, Sheriff. You'll find a big operation there. I went up there while he was out of town and saw it for myself. He's got enough stuff just in kegs to supply everybody in North Alabama and two stills to keep on doing it."

"Tell you what, Bobby Joe, let me take the little wife here home and I'll come back and get you. You can show it to me yourself."

"Sure thing, Sheriff. I'll wait right here."

As Mark and Sue Halbert drove up the mountain, Sue said, "What are you going to do about Bobby Joe Baxter's mouth?"

"I don't know, Honey. I've got to call Daddy Bug and see how he wants to handle it. We sure can't get everything hid quick enough, and if I don't go back and get him, he just might go to the Feds right away."

"What do you think he's got against Daddy Bug anyway? Sounds to me like he wants to turn him in just for spite."

"That's what it is. He's jealous of Daddy Bug and his power and he's trying to bring him down. I guess the two of them have had a few altercations in the past. I'm sure it was no contest as to who got the upper hand."

"Vanessa said something to me on the phone about Bobby Joe being the one who gave them that dead rat for a wedding present. She said Daddy Bug told her when he got home from his trip the other day."

"That little bastard. I'll tell you another thing. He's been making remarks around town about Precious, too. I hear he's been telling people how she was getting to be quite a babe."

"That does it. I want him gone. Away from here," Sue said. " He's already done time for rape and I don't want his filthy hands on my daughter. Get rid of him."

Mark drove into the circular driveway of their newly painted house and put the cruiser in park. He got out and opened the passenger door for her.

"Don't worry Honey, he won't get his hands on Precious and he won't turn Daddy Bug in. Just trust me."

Sheriff Halbert walked into the remodeled kitchen and walked to the phone on the kitchen desk. He dialed Daddy Bug's number and waited for the phone to ring three times. He hung up the phone and dialed again. That was their signal that something urgent was in the air.

Daddy Bug picked up on the first ring. "Yeah, Mark," he said.

"Daddy Bug, we've got some trouble with Bobby Joe Baxter. He said he came up and saw your operation while you were out of town with your distributors. He wants to turn you in to the Feds. Like, I mean, right now. How do you want to handle it?"

"Take him out. Figure out some way. This guy has been on my case for a long time. I want him out of my life. A dead rat is enough for me. Do you need some help from me or can you do it alone?"

"I'll figure it out, Daddy Bug. Don't you worry none. We'll call you."

"Under no circumstance are you to let Vanessa know how you do it. Sue can't tell Vanessa, no matter what good friends they are. Vanessa remembers when he called her a squaw in High School and she would know that I had something to do with it."

"Leave it to me, Daddy Bug, I know what to do."

"Sweety, I'm going to take a nap," Sue Halbert called from the master bedroom. "Princess is spending the night with her friend, so I have to get my beauty sleep if we're going to the Country Club tonight. Wake me in an hour."

Sheriff Mark Halbert made sure his pistol was loaded

and he had extra bullets. He got in his cruiser and started it. Switching on his radio, he called for backup.

"This is Sheriff Halbert. I'm on my way to a 10-32. A suspected rapist is having coffee at the Lake Chastain Cafe. I want to take him in with no trouble. Cy Davis, meet me in the front. We're taking in Bobby Joe Baxter for an attempted rape of my step-daughter, Precious. Don't believe a thing he says. He's a pathological liar, and Precious will pick him out of a lineup."

Mark was doing his usual thorough job. He was taking care of business, both Daddy Bug's and his own. He hoped his friend was listening with his police scanner. Knowing Daddy Bug, he just might drive into town and watch the excitement.

The Sheriff and his backup quietly surrounded the Lake Chastain Cafe while Bobby Joe Baxter drank coffee and talked to Wilma, the waitress. The door to the Cafe was open and Mark could hear him brag in his loud voice.

"I'm gonna be a big man in this town when Daddy Bug goes to jail, Wilma. The Sheriff is gonna send him off and then I'm gonna be kingpin in this town. You could go along with me if you want to. Bug's wife is hot for me, but I won't go with no squaw. I kind of like women like you. Blond, hot and ready to go. What say, Wilma?"

The Sheriff saw the worried look on Wilma's face when she observed the cars surrounding the cafe. "Yeah, Bobby Joe, like I said, I have to take the garbage out back. Be back in a minute. Don't go nowhere."

"I'm only waiting for you, love. Hurry back," Bobby Joe said as she disappeared through the back door.

Sheriff Halbert got on his radio and said, "Let's give him a chance to give up, but if he doesn't, don't spare the bullets. This man is dangerous. He's already had one conviction for rape and for all I know, he could be capable of murder. Cy, go in an put the cuffs on him."

Cy Davis, Deputy Sheriff, entered the Lake Chastain Cafe and approached Bobby Joe Baxter from the rear.

"Bobby Joe, you're under arrest for attempted rape. I will read you your rights. You have the right to remain silent. You have the right to an attorney. If you cannot afford an attorney, the court will appoint...."

"You sumbitch, you don't know who you're messin' with. I'm Bobby Joe Baxter. The Feds are my friends, or soon will be when they hear what I got to tell them."

Bobby Joe turned to strike Cy Davis in the face, but he was too late. Cy had drawn his gun before entering the cafe and his finger was on the trigger. Before Bobby Joe could hit him, Cy pulled the trigger and Bobby Joe crashed to the floor with his hand over his heart.

Well, thought Mark, who had witnessed the whole thing. Another one of Daddy Bug's worries was over. He saw that Daddy Bug had a ring side seat watching from the pickup he had parked across from the cafe.

Bobby Joe's momma and daddy called Mark after his funeral and wanted help in finding out who put a J. C. Penney box with a dead rat in it on his grave. Who would do such a thing? It was a sacrilege to them.

Mark decided that an old score was settled. He found out recently that Bobby Joe Baxter ruined Daddy Bug's wedding day, and he had saved that J.C. Penney shoe box for just such a settlement.

# 16

After Bobby Joe Baxter got killed, and the weak link in his network died, Daddy Bug's world started to settle down. The Feds finally gave up trying to pry any information from the people who got sick. Jimmie Haywood was proving to be a great brother-in-law and a help in the business.

Daddy Bug decided he would have to be more careful with the aging and quality of his recipe, so he put yet another still in operation. In that way, he could supply the ever increasing demand for white lightning without sending it out prematurely.

Due to the efforts of President Lyndon Johnson and Martin Luther King, the civil rights movement was penetrating all the towns and cities in the South. Lake Chastain was rather isolated from the movement since there was only one black man in the town. No one treated him any different than anyone else and when he sat at the lunch counter in the local cafe, he joked and laughed with the white merchants. They, in turn, would hire him for different jobs and pay him a fair wage.

This was not the dominant attitude elsewhere in Alabama, however; Daddy Bug was aware that there was a great stress between the races. The violence continued in the form of cross burnings, bombings and homicides of blacks. It was a volatile era that caused much tension in Daddy Bug's territory, which naturally caused his customers to drink more.

His business was booming.

Further, the Vietnam war was still raging and there were over half a million United States troops fighting in the jungles. More and more of the families of Lake Chastain were getting notification that their sons were dead, missing in action, or prisoners of war.

The same notifications were going to people across the United States. A new attitude was prevailing in the land; an idea that we must have peace and withdraw from an unbeatable war action.

Some people drank to forget those sorrows and the hippies got stoned on LSD and stronger drugs. The flower children were living in communes and practicing free love as their means of protest to the war.

Although there were no hippies or flower children in Lake Chastain, it was not uncommon to see men, and occasionally women, stumbling down the street with a pint jar open in their hands. Sheriff Halbert would never arrest them; just put them in the jail to sleep it off and send them home. He did this at Bug's suggestion.

On Friday, October 30, 1971 at 1:00 P.M., Juggie, Tessa and little Jimmie, Jr. were at school. Lydia Anne was shopping. Daddy Bug and Jimmie were out buying supplies for the recipe. Vanessa was home alone when her parents came to the house with the news that her brother Stan Henderson was missing in action.

Vanessa had always been close to her only brother. He had been her protector until Bug Garland came into her life. Her grief was acute, since she knew that "missing in action" usually signified death.

With tears in her eyes, she sat at the kitchen table and opened a jar of the recipe. Her parents were aghast as they had never before seen her drink anything stronger than ice tea.

"Vanessa, what are you doing?" Mrs. Henderson cried.

"Momma, I have to have something for my nerves," she whispered.

"Girl, I've never said a word about what Bug did for a living. I've never interfered, but it breaks my heart to see you start that drinking. It won't bring Stan back and it's a bad thing to get started with," Mr. Henderson said.

Mrs. Henderson interrupted, "He knows for a good reason. It's not on his side, honey. Even though everyone says that it's in the Indian blood to become an alcoholic, that's not true. It's on my side. No matter what your nationality is, if you have a bent for it, it gets in the blood and you can't stop it. My Daddy almost died of it and that's why you've never seen me take any of it. Your Daddy never had the taste for it either."

"I'll only have just a little bit. A little bit can't hurt me, Momma."

"A little bit can kill you. Don't you know that if you drink one drink, it can lead to another and another. Both your brother and your grandfather had the problem. Your granddaddy took the cure when you were little. You're brother got cured in the Army during boot camp."

"I never saw Stan drunk, so don't tell me he was a drunk."

"Don't you understand. Different people can drink different amounts and you can't always tell, but the fact remains that they have to have it. They can't stop once they start."

"Alright," Vanessa said. "I won't have any. Why don't you two go on home and I'll just lay down awhile before the kids get home."

They all hugged good-bye and Vanessa found herself sobbing aloud again. Her brother was gone and she knew he would not come back. She sat at the table, head in hands, long black hair hiding her heart-shaped face.

She looked again at the jar of moonshine. It was still cold from the refrigerator, she noticed as she put her hands on it. She opened the jar and poured a small amount into the glass that stood on the table.

Sipping the clear bright liquid, she leaned back in the chair and closed her eyes. Her bodily seemed to visibly relax. She had never tasted it straight. Daddy Bug had always mixed just a drop with a soft drink for her, and it had always relaxed her.

She did not know how long she sat there but suddenly she realized someone was shaking her arm. She opened her eyes to see who it was.

"Momma, wake up," Juggie said.

She opened one eye and looked at her son. He's growing so big, she thought. At ten years old, Juggie Garland was tall for his age.

Standing next to him were Tessa and Junior with puzzled looks on their faces. She had never been asleep before when they came home from school. Cookies and milk were usually set out on the table so they could have a snack before starting their homework.

"I'm sorry, kids. I must have fallen asleep. I'll get you a snack right away." She looked with alarm at the empty jar. She picked it up, along with the fallen glass.

The wall clock in the parlor rang four times. It was four o'clock and she had been asleep for over two hours.

How could I have drunk the whole thing, she thought. She remembered that she had taken another half glass after the first one, but she didn't remember anything after that. Her head was throbbing and she was nauseated.

She went to the sink and splashed cold water on her face. Then she searched for some aspirin. She would have to get herself in shape before Daddy Bug came home.

Quickly, she downed three aspirin and something to settle her stomach. Then she grabbed the empty jar, washed it and put it with the rest of the supply in the pantry.

"Momma, can we have our snack now?" Tessa said.

The children had been sitting at the table watching her every move. She could tell they knew something was wrong with Momma, she acted like she was sick. Anyway, they had never seen her like this.

She prepared the snacks for the kids and set them out on the table; her hands shook and her face started to sweat. What was the matter with her? She knew she was about to be violently ill and ran from the kitchen to the bathroom.

She kneeled by the stool and grasped its base. She heaved and heaved until she had voided everything she had eaten that day. Then she started dry heaving until the stool was filled with bloody water.

Finally, her feeling of nausea subsided. She rinsed off her face in the sink and looked at herself in the mirror. Her eyes were bloodshot from the strain and her face was pale and tired looking.

Just as she was wiping her face and hands to return to the kitchen, Daddy Bug appeared in the doorway. He looked at her with alarm.

"What's the matter with you? Are you sick?" he said.

"I'm not sure what's the matter. I've been throwing up," she said.

Bug went in the bathroom and put his arm around her shoulders. He could smell the rancid odor of the alcohol on her breath.

"Have you been hitting the sauce, Vanessa?"

"I was only going to have just a little, but I must have drank the whole pint. I just don't remember."

"Good God, woman. Why the hell would you do a stupid thing like that?" he shouted and turned her to face him. "Are you trying to kill yourself?"

"Momma and Daddy came over and told me that they had word that Stan was missing in action. I just wanted to have a small bit to help me relax and deal with it."

"Don't you know that drinking that much when your not used to it can kill you? You can die from it," he said.

"I promise I won't do it again, Daddy Bug. I'll just have a drink when you make it like you always do."

"It's too bad about Stan. He might be alright though. You never know. Maybe he's a prisoner of war or something. We'll just have to wait and see."

He was disturbed by Vanessa's bout with the pint jar. She had never liked the taste of the white whiskey without a mixer. After talking to her about Stan for an hour he changed the conversation to her.

He realized that she had experienced a blackout. How had she managed to drink the whole jar without passing out before it was finished? When he made a drink for her, he put a tiny splash of it in a tall glass of mix.

She had excused herself and gone to their room after he had shaken her and yelled at her about it. He didn't go after her but started to make supper for the kids since Lydia Anne hadn't returned from shopping.

After they ate, he sent them out to play while he talked to Jimmie, who had eaten supper with them.

"What do you think came over Vanessa this afternoon?" Jimmie asked.

"I sure don't know, but I'm going to keep an eye on her. A body can't let some bad news turn them into a drunk. I've seen a lot of people get bad news and the last thing they want to do is drink."

"Vanessa just doesn't seem like the type of person who would become an alcoholic. She's too kind and good."

Daddy Bug paused for a minute and reflected. "That's exactly why I'm worried. People who are too kind and good are the ones who can't take any kind of pressure or bad news. They just aren't equipped for it."

"Well, anyway, I hope Stan comes back. Then, maybe everything will be all right," Jimmie said.

"She promised me she would never take a drink again unless I made it for her. I hope she doesn't because Stan and her old granddaddy had a problem with liquor and I don't want to see it happen to Vanessa."

"I tell you what. If you want, I can help you take all the pints in your house and we can lock them in the shed down by the stills. Then when you want to have a little snort, you can just go down there and get one."

"That's a great idea, Jimmie boy. Let's do it right now."

They went out to the back porch to get some cardboard boxes that they used to carry the jars to the distributors.

"How many do we need, Daddy Bug"

"Two will be enough. I only have a couple dozen jars in there."

Back in the kitchen, he opened the pantry door and surveyed the shelves. He loaded all of the pints in the boxes and the two men carried them to the shed.

Vanessa heard the exchange between them and she was ashamed. She had never wanted to be a problem to Daddy Bug and now he was worried that she would start drinking. What had she come to in her life?

Looking out the window, she saw Daddy Bug and Jimmie coming out of the woods in the back carrying the empty cardboard boxes. They walked closely together as if they were conspirators. She knew they were discussing her.

She heard Lydia Anne come in the house from her shopping trip, and call her name. She sat up straight on the bed.

"I'm in here Lydia Anne ," she called.

"Well, girl, what's the matter with you? Where are the men?" Lydia Anne, loaded with packages, stuck her head through the open door.

"They're coming in the back right now to answer your second question, and I'm a little bit too sick to answer your first."

"You don't feel well? You do look a little green around the gills. What happened to you?"

"I guess I drank too much of the mist, and then I went to sleep. When I woke up, I started to throw up."

The family had long ago taken up Sue Halbert's word for moonshine, and referred to it as "the mist" or "the recipe" around the house when the children were around.

Lydia Anne peered closely at Vanessa's puffy face and dull-looking eyes. "What brought that on."

"Momma and Daddy came over and told me that Stan was missing in action. I was so overcome, I thought I'd take a little drink to calm me and I don't remember anything else until I woke up about an hour ago."

"I feel real bad about Stan, Vanessa, but I'm concerned about you. Doesn't do any good to worry about Stan. I'm sure you'll hear from him soon."

"Anyway, you know Nixon's pulling all of the troops out of Vietnam and part of the deal is that we get any prisoners back. And I hate to say this, we'll also get any remains; it said on the radio. We'll know soon enough."

Vanessa looked at Lydia Anne and started crying again. As Lydia Anne hugged her in sympathy, Vanessa was sure she would never see her brother again. Her only brother may be lying dead or alone in a jungle in a place that had become hell on earth.

When the Southern boys started to return to their homes in North Alabama, Vanessa peered anxiously for her brother's name in the Birmingham newspapers. Stanley Henderson was not listed as returning from Vietnam.

# *17*

It was not until March, 1973, that the United States forces were completely withdrawn from Vietnam. During the year and a half between Vanessa's first black out and that historic occasion, Daddy Bug knew she worried constantly about Stan. To allay that feeling, she drank.

She covered it well. Bug suspected it at times but couldn't be sure. She never acted drunk and none of his supply in the shed was missing. He was just curious that she seemed to act cheerful all the time.

Then, when it was broadcast that all of the prisoners of war had been released and they had not heard from Stan or the Army about his fate, Daddy Bug saw a change in Vanessa. Gone were her bright smiles and sunny disposition.

She moped around the house in her bathrobe from morning until night, dressing only for her occasional mysterious walks in the woods. Her efforts at housecleaning were minimal and she made the plainest meals; unusual, since she once prided herself on her excellent baking and cooking.

Daddy Bug tried to talk to her about her decline, but received no comment other than she wasn't feeling good. He talked to her parents about what was happening to her and they offered no help except to sympathize. They were also grieving about Stan.

Finally, he could stand it no longer and decided that she must get some help. He came in the house and went straight to their bedroom. He knew she would be laying in the bed staring at the ceiling.

"Vanessa, I need to talk to you," he said in his sternest voice.

"Daddy Bug, I don't feel good. Can't it wait?" she murmured.

"No, it can't wait. I'm sick of what's going on around here and it's got to change. I'm taking you over to see Doc Parsons right now. Get up and put some clothes on."

Without a word, Vanessa got up and started putting on an old soiled cotton dress. Daddy Bug grabbed it and threw it on the floor.

"Get something clean out of the closet and put it on. No wife of mine will be seen looking like she don't know anything about soap and water. And go comb your hair and put on some lipstick."

Vanessa merely looked at him and complied. She was presentable when she came out of the bathroom. She even put on nylons and her good sandals.

Bug glanced at her and noticed how thin she had become. She had long since given up pretending to eat even a meager meal. Her appetite was gone.

She moved like a shadow out the front door and toward the car. Bug walked ahead of her and opened the door on the passenger side.

Soon, they were on Stop Gap Road headed toward Doc Parsons' house. He had his office and examining room on the lower floor and lived on the top floor with his wife.

As they drove in the driveway, Mrs. Parsons came to the door of the office and waved. She acted as receptionist, assistant, and general goodwill ambassador for Doc Parsons.

She smiled in her cheerful, grandmother way and escorted them into the office. "Now, tell me, which of you is the patient today?" she said. She stood behind the tall counter inside the door and looked at them.

"It's Vanessa, Mrs. Parsons. She's just not herself and I think she needs a check-up. Something's not right with her."

"You just come with me honey and we'll get you ready. Doc is upstairs finishing his lunch and he'll be right down."

She opened the door to a small room which held an examining table, a sink, a desk and a metal cabinet. Daddy Bug followed close behind. He wanted to hear every word said.

Closing the door behind them, she said to Vanessa, "Just get undressed and put on this little gown. Here's a magazine to read and Doc will be here in a minute. Daddy Bug , you can sit over there."

Daddy Bug complied and watched Vanessa nod to Mrs. Parsons as she left the room. She turned her back, undressed and put on the gown.

Sitting on the examining table she glanced idly at the magazine and set it on the end of the table. Then she stared at the charts on the wall in front of her. Bug said nothing to her. He felt he had earlier been too harsh, but he couldn't help it

"Hi Vanessa. Hi Daddy Bug. What seems to be the problem?" Doc Parsons said when he bustled into the room.

His naturally rosy cheeks seemed even redder than usual. He took his stethoscope off and shook Vanessa's limp hands in his. He peered at her pale face as she spoke to him.

"I'm not sure Doc Parsons. I'm all drug out and can't seem to find any energy. I keep thinking about my brother not coming home from Vietnam and I guess I'm kind of depressed. Daddy Bug is real down on me, too."

Before Daddy Bug could say anything, Doc Parsons said, "I'm sure he's not down on you, sugar. He's just concerned because your not yourself. Let's have a look at you."

Doc Parsons listened to her heart and lungs; looked in her eyes and ears with his instrument. He said he could see nothing out of the ordinary, except he was worried about her pasty complexion and her trembling demeanor.

"Have you been eating right or taking any over-the-counter medicines?" He asked.

"I just don't have any appetite, Doc. I haven't been taking much of anything except for my sinus problem."

"Let's draw some blood and I'll send it to the lab in Lake Chastain. That should tell us what's wrong. I suspect you're a little anemic. That could be the cause of everything."

He drew a vial of blood from her arm and told her to get dressed. Sitting at his small desk, he wrote a prescription.

"I'll have these tests back in about five days. In the meantime, I want you to get this prescription for iron tablets filled and start taking them. Don't worry none and try to start eating right."

Doc Parsons walked the couple to the front area and shook hands with Daddy Bug.

"Daddy Bug, I don't see anything seriously wrong. I'll have the results of the blood tests back in short order and we'll get your misses back to normal"

"Thanks, Doc. Come on Vanessa, let's go home. I've got a lot of work to do," he said. He opened the office door to leave, guiding Vanessa to the car by her waist..

Driving to the drug store in Lake Chastain, Daddy Bug seemed pre-occupied. He finally broke the silence between them. "Vanessa, I want you to know that whatever it is that you have wrong with you, I'll stick by you until you lick it. My Daddy and Momma were always together on everything and I hope that we can be that way too."

"Daddy Bug, there's nothing wrong with me that seeing my brother alive won't cure. But, it means a lot to me, what you just said."

After they got the iron tablet prescription filled, Daddy Bug stopped in front of the Dairy Barn and went in to get an ice cream cone for Vanessa. Once inside, he ordered two vanilla cones, then turned and saw Sue Halbert sitting in a booth eating a chili dog.

"Hey there, Sue. How's Mark doing these days? I haven't seen y'all for a couple of weeks. I guess the Sheriff of the County keeps busy with all those hippies coming through nowadays."

"We're doing just fine, Daddy Bug. Mark's got his hands full with that new commune that they set up on Kryder Mountain. All the farmers there claim they've been stealing their chickens and robbing their gardens for food. He's keeping busy checking out all the complaints."

"Well, you come and see us whenever you get some free time. I think it would do Vanessa good. She's a little under the weather right now."

"Daddy Bug, sit down just a minute. I wanted to talk to you about Vanessa. I think she's been drinking on the sly. I hate to be the one to tell you and don't you dare tell her I did. I'm getting worried about her."

"What makes you think she's drinking, Sue?"

"Mark said he's heard that Vanessa set up a connection with one of your own distributors and she's buying it up as fast as he can deliver it. She meets him in the woods behind your house twice a week."

"Who's the man?" He asked.

"I can't say. It could be just gossip, but you might want to keep an eye on her when she goes for a walk. I'm just telling you because she looked so poorly last time I saw her."

"You mean to tell me she's been buying my own stuff? I wonder where she's getting the money."

"I don't know, but I can try to find out for you. I know her mother and father go over there sometimes when you're gone. Maybe she's crying poor-mouth and they give it to her. She could just tell them that she didn't want you to know she was getting money from them. You know, a man's pride and all."

"Thanks, Sue. Keep your ears open for me. I've got to go but don't be a stranger at our house."

Daddy Bug got up from the booth, paid for the ice cream cones and went out to the car. He handed one of the cones to Vanessa and said, "I don't want you going for no more walks in the woods unless I'm home, Vanessa. I'm worried you might get hurt and there would be no one to help you. Remember what happened to my Daddy?"

"What makes you think I'm walking in the woods, Daddy Bug?" She said.

"Lets just say I'm psychic, honey. My mother was too and she passed it on to me."

Vanessa did not look at him, but turned to gaze listlessly out the side window. Bug started the car and turned to go back up the mountain.

His thoughts were racing trying to think of which distributor would dare sell his wife liquor behind his back. It surely couldn't be any of the four regulars. They would know that if he found out, he would make them sorry as sin.

He wondered about the new one he had found to replace Bill Edwards. After a long search, he had finally settled on a partially disabled Vietnam veteran named Arnold Matheson. Arnold had been highly recommended to him by all of Bill Edwards' customers.

He had come to the Garland house to talk about the position. Daddy Bug was very impressed with the soft-spoken man and recruited him on the spot after making sure he didn't gossip and could keep his mouth shut.

He seemed quite taken with Vanessa at the time, but acted as a perfect gentleman in front of her. Vanessa was shy and retiring, as always, and quickly left the room when they started to talk business.

They pulled into the drive of his house and he shut off the motor. Then turning to Vanessa, he said, "Have you talked to Arnold Matheson since I hired him?"

The pale complexion of her face turned suddenly pink. She looked down at her knees and mumbled, "No."

Bug left her sitting in the car and rushed in the house to the kitchen phone. He dialed Arnold Matheson's number.

After several rings, Arnold answered with, "Arnold here."

"Arnold, it's Daddy Bug. I need some straight answers from you. Have you been supplying my wife with liquor behind my back?"

"What make's you ask that, sir?"

"I said straight answers. I'm asking you one more time and then I'm coming over to your house and take the answer out of your hide if you don't tell me right now."

"She called me and told me she was buying it for her brother and you wouldn't approve. She arranged to meet me in that clearing way back of your house. I told her I didn't like the situation, but what else could I say to the boss' wife?" Arnold blurted.

"Her brother didn't make it back from Vietnam. He's probably dead. You should have come to me right away. She's been drinking it all herself."

"I'm sorry, sir. You're right, I should have asked you about it. I won't bring her any more of it."

"You and I will talk no more about this. Just keep doing your job and the only time I want you at this house is when you pick up your supply from me, and under no circumstances are you ever to come for your supply unless you're sure I'm home. Got that?"

"Yes sir, I got that sir."

Daddy Bug slammed the telephone back to its cradle and strode out to the car. Vanessa was still sitting on the passenger side looking straight ahead, tears running down her cheeks.

Opening the door, Bug took her hand and drew her from the car. He pulled her close. "Honey, I know all about it. I pulled it out of Arnold just now on the phone. We'll get you some help. Let's go in the house."

He walked her in the house and led her into the bedroom. "I'll be back in shortly, honey."

Back in the kitchen, he dialed Doc Parsons' number. "Doc Parsons, it's Daddy Bug. I think I know what Vanessa's problem is. She's been hitting the sauce behind my back. We need to get her some help."

"Surely, that sweet girl can't be drinking," Doc Parsons said.

"I think she is. She's all upset over Stan not coming home and I think she's drinking to forget. Now, what can we do to help her?"

"Well, if you think it's that bad, we could admit her to the hospital for a while. That way, we can make sure she eats right and can't get her hands on any liquor. Also, if she is drinking heavily, it will be extremely important to observe her during detoxification."

"I'm bringing her to the hospital right now, Doc. I want to take care of this problem as soon as possible. I'll meet you there in twenty minutes."

When Daddy Bug hung up the phone, he turned to go back to the bedroom to collect Vanessa's things and put them in a suitcase. Vanessa stood facing him from the kitchen doorway.

"I'm not going to the hospital, Daddy Bug. I'll kill myself if you lock me up in the hospital."

"Honey, it's not the nuthouse hospital. It's the medical hospital in Lake Chastain. You'll be just fine once you're in there. I'll come and see you every day and so will Lydia Anne."

Bug was used to dominating people and having his way, but he was smart enough to know he wasn't right all the time about everything. This was not one of those times. This time he was sure he was right.

# 18

For the third time in his entire life, Daddy Bug's heart was broken. The first time was when his own Pa had died, or as he concluded, had been murdered. The second time was when his Momma died, the result of grieving for his Pa. Now, his own Vanessa had to be hospitalized for drinking too much, because of worry about her missing brother.

The Doctors of Psychiatry and specialists in alcoholism had not been optimistic when he told them that alcoholism ran in the family. They recommended that he commit her to the State of Alabama Rehabilitation Center, surmising that she would be able to come home in a month.

At the center, they would dry her out and treat her for her depression and lethargy. It would be the best thing for Vanessa and the family, he was told. It would never do for her to stay around the house. She would only get worse. Besides that fact, it was better that the children not see her in that condition.

The month came and went and she did not get better. She seemed to be in a stupor and would speak to no one. She stared straight ahead when he came to visit her. Sometimes, he noticed dry spittle below her lips and he knew that she had been drooling.

For almost a year, he kept the family together and paid a weekly visit to Vanessa. It seemed she had given up on life. He got no response from her no matter what he said or did. In the beginning, she begged him to take her home. She sobbed and promised not to drink anything if she could only come home. The Psychiatrists at the Center decided she had a form of depression and needed further treatment.

Now, nearly a year to the day, since she had been admitted to the Center, Daddy Bug sat with her in the sunroom. He was getting impatient.

"Honey, you've just got to snap out of it. I can take no more of this. The kids miss you and Lydia Anne's got her hands full trying to take care of Juggie, Tessa, and her own Junior. And then, there's the house needs looking after."

Vanessa looked at him vacantly and then stared out the window behind him. She had disconnected from the world.

"Vanessa, I ain't about to keep coming here to visit you if you don't try to listen to the Doctors and get better. You just ain't trying and you better start because we've all been going through a tough time."

She hung her head and looked at a shredded tissue she held in her hand. Then, she got up and walked slowly down the hallway to her room.

"Honey, I'm warning you. Next time I come back here, I want to see a smile on that face and I want you to talk to me. Don't you care about anything? Don't you miss the kids?" he shouted.

Vanessa quietly closed the door to her room as Daddy Bug started after her. There were no locks on the door, so she crawled under her bed and lay facing the wall, her raven hair covering her face. Suddenly, Daddy Bug burst in, followed by a floor nurse.

"Mrs. Garland, you must come out of there," she said as she got down on her hands and knees and stroked Vanessa's shoulder.

"Honey, come on out and stop this foolishness. Here nurse, let me get her." Daddy Bug stooped down, grabbed one of Vanessa's hands and pulled her unresisting body to him.

"You'll have to leave now, Mr. Garland," the nurse said. "Mrs. Garland needs her medicine and then she must rest."

Daddy Bug surrendered Vanessa to the nurse's supporting arms and looked at the blank eyes of his beautiful wife. He turned slowly and left the room, shoulders sagging as if he carried the heavy burden of the world's troubles upon them.

He drove from the manicured grounds of the Center with one thought in his mind. He knew that unless something could snap his wife out of the stupor she was in, she would be lost to him and the kids forever. That something would have to be found quickly, as it seemed to him that she was more withdrawn every time he came to see her.

The Doctors told him that a trauma, physical or emotional may have pushed her over the edge. Her sickness was hidden by the alcohol which acted as a tranquilizer. When they removed the alcohol, the doctors were able to properly diagnose her and start her treatment.

But she wasn't getting better, he thought, as he drove along the tree lined highway toward Lake Chastain. All the medicine and therapy were only making her worse.

The Doctors told him that they weren't sure, but they thought her illness was genetic in nature. Many times it did not surface until something tragic happened. Daddy Bug was sure that it was the almost certain loss of her brother in Vietnam that caused the trauma.

He remembered when she had heard that all the P.O.W.s had been released. He knew that was the shock that could trigger the sickness that would change his Vanessa to that hollow shell he had just left behind in the hospital.

The sun was setting by the time he pulled the car next to his house. He saw that the lights were on in Lydia and Jimmie's house and walked toward it.

Juggie and Tessa were playing with Junior on the swing that he had hung from a big oak tree. He watched them as he approached and thought of their loneliness.

They had not seen their mother for over a year. He wouldn't let them see her in her mental state and they cried for her for the first few months. Now, he knew they carried a silent grief within them, but they no longer cried.

Little Junior was eleven; Juggie was almost fourteen; and Tessa was twelve years old. How they had grown, he thought. What would they do if their mother did not get better?

His son, daughter, and nephew all saw him coming toward the house at the same time and ran to meet him. "Hi, Daddy Bug," they cried in unison.

"How's Momma, Daddy Bug?" Juggie said, taking his father's hand and walking by his side toward the house.

"She ain't doing so good, Son," he replied. "I've got to make something happen soon so she can get better and come on home, but I don't know how."

They entered Jimmie and Lydia Anne's small house, and heard Lydia Anne call to them from the back that supper was on the table. At that moment, the phone rang.

Jimmie went to answer it and Daddy Bug could hear his brother-in-law's excited voice, "You can't mean it! I can't believe it! Yeah, he's here right now. Just hang on a minute."

Daddy Bug saw Jimmie motion for him to get the receiver. He put the receiver to his ear and heard the voice of his mother-in-law say, "Daddy Bug, we just heard from the U. S. Army that Stan may still be alive in North Vietnam. There's this man who specializes in finding M.I.A.s and P.O.W.s and he thinks he's got a lead on where Stan could be."

"Who is this guy and how can he know anything?" Daddy Bug spoke softly.

"He's an Asian who's working undercover for the Army. He said he's got inside information about the Viet Cong and he knows where they're keeping some of the prisoners. It's in a remote region in North Vietnam. He said a lot of the prisoners have been brainwashed to want to stay and help reunite and rebuild Vietnam and Stan might be with them."

"Don't tell Vanessa anything about this. I don't want to get her hopes up if Stan doesn't want to come home. For all we know, this guy could be wrong and Stan could be dead."

"I thought it might help her if she could have some hope that Stan might be alive. Maybe it would help her to come out of her madness."

"Like I said, don't you say anything to her. I need to think about this some more. I'll talk to the doctors and see what they have to say," Daddy Bug said, and hung up the receiver without a goodbye.

He went to sit at the table with the rest of the family. His mind was racing with frustration at the new information. If this Asian guy really had a line in with the Viet Cong, he would be able to get more information soon. If he didn't, he was just blowing smoke and trying to get attention. More than likely, the Army was paying him some big bucks and he would try to make that last as long as he could. In any case, it was too soon to say anything to Vanessa.

"Daddy Bug, is the news good? Is Stan coming home?" Lydia Anne rousted him from his thoughts.

"I don't rightly know what's going on, Lydia Anne . I'm not sure if this dog's gonna hunt or not. It all sounds too iffy to me and it's sure not something I'll run to Vanessa with.

"I don't think she could take another shock or trauma. You know what I mean? Getting her hopes all up and then nothing comes out right and we find out Stan ain't alive. Let's put it on ice until we know more."

"Lydia Anne , let's eat and let Daddy Bug quit worrying about everything. Kids, eat up so Daddy Bug can get some rest. He looks plumb tired out," Jimmie said.

"Thanks, Jimmie, I sure am tired. It's almost more than I can stand to see Vanessa like she is. I think I'll call the doctors tomorrow and see if they can start giving her those shock treatments. They've been wanting to do it for months and I said no. Now, I think it might be the only thing that can help her. Nothing else is working."

The family ate the rest of the meal in silence. Bug knew he was not alone in his worry. Each of them had their own thoughts. Each of them worried about Vanessa and hoped that the call from the Army might soon develop into the homecoming of PFC. Stanley Henderson, United States Army, P.O.W./M.I.A.

Daddy Bug Garland cried before he went to sleep that night. If only Stanley could come home, maybe his Vanessa would get better. His bed felt especially empty as he lay and watched the foggy mist rise and envelop the moon-drenched mountain near his boyhood home.

# 19

Daddy Bug prospered in his business for many years. Even during the three years after the Federal Government set up the Bureau of Alcohol, Tobacco and Firearms Bureau in 1972, he had not been bothered by their agents. His good friend, Sheriff Halbert, kept him informed of the State agents' whereabouts, and all his distributors were loyal and trustworthy.

He should have been happy as a pig in mud, as the mountain folk liked to say. He wasn't. His Vanessa was suffering and fearful of the shock treatments at the hospital.

It had been six months since they started to administer the treatments, and the most that could be said was that she was showing some emotion. That emotion was terror when it was her scheduled time for "shock therapy."

She cried and screamed and threw herself on the floor when they came to get her to strap her to the table. She returned to her room silent and withdrawn, curled into the fetus

120

position on her bed, and would stay that way until they came to get her for meals.

On one such occasion, Daddy Bug was visiting when they came to get her. He held her in his strong arms to stop her terrible thrashing, murmuring over and over that it would be all right.

He looked at the orderlies who stood patiently waiting. "Does she act this way every time you come to get her?"

"Yes, sir. Most of the time it's a lot worse. We have to put the strait jacket on her to control her," said the older of the two.

"Well, I want to talk to the Doctor right now. Can you go get him?" Daddy Bug continued to hold the now-trembling Vanessa tightly in his arms.

"Yes sir. Do you want us to take her for treatment now?"

"No, I'm keeping her here. Now go get that Doc," Daddy Bug said in his no-nonsense voice. "And both of you get out!"

Both men rushed out the door at the same time bumping into each other on the way. They knew they should not contradict this man with the steely voice and the bulging eyes. Although he appeared younger than they, he looked much stronger and menacing.

Within five minutes, Dr. Graben came into the room. "Look here, what do you think you're doing? Mrs. Garland is supposed to have electro-therapy and we're behind schedule. Now, what is the meaning of this?"

"Doc," Daddy Bug began slowly, "You've been shooting electricity into my wife's brain for six months now and it looks to me like she's getting worse. What else can you do that won't scare her so bad?"

"Mr. Garland, we're using all the latest recommended techniques and medicines for your wife's condition. We've even called in specialists to examine your wife and give their opinions. Everyone agrees that we're doing everything possible for her."

"Well, it's not enough, is it? Have the nurse get her things together. I'm taking her out of here. She's going home where at least she can see her kids in familiar surroundings - in her own house."

The Doctor appeared disturbed by this announcement. "She's a threat to herself and others. We're sure she is capable of hurting herself or maybe even her children. If you dismiss her, we can't be responsible."

"Don't nobody have to be responsible for my wife except me. I just thought you could help her, but I see now that you can't. Just get her things packed up." Then, Daddy Bug turned to Vanessa and said, "I'm taking you home, honey. Get some clothes on and we'll go."

Vanessa looked at him intently. Slowly, the dullness in her eyes lifted and tears ran down her cheeks. She smiled faintly and sagged to the bed. Then, she gathered her slacks and blouse and went into the bathroom.

"I wish you would reconsider. We feel we're close to a breakthrough with Mrs. Garland. We'll stop the electro-therapy if you want. We'll treat her with group therapy and the medicines."

"Doctor, the only treatment she's going to get is a whole lot of love and attention at her home. My family and I will take care of her. She ain't going to hurt anybody. She's never killed a fly in her life. I can't stand to see her this way anymore."

"I don't think you understand her illness, Mr. Garland. She's a much different person than you think. She needs therapy in a professional environment in order to get better."

At that moment, Vanessa, now dressed, came out of the bathroom and looked at Daddy Bug. "I'm ready to go home now," she said.

This was the first complete, logical sentence she had spoken since she had started the shock therapy. The first in six months.

Daddy Bug and the Doctor looked at her in surprise. She had washed her face and combed her hair. Her eyes were bright and she smiled at them.

"Well, look here at my pretty girl." Daddy Bug stepped forward to take her hand.

The Doctor, seeing the change in Vanessa's appearance, said in his most authoritive manner, "You'll have to sign some papers at the front desk. I'll sign her release now and then you can take her." He turned and stalked out.

The nurse completed the packing for Vanessa and handed the suitcase to Daddy Bug. She turned to Vanessa and put her arms around her waist.

Holding her cheek to Vanessa's, she whispered, "We all love you Vanessa. Remember that if you ever want to come back, we're here for you. Take care of yourself."

Vanessa looked directly into the nurse's eyes as she said, "I thank you, but if I ever have to come back, it won't be because I want to. Good-bye. You can come to my house and see me if you want."

The nurse merely smiled, and giving Vanessa one final pat on the shoulder left the room. Vanessa turned and looked at the room for the last time before taking Daddy Bug's arm and pulling him out of the room.

Daddy Bug signed the papers at the front desk and, hand in hand, Mr. and Mrs Billy Unger Garland walked out the front door, got in their car and started home. Daddy Bug held her hand, but said little, during the drive.

His mind was in a quandary as he drove. He would have to arrange for someone to be with her all the time. Lydia Anne was busy with her job at the drug store and taking care of Jimmie and Junior. Juggie and Tessa were busy with all their school functions, both day and night.

Both of them were active teenagers and were highly popular in Lake Chastain High School. They became staunchly independent after Vanessa was admitted to the hospital and soon arranged rides to and from their numerous school activities.

The city school bus now came up the mountain to pick them up for regular school. It appeared that Sheriff Halbert did not like it that Sue had to drive Precious to school every day when she was in high school and made a few phone calls.

Somehow, he would find someone to care for Vanessa, Daddy Bug decided as he pulled in the driveway to his house. It was just good to have her home with him.

He opened the car door for Vanessa and noticed Mr. and Mrs. Henderson's car parked in Lydia Anne and Jimmie Haywood's driveway.

"Honey, you're parents are over at Lydia Anne's Shall we go over and see them before we get you unpacked?"

Vanessa said nothing but turned toward her sister-in-law's house and started forward. By the time she reached the front porch, she was almost running.

Daddy Bug stepped ahead and opened the door for her. She went into the living room and let out a shriek. Daddy Bug rushed in behind her and looked around the room.

Mr. & Mrs. Henderson, Lydia Anne and Jimmie sat on the sofa. Stretched out in the over-stuffed chair, Stanley Henderson smoked a cigarette and grinned. "Hello little sister," he said. Stanley Henderson was thin and pallid, but otherwise in good condition.

After the initial hellos were over, he spent the evening recounting the horror of his years as a P.O.W. in North Vietnam. As frightening as it was, he said he would go through it again for his country.

Listening to Stanley, Bug knew his homecoming was the answer to his prayers and hopes. He watched Vanessa who sat by Stanley's chair, huddled on the floor with her arms encircling her legs. She said little, but stared at him as he talked. It was if she were seeing a ghost, so intently did she concentrate on his features.

Finally, at midnight, Mr. and Mrs. Henderson said good-by. The children had long since gone to bed, Juggie and Tessie begging to spend the night with Junior. Vanessa, Stan and Daddy Bug bid goodnight to Lydia Anne and Jimmie Haywood and made their way to their house next door.

Wide awake with the excitement of Stan's return, Daddy Bug made coffee and the trio settled around the kitchen table to reminisce.

Stan asked, "Wha"s been going on around here since I've been gone?"

Vanessa looked quickly at Daddy Bug and very slightly shook her head. Then, she looked at the floor.

""Well, Stan," Daddy Bug said, "the business is going as good as can be expected. We haven't had any trouble with the revenuers. All the distributors are doing their jobs and things are going fine."

"I figure to come back in with you if you'll have me, Daddy Bug. I don't feel strong enough to get a job doing any physical work yet. Maybe I can do your collections for you."

"I've got Jimmie, Lydia Anne's husband, helping me with that Stan, but you can help me with the book work. I'm buying sugar in bulk direct and I need someone to go pick it up and keep a tally on it. It might cause suspicion if anyone saw the manufacturer's truck pull up to the house. They can load it for you there and Jimmie and I can unload it when you get it here."

"I'll do anything you want me to, you know that. Just tell me what it is and I'll do it. Little Sister, what have you been doing while I've been gone?"

Vanessa looked down at her coffee cup and said, ""Not much, Stanley. I'm keeping busy." Then changing the subject, "We were sure scared that you were dead all these years. It's good to have you home."

Daddy Bug knew that Vanessa did not want Stanley to know about her stay at the hospital. He decided not to tell him about it until a later day, with the hope that Vanessa's mother and father had not said anything to him about it. Instead, he broke in, "Well, it's getting late so we better hit the hay. Big day tomorrow."

Vanessa jumped to her feet and started to clear the cups away. "You can sleep in Juggie's room, Stanley. I'll change the sheets right away." She ran from the room.

"What's the matter with Vanessa, Daddy Bug? She's acting awful funny. Lost a lot of weight, too" Stanley said.

"I'll tell you more about it tomorrow, Stan. Fact is, she doesn't want you to know she's been sick. Still is. But let's wait until tomorrow and I'll tell you."

"I knew something was wrong the minute I saw her. She doesn't look like the sister I left when I went to the Army."

"I'll get you up around eight. You can sleep in," Daddy Bug said and he went to his bedroom.

Vanessa came into the bedroom and started to undress for bed. She had not had any medicine for eight hours and she was starting to be shaky and tremulous. Could she make it through the night without her pills, he wondered. "Come on to bed," Daddy Bug spoke from the darkness. "It's been a long night and we need to get some sleep. I have to get up in about four hours."

"Yes, Daddy Bug," she said crawling in beside him.

He wrapped her in his arms and cradled her head on his shoulder. She was shivering slightly and he held her tighter, pulling the blankets around her shoulders.

"What's the matter, honey? Are you cold?"

"I'm just wishing I had some medicine. I get too nervous without it."

"Well, I'll call Doc Parsons tomorrow and we'll get you some. Now, just go to sleep."

He could feel her body go limp while he rubbed her back. Soon he heard her even-paced breathing. She was asleep for now, but what would he do with her tomorrow, and the day after that? Who could he get to keep an eye on her? She had to be watched all the time.

He lay awake and worried. Then, a solution came to his mind. Stanley Henderson would stay with them. Stanley could watch Vanessa during the times when he couldn't. With that problem solved, he fell into a dreamless sleep.

# 20

Daddy Bug was as happy as could be. Vanessa progressed rapidly in regaining her sweet, happy personality. She seemed to thrive on the love and affection showered upon her by her family. He noticed that she especially enjoyed being around her brother Stanley, following him around the house as if she had to make sure he was still alive.

Stanley, too, gradually gained back his strength and enjoyed taking walks in the cool mountain air. During those times, Daddy Bug and Vanessa would accompany him, all the while directing their conversation to the activities and occurrences of the years since Stanley's disappearance.

Vanessa always bowed her head in shame when they spoke of her addiction and subsequent illness. She smiled gratefully when they praised her for her recovery.

One cloudy day, they walked to check the progress of the distilleries, enrapt in their own thoughts. They suddenly saw a figure dart through the bushes to their left.

Daddy Bug shouted, "Stan, someone's been messing around the stills. Let's get him."

He took off in pursuit, with Stan following closely behind. As they neared the figure, Daddy Bug recognized his nephew, Junior.

"What are you doing here?" He yelled. He grabbed Junior by the back of his shirt and spun him around.

"I just wanted to see the stills. Some of my friends said you were a bootlegger and I wanted to see where you made the whiskey."

"You know this is off limits back here, Junior. I told you never to come back here. Besides, who told you I was a bootlegger?"

"Precious Halbert told Tessa you were and she told some other people, too. That's how my friends found out."

"Well, I guess I'd better have a little talk with the Sheriff's daughter. She's got no business spreading rumors about me or anyone else. Now get back to the house and stay there. I'll tend to you when I get back."

Junior ran back along the path to his house. Vanessa, Stanley and Daddy Bug watched his sturdy figure retreat. He loped along like a frightened, wounded animal.

He had just turned thirteen years old and he was already approaching six feet tall. Active in sports, his muscular body belied his young age.

Daddy Bug, and Jimmie tried their best to teach him the virtues of a Spartan lifestyle but he rejected their advice; leaning instead to the clowning and teasing manners of the other boys his age. Life, for him, was full of temptations and curiosity, some of which took him into situations that were risky and dangerous.

Jimmie came to Daddy Bug on numerous occasions seeking his counsel on what he should do to correct Junior's ways. Daddy Bug knew his young nephew would be a problem one day if he didn't do something to put him on the right path.

As Stanley, Vanessa and Daddy Bug walked slowly back to the house, Daddy Bug broke the silence.

"I'm gonna have to do something about that boy. He's getting completely out of hand. If I don't he's gonna end up a no-good."

"What if we let him start helping in the business - like after school and on Saturday?" Stanley said.

Vanessa looked at her brother and said, "Lord knows, he's big enough and strong enough to do some of the heavy lifting."

They approached the back door of the cabin, and Daddy Bug opened the door and went inside. Then turning to face the other two, he said, "Go next door and tell him I want to see him out on the front porch in exactly ten minutes. Don't say anything to him about this. I'll just have to think about it."

Daddy Bug settled into the rocking chair on the front porch and looked out over the mountain. The green of the fir trees contrasted sharply with the bare limbs of the hardwoods, making a panorama of green and brown. Why couldn't everything work as simple as Mother Nature's miracles, he thought?

He felt the chill in the air. Winter was upon them, which meant the cold damp rains, fog and the occasional ice storm would soon be the norm - rather than the exception. He was not looking forward to it.

Then his thoughts turned to Jimmie Haywood, Jr. There was something different about Junior, but he just couldn't figure out what it was. He was a clean-cut kid, but there was a wildness in him that Daddy Bug had to strip out.

As if he had read Daddy Bug's thoughts, Junior came walking up the porch steps and said, "I'm sorry I went down there. I promise I'll never do it again."

Daddy Bug looked up at the handsome face with the dimple in its chin and managed a smile. "Boy, you always could charm Daddy Bug, but I'm gonna hold you to that promise unless I decide differently. Now, boy, I want you to sit down on those steps. We've got some talking to do."

"Sure thing, Daddy Bug. What did you want to tell me?"

"I want you to start settling down and get a little bit serious about life. When I was your age, I was helping my Daddy all the time.

Now, what you saw today was what we call the family business. We don't cotton to anyone calling us bootleggers. There's nothing wrong in what we do. There's a need for it. We don't hurt anybody and it's how we make our living; how we pay for all your food and clothes, plus the spending money we give you."

"Yeah, but my friends say it's against the law."

"It may be against some laws, but it's not against mountain law. Those Federal and State boys just want to regulate it so they can tax it. I don't want you to ever discuss it again with anybody but me."

"But what if someone turns you in? What would happen to all of us."

"Nobody that knows me will turn us in. That's why I told you not to talk about it. If your friends say anything to you, just tell them to mind their own business or Daddy Bug will come and have a prayer meeting with their parents."

"Why would you have a prayer meeting with their parents."

"So they can pray their kids will keep their mouths shut and pray I don't shut off their supply. This is a dry county and most people don't want to drive to Atlanta or Birmingham to get what they can get right here - and a lot cheaper."

"I'll tell them what you said, Daddy Bug. Is that all you wanted to talk to me about?"

"No, I want you to drive on over to Sheriff Halbert's house with me. I need to have a talk with Precious and she's home from medical school for the holiday. She's smart as a whip, but she's got a mouth on her that won't quit."

"Why do I have to go with you, Daddy Bug?"

"Because I want you to start helping in the business and you have to learn how to handle people. Better sooner than later. Maybe you can pick up a few pointers by listening to how I handle the situation."

Daddy Bug poked his head in the front door of the cabin and yelled to no one in particular that he would be back later and that Junior was going with him. Then the two, uncle and nephew, climbed into the pickup truck and headed to Stop Gap Road.

As they drove along, Daddy Bug was deep in thought. He glanced at the passenger side of the car and noticed the clean profile of his nephew. He would surely be a handsome man when he grew up.

"Junior, there are few things in life more important than your family. I don't just mean your Momma and Daddy. I mean all your blood kin. Don't ever talk about them to anybody else and don't ever allow anybody else to talk about them to you, unless they want to say something good."

"You mean like when my friends called you a bootlegger?"

"Yes. You should have whooped them good, right there and then."

"But Daddy Bug, there were two of them and only one of me."

"Junior, you know that when it's two against one, you have to get an equalizer. By that, I mean you need to pick up a stick or go get an ax handle and use it."

"I just don't think I could hit anybody with an ax handle. I don't even like to fight much."

We'll just have to change his mind about that, thought Daddy Bug as he turned onto the circular drive in front of Sheriff Mark and Sue Halbert's house. Can't have him growing up a sissy.

Sue Halbert answered the door to his knock. Middle age was kind to her. Her figure was still trim and her face bore only the finest lines around her eyes.

"Hi there, Daddy Bug - and you too Junior. Come on in. Mark's not here but I can call him to come on home if you want."

"I'm not here to talk to Mark, Sue. I want to have a word with Precious if you don't mind."

"I don't mind, Daddy Bug, but why on earth would you want to talk to Precious?"

"Well, Sue, it seems Precious has been running her mouth about my operation and now some of Junior's friends are talking, and telling him I'm a bootlegger." Daddy Bug spoke in his most casual voice. "I can't have a lot of talk getting out to strangers. I'm sure you can understand that."

"Are you sure it was Precious? She's upstairs right now. I'll call her down." Sue stood at the foot of the staircase and yelled, "Precious, get your little hiney down here, right now."

Precious peered over the upper bannister and saw her mother, Daddy Bug and Junior staring up at her. Her beauty defied description. Daddy Bug assumed that she was accustomed to men staring at her, so he tried to make his expression forbidding and stern. The look mirrored in Daddy Bug's eyes would let her know he was upset with her.

"Hey there, Daddy Bug. Hey, little Junior. What's going on?" She called down the stairs.

"Precious, Daddy Bug wants to talk to you. Come on down to the kitchen," Sue said. "Come on, Daddy Bug. I'll make some coffee for us. Junior can have a soda."

Daddy Bug and Junior settled around the kitchen table and watched Sue scurrying around making coffee. Precious joined them within minutes.

"Well, what do y'all have to talk to me about?"

"Precious, it's real hard for me to call you on this, but I understand you told Tessa and a few other people I was a bootlegger. Now, I'm not a bootlegger and you know it. I provide a service for the good people and they all appreciate it. What do you have to say for yourself?"

"I don't have to defend myself to you Daddy Bug," she said with eyes blazing. "It's a free country and if I did say you were a bootlegger - which I'm not admitting I did - you couldn't stop me."

"You watch your mouth, Precious," Sue yelled. "You show some respect for Daddy Bug. I won't have you smarting off to him."

"Momma, in order to get respect, you have to show some. He can't just come in here and accuse me of something."

Daddy Bug looked at Precious and slowly rose to his feet. "Sue, you and Mark need to do some restructuring of this girl's thinking. She seems to be taking on some high-falutin' ideas at that fancy college. I'll be back to talk to you and Mark after the holidays."

"We'll make her understand about her mouth before she goes back to school. Don't you worry none about it, Daddy Bug."

"In the meantime, Precious, listen to me good. I'd better not hear that you talked about my business with anybody else. Your mom and dad stand just as much to lose as I do. And if they do lose, then it stands to reason that you'd lose and wouldn't be able to finish that wonderful education of yours."

Precious was on her feet, hands on hips, by the time Daddy Bug had finished speaking. She jerked her head around and looked at her mother

"Momma, what is he talking about?"

"Just listen to him, Precious. Daddy and I will talk to you about it later." Then turning to Daddy Bug and Junior standing by the already open front door, Sue said, "We'll take care of everything. Don't worry."

Junior and Daddy Bug waved at Sue, who watched them as they drove away. Junior' brows were pinched together in a questioning look and he glanced at Daddy Bug who stared straight ahead and whistled.

"I've just got to know what you meant back there. You said Sue and Mark would lose if you lost, and if they lost, Precious would lose. What did you mean, Daddy Bug?"

"I meant that Mark is my silent partner and if I was put out of business and went to jail, then he would go right with me."

"What do you mean, silent partner?"

"I mean I pay him to be silent and keep everybody else silent about my business. If he didn't get the money he gets from me, he couldn't send Precious to college. If he couldn't send Precious to college, she couldn't become a fancy doctor like she wants."

Out of the corner of his eye, Daddy Bug saw Junior leaning his head against the back of the seat. He smiled to himself, knowing full well that Junior was thinking about what he had just heard. He hoped this would make Junior understand the man he called Daddy Bug.

Daddy Bug was kind to most people in return, but he displayed the side of him today that was ominous. He became a dude that you didn't mess around with.

The mountain man did the thing he was supposed to do. Teach a member of his family about life. He knew that Junior had learned more about life and people in four hours in his company than the boy had learned in all of his previous years, a four-hour period he likely wouldn't forget. His own daddy had taught him the same way.

# 21

Daddy Bug continued to teach him. Jimmie Haywood, Jr. or as everyone called him simply "Junior" quickly learned the business. He got acquainted with all of Daddy Bug's distributors and knew the recipe by heart.

People in town started to refer to him as Daddy Bug's shadow. He spent every spare minute under his Uncle's guidance.

Daddy Bug was happy at the turn of events. Juggie had been snowed under with high school and school activities for the past few years and lost interest in anything related to the business. He also informed Daddy Bug that he intended to go off to college when he graduated and he lost no time enrolling at the University of Alabama after graduation. Daddy Bug missed Juggie but he was happy he was doing well at college.

Since Tessa had never helped him (he didn't believe in involving women folk), he knew his timing was right when he'd explained the nature of things to Junior two years ago. He'd taken to it like a duck to water.

Stan was not much help to him anymore. He suffered from nightmares about his tour in Vietnam and the torture he received at the hands of the Viet Cong. Vanessa and Daddy Bug heard his screams in the night and rushed into the bedroom to find him covered with sweat, staring straight ahead. After Vanessa soothed and quieted him, they would hear him pacing back and forth in the parlor.

So, it was with pride that Daddy Bug introduced his nephew to his distributors. The distributors treated Junior with the same respect that they showed for Daddy Bug - and the same deference.

Junior watched him closely and tried to emulate his walk and mannerisms. He even practiced getting red in the face and glaring with his eyes. Staring in the mirror, he tried to imagine that someone had wronged him. The sweet expression of his face melted away and in its place, an image of a dark-haired, irate Daddy Bug appeared.

At sixteen, he was as tall as his Uncle, but was bulkier than any of the men in his family. He worked out at the school gym and was active in football. He knew he was considered a jock. The girls looked at him with envy when he took to the field. The Announcer called his name as he ran to the fifty yard line; the cheerleaders did their special back-flip and threw their pompoms in the air.

His jet-black hair glistened in the sun. He knew how to toss it a certain way so he would appear masculine to everyone, yet connote a certain air of sincerity to the audience. He was a born-again politician.

None of this was lost on Daddy Bug. He watched every

game with fatherly pride, even though this was his nephew. His own son, Juggie, was a victim of the system. Junior was living again in him. Daddy Bug could mold him and shape him to be the man that he was - and the man that his own Daddy was - a true mountain man.

Daddy Bug figured that Jimmie Haywood, Sr. was a good person, but he was weak. He didn't have the fiber in his bones to be the strong person that Daddy Bug was. But, Junior inherited the grit of Jake Unger Garland and Billy Unger Garland. Thank God, some of it passed through the blood line. Lydia Anne was the link. She carried her father, Jake's, good blood to her own son.

It was a cold, spring, Friday night and Daddy Bug had just attended one of Junior's football games. It was the night that Junior proved he was a Garland. The team was competing in the Dixon County football finals. Junior was the split end. He caught the pass and was going for a touchdown. It was the winning touchdown with two seconds to go in the game. A Calumet City defensive end tried to tackle him and he elbowed him in the mouth, turned and said "Say amen, brother" and made the touchdown. The crowd went wild.

On the way home from the game, Daddy Bug, who was driving him home in the pickup, said, "You did right well out there son. What made you give it to him in the teeth?"

Junior smiled and said, "Daddy Bug, I've been watching you. You never take anything from anybody and I won't either. I learned from you that you have to set your own pace in life. And, I also learned from you that you have to teach people a lesson, one time - and make it stick. That guy will hesitate before he tries to tackle me again. He won't forget that elbow I put in his teeth and he'll spread the word."

"You're a good boy, Junior. You learn quick and you learn good. Now, I want you to go with me on a run tomorrow night. There's a distributor that did me a disservice a couple of years ago. I want you to help me to teach him a lesson - and make it stick."

"Whatever you want, Daddy Bug. I've got to get back relatively early though, because I've started to go to the Presbyterian Church with my girl. It was a promise I made her when we decided to go steady and I need to get to bed early."

"You're only sixteen years old. Who is this girl and why the Presbyterian Church?"

"She's the prettiest girl you every saw. She goes to that church and that's the only way her parents would let us go steady. I have to go with them on Sunday. Don't worry none. I haven't mentioned the business."

"Who is she?"

"Her name is Mona Lisa Skruggs. Her father is the preacher of the Presbyterian Church, the Reverend Abraham Skruggs, and she's the head cheerleader. You saw her tonight."

"Good God in Heaven. You picked a preacher's daughter to date steady?"

"All you have to do is look at her and you can tell what I see in her. She's real sweet and totally gorgeous. Plus, all the guys are trying to date her and she won't have no one but me."

Daddy Bug grimaced with displeasure. "Son, sooner or later, her Daddy is going to say something to her about the business and then she'll try to persuade you that it's wrong to take part in it."

"Daddy Bug, ain't no girl, no where, will ever tell me what to do. I won't let her pussy-whip me if that's what you're saying."

"That's exactly what I'm saying. Her Daddy is not one of my best customers, but he's good for a few dollars a year. We just keep it a big secret and I'm sure his wife and daughter don't know about it."

"I'll just tell her not to try to run my life if she says anything."

"Famous last words. She's already getting you to go to her church. You never went to church before, except for funerals and weddings. Next, you'll want your daddy to buy you a suit."

"I swear, Daddy Bug, right here and now, I won't let her persuade me to quit working with you. Now, tell me, where are we headed tomorrow night?"

"I'll tell you all about it tomorrow on the way to his house. In the meantime, never change the subject on me. When I want the subject changed, I'll change it."

"Sure thing, Daddy Bug." The tone of Junior's voice told Daddy Bug that he knew better than to cross him. "I didn't mean to change the subject. I was just curious about tomorrow night because you trust me enough to take me along."

"I'll get to that soon enough. Right now, I want to talk a little more about that Mona Lisa Skruggs girl before we get home. Does your Daddy and Momma know you're going steady with her?"

"No, they just think I'm going out with the guys when they let me take the car. You're the only one I've told in the family."

"Good, keep it that way for now. I want you to invite her over for supper one of these days. Then we can all meet her at once. Are you pretty hooked on her, then?"

"Yes, sir."

Daddy Bug turned off Stop Gap road onto the road to his house. He braked the car in the driveway and shut off the ignition key.

Turning to Junior, he said, "I'm going to tell you this just once and then I won't mention it again. I'm going to give you a sermon that you need to take to heart.

"Always remember that you have a family and the family should be the most important thing in the world to you. They're the only ones you can trust to love you no matter what happens. Don't ever let anybody turn you against the blood family you've got now."

Junior looked at Daddy Bug. "Why would I ever do that, sir?"

"Because I know what a pretty girl can do to a man. He gets all his priorities wrong when his head's not on right. When the love bug bites you, you don't know where to scratch sometimes, and you end up scratching somebody else. There are certain women that give off this odor or attraction. It's like a bitch dog in heat. Men can't resist it. The bitch dog won't take on all comers, but she takes for keeps the one that can provide for her and feed her; the one that she sees the best in and that she can control. She hates all other females and tries to get rid of anyone connected with that man she's chosen.

"She wants to control and dominate him and he smells that smell and can't say no. He gives up his friends and family and she's still not satisfied. She's a cannibal and wants to eat him up - alive.

"I met a lot of females like that and I steered clear because my Pa told me about them. That's why I'm telling you now and that's why I married a clean, honest woman like your Aunt Vanessa. She has that one weakness, but she's loyal and honest and true. She opens her heart to everyone. She's one in a million and I hope you find someone just like her to marry and to be the mother of your children. Anything less would be a scab on you and all of your family, including me.

"Mark what I tell you here and now. Be true to your blood family and yourself. And with that, this little prayer meeting is over. Let's get on in the house. I'm tired to the bone."

# 22

On Saturday night, Junior and Daddy Bug went to visit the distributor who had done Daddy Bug wrong a couple of years back. Seems he had held some money back, by explaining that one of his customers couldn't pay. Daddy Bug would often overlook someone paying if he was having hard times. People needed the recipe more than anything during hard times.

Daddy Bug told him that two years later, he met the customer in the cafe in town and asked him how he was getting on with his business. The customer replied, "Never better."

Daddy Bug asked him how his business had gone two years ago. His reply was, "Never better."

On Saturday night, Junior watched as Daddy Bug took the distributor by the neck and forced him to cough up the fifty dollars he had shorted him two years ago. Daddy Bug's first words to the distributor were, "I met Brian Reed in town the other day. He says his business has never been better -

142

and that goes for two years ago, too. Where's my $50.00?"

The distributor reached into his pocket, struggling for breath with Daddy Bug's grip around his throat, and handed him fifty dollars in cash.

Daddy Bug's last words to the distributor were, "If I ever hear of you trying to cheat me again, I won't be so polite as to pay you a personal call to collect. You just won't know when or where something could happen to you. Have you got that straight? No advance warnings. Nothing."

Junior watched in awe as Daddy Bug stuffed the money in his pocket, released the scarlet-faced distributor and turned to go back to his pickup.

"Come on Junior, let's get back to our families. You don't need to be exposed to any more of this tonight."

The experience of that night and the night at Precious Halbert's house stuck in Junior's mind as he proceeded through high school.

The night Mona Lisa Skruggs came to supper at Daddy Bug and Vanessa's, she was silent except for one-word answers to their polite questions. She stared at the table and the floor and after supper called Junior outside for a walk. She hadn't bothered to offer help to prepare supper or offer to help clean up afterward.

She stood up after the meal, looked at Junior and said, "Let's go for a walk in the moonlight."

Daddy Bug noticed that Junior offered no resistance as they left the house and walked down the mountainside. He knew that it would take all of Junior's will power to overcome the strong egocentric selfishness of the Preacher's daughter. That girl is totally self-absorbed, he thought. Would Junior listen to his natural good sense that Daddy Bug had helped him attain, or would he let his out-of-control hormones rule the roost?

To Daddy Bug's mind, Mona Lisa Skruggs was rather plain looking and not too intelligent, but he could tell she had a hunter's instinct for what she wanted. To that end, she would use her allure to make all of the animal instincts in Junior come alive and burst to the surface.

Daddy Bug knew that she wanted Junior because he was a handsome, intelligent young man who had a future. She was smart enough to know he would go some place, and be able to provide for her in a top-notch way. He would make a good meal ticket for her.

He imagined that she was jealous of the way Junior and his family lived and how close they all were. It wasn't that they were rich. It was just that the Preacher's family lived in relative poverty, while Daddy Bug's clan lived in comfort and needed nothing after all their years of hard work. They drove good cars and trucks, wore sensible but good clothing, and ate the best food that Lake Chastain and Huntsville had to offer.

Many of the preachers and ministers lived only on what they could get from tithes and offerings in church. Bug knew it couldn't be that much since most of their families were forced to live in practiced dignity with their mended and hand-me-down clothes and less than adequate food.

Daddy Bug suspected that Mona Lisa Skruggs looked down her nose at his family business, but he also allowed that she wanted to make sure that she had a way out of her poverty and hopelessness. To that end, she would try to ensnare Junior. He was not only handsome, but he would some day share Daddy Bug's good fortune.

After Mona Lisa and Junior left the house for their "walk in the moonlight," Daddy Bug sat at the table with Vanessa. He looked at his wife whose hair was liberally sprinkled with gray and thought how lucky he had been to get such a beautiful, gentle woman. She had gone through a lot with him, always with his interest at heart. Life had painted its portrait upon her face, but every gray hair and every line were precious to him.

She looked back at him and before he could say anything, she said, "I get the feeling you don't care much for Mona Lisa Skruggs, Daddy Bug."

The woman could read his mind. "What makes you think that, honey?"

"Well, you keep looking at her out of the corner of your eyes. And you gave Junior a funny look when he asked me if he could help clear the table, and she didn't offer to help with anything."

"There's something sneaky about her. She tries to act like she's too good for us, and so smart about subjects in school. I know for a fact that they live over there in a shack that I wouldn't have my dog live in. Terence, at the grocery store, said he doesn't know what they eat because they hardly ever buy any groceries. Plus, the principal at the high school told me the teachers just barely pass her because they don't want her in their classes next year."

Vanessa wiped and put away the last of the dishes. She poured a cup of coffee for each of them and said, "It sounds like you've been asking around about her. You don't think Junior is getting serious about her, do you?"

"I more than think he's getting serious about her. He came right out and told me he was going steady with her. He's started going to her father's church. She hen-pecks the hell out of him and he acts like an old coon dog that's just been fed a bone. He licks up to her like she's been sent from heaven. That boy doesn't have a backbone when she's around. It's downright sickening."

"Well, what do Lydia Anne and Jimmie have to say about the situation?"

"I haven't told them yet and neither has he. They don't even know we had her here for supper tonight. I deliberately waited until they had to be gone for the night before I had her here. I wanted to check her out before he told them so I could talk to him a little bit. Lydia Anne and Jimmie won't like her,

I'm sure. They're just plain, good folks and this girl puts on airs like she's the Queen of England."

"Well, whatever happens, we can't interfere in their business," Vanessa said..

"Honey, Junior is our business. I'm taking him in the business full-time when he gets out of high school. He's got a knack for getting along with everyone. He's sharp as a tack and I won't let no two-bit bitch in heat make him into a brainless idiot that can't say, 'I'm a man.'"

As the words "I'm a man" poured from the opened window, Junior and Mona Lisa opened the back door and entered the room. Something was obviously wrong. Junior looked sheepish and Vanessa looked disheveled. Her lipstick was completely gone, her hair was mussed, her bra strap hung on her upper arm. She looked down at the floor and said, "I need to go home now."

Junior looked down at the same floor and said, "I'm gonna drive Mona Lisa home if it's all right with you, Daddy Bug. Can I use your pickup truck? The folks are gone for the night and I don't have any other way to get her home."

"Son, you can use my pickup any time for a good reason, and I guess you've got as good a reason as any to use it now." Daddy Bug tossed the keys to him and the youngsters went out the door.

Daddy Bug smiled to himself and motioned for Vanessa to come to bed with him. "Come on, Vanessa, let's go to bed. It's no use to wait up for them. I think they have some talking to do and likely won't get home before dawn."

He was pleased with himself. He understood what Junior was going through. Junior had himself a preacher's daughter who didn't know how to say yes without saying no. He would talk with Junior about it when they made their rounds in the morning.

Vanessa stood to go to their bedroom with him and smiled at him. He guessed correctly that she had recognized the passion that had erupted between Junior and Mona Lisa on their moonlight walk - she had recognized it and missed it. She took his hand, smiled into his eyes and guided him into their bedroom.

Her dark eyes were shining when she led him gently to the bed. Never had he loved her so much as he now did. He felt like putty in her hands as she gently lay him on the hand-knitted coverlet. Her hands seemed invisible when they urged the shoes from his feet and removed his other garments.

She came to him with an urgency he had never known. It seemed that in an instant she was nude and towering above him with her curtain of hair cascading over his body. Surely, he was dreaming. She pressed herself against him and he felt her creaminess. He felt as if he were in a phantasmagoric revelry. Who was this person? What was she doing?

He decided to give in. He could not always be the leader. He could not always be on top.

She felt his surrender. Never had she felt more power within her body. She wanted him. He was not taking her. She was not just succumbing to his desires and needs. She was making herself and him happy, because she wanted him - and he was letting himself be taken - for once in his life.

Vanessa placed herself upon him and felt his thrust, tentative, then with a slow urgency that radiated to her innermost being. She moved gently at first, her body somehow swaying as if to the invisible beats from the drums played by her Cherokee ancestors of long ago.

Then, with an increasing passion, she moved to the quickening rhythm she heard inside her head. Her feelings rose to a storm within her and she thrust herself upon him, crying aloud when she could no longer bear the ecstasy she felt.

She lay upon him and felt the mutual throbbing of their bodies subside. She remembered the song that her grandfather taught her. The song of togetherness. The prayer to the distant gods of her people. She was at peace.

Daddy Bug felt as if he had never before known such love. What had come over his dear and faithful wife. He had loved her before, yet she had never shown the passion, the love, that he knew tonight.

He gave himself to her and she had taken him. He would never tell anyone about tonight. They would never believe it.

He had held her in his arms for a long time when he heard Junior come in the house. He heard the keys to his pickup land on the kitchen table and the kitchen door shut. Strange, he wasn't gone as long as Daddy Bug predicted. Tomorrow, he would talk to him about Mona Lisa Skruggs. Tonight, he just wanted to hold Vanessa and shut the world and all its troubles out.

# 23

As they made the morning rounds, Junior told Daddy Bug why he came back so soon from the trip to take Mona Lisa Skruggs home. It seems her Daddy was waiting up with the porch light on, and kept blinking it off and on as they sat in the pickup.

Preacher Skruggs finally opened the door as if he were coming outside to jerk her out of vehicle. Mona Lisa quickly straightened her clothes and hair, dabbed on some lipstick, got out and ran for the house. Junior laughed when he told Daddy Bug that he waved and shouted "goodnight" at Preacher Skruggs. Preacher Skruggs slammed the door shut without returning the greeting.

"Guess I've got some fence-mending to do," he said.

"You'll do no such thing, Son. It takes two to tango and he should be as mad at his daughter as he was at you. But if you're really worried, what you could do is go to church with his daughter, then when you shake hands with him after the service, you tell him what a fine sermon it was. He'll forget all about last night and you won't have to do any fence-mending."

"I guess that might work all right. I just hope Mona Lisa didn't get too much heck when she got in the house."

Daddy Bug thought for a while, then said, "Son, I may as well tell you the truth. I'm not too crazy about Mona Lisa. I've always told you the truth and I smell trouble if you continue to go steady with her. Your Momma and Daddy won't like her either. I'm sorry to say it like this, but I sure hope you don't want to get married to her."

"We haven't talked about anything like that yet. It really hurts me that you don't like her, though. What's wrong with her?"

"She's got a self-important attitude about her. She doesn't know how to carry on a conversation about anything but herself. Besides, I don't think she's too bright."

Junior looked at him with a frown, but said nothing as Daddy Bug continued, "You can tell a lot about somebody when they eat a meal with you. The way my Daddy used to put it, they either break bread with you or they don't. What he meant by that was, you either have communion, meaning togetherness, or you don't. She didn't offer to be sociable or even polite, so I figure she didn't want to break bread with us."

"Sir, I don't want to disagree with you, but Mona Lisa is just shy. She didn't know what to say to you and Aunt Vanessa."

"How about something like, 'How are you?' or, 'Can I set the table?' or, 'That supper was good. She has no sense of what's right, that I can see."

"Just give her a chance, Daddy Bug, I know you'll like her when you really get to know her."

Daddy Bug said nothing but he knew that if Junior kept company much longer with Mona Lisa, it would bode nothing but trouble. Already, he was defending her bad manners and attitude. Shy, indeed.

The silence in the cab of the pickup was deafening. Each of the two men were deep in thought as the car turned off Stop Gap Road toward their houses.

Suddenly, Stanley Henderson appeared from the trees at the side of the road. He stumbled, then fell - face down - in the road. Daddy Bug slammed on the brakes and jumped from the vehicle, followed by Junior.

He kneeled by Stanley's inert body and rolled him over. His face was a ghastly gray tone. His eyes were closed, his mouth hanging open. There was no sign of trauma.

Junior felt for a pulse in the vein in his neck. He could not find one. He looked at his uncle with consternation and urgency.

"Daddy Bug, I learned mouth to mouth resuscitation in school. Let me work on him while you go up to the house and call the doctor."

He quickly got to work on his Aunt Vanessa's brother without waiting for Daddy Bug to answer. The older man watched with amazement as Junior put his finger in Stanley's mouth to see if there was anything in it. Then he moved to a position beside his head, grabbed the nape of his neck with one hand and his forehead with the heel of his other hand, pressing down to elevate the chin.

Daddy Bug stood fascinated as Junior pinched Stanley's nose shut, put his own mouth over Stanley's and blew four quick breaths. He then proceeded to blow one breath every few seconds. Stanley's chest rose and fell each time.

"Hurry, Sir, go call the Doc," Junior shouted. "I think he's got a pulse now, but we better have the Doc look at him. I'll keep working on him."

Taking orders was not one of Daddy Bug's favorite things to do, but he was so shaken he turned immediately and started to obey his nephew. He drove the short distance to his house, his mind racing with a thousand questions. What happened to Stanley? How did Junior learn how to do the mouth to mouth? What would he say to Vanessa?

He ran through the kitchen door, went directly to the phone and dialed for Doc Daly. He was young, but had taken right over when Doc Parsons passed away. Plus, he knew all the latest techniques and lived nearby.

Mrs. Daly acted as receptionist, nurse and assistant, as Mrs. Parsons had done for Doc Parsons. She answered "Doctor Daly's medical office" on the second ring.

"I have to talk to the Doc." It was not a request, but an order from the frightened man.

"I'm sorry, but Doctor Daly is out on a sick call. This is Mrs. Daly. Can I help you with anything?"

"Ma'am, Vanessa's brother, Stanley, just fell in the road. He wasn't breathing but Junior started blowing in his mouth and he started breathing again. He looks mighty bad - all gray and everything. It looks pretty serious. Where did the Doc go? I'll go get him." His words came out in staccato gasps.

Mrs. Daly recognized Daddy Bug's voice and noticed his urgent tone. "Calm down, Daddy Bug, I'll call Doc and tell him to come right over. Take some cool cloths down and bathe Stanley's face. The Doctor is only a few minutes away from your place. Hang up now so I can ring him."

When Daddy Bug hung up the phone, he heard a moan coming from the rear of the kitchen. Turning, he saw Vanessa standing by the door with a look of terror on her face.

"What's happened to Stanley?" She whispered.

"Honey, I don't know. The Doc's on his way. Little Junior is with him. Where were you, anyway?"

"I was just next door at Lydia Anne's. Where is Stanley now?"

"Get some towels and wring them in some cold water. Then, we'll go down to where Stanley is."

Vanessa rapidly dumped ice into the kitchen sink and filled it with water. She threw four kitchen towels in the water and wrung them. Within three minutes, she was ready to go, cold towels in hand.

The couple got in the pickup and sped to the site where Stanley lay close to death. Just as they pulled up, the Doctor turned into their road off of Stop Gap road.

Stanley still lay upon the ground with Junior holding his head. His head was pillowed upon the young man's coat. He was not moving, but his eyes were open and he appeared alert.

The Doctor, with his bag in his hand, rushed from his car and bent to Stanley's side. "What seems to be the matter here?"

He opened his bag and took his stethoscope out. Fitting the instrument to his ears, he listened to Stanley's heart. The beat was faint, but steady.

Vanessa knelt on the other side of Stanley, holding his hand. The cold towels lay on the ground beside her. She said nothing, but watched her brother with a worried look on her face.

Daddy Bug waited nearby as Junior explained to Doctor Daly how they saw Stanley fall in the road, that he didn't have any pulse, and how he performed the mouth to mouth resuscitation.

The Doctor listened intently, watching Stanley's face closely. Then, he said, "Stanley, are you on any medications?"

"Yes I am, Doc. I take two different kinds for my nerves. See, I still have nightmares and things from my stint in Vietnam. The V.A. Doctors gave me these pills to calm down my nerves and make me sleep at night."

Doctor Daly put his stethoscope in his bag and closed it. He looked up at Daddy Bug and said, "Daddy Bug, I'm going to admit him to the hospital for observation overnight and some tests. I think he's strong enough to ride in the car laying down without calling an ambulance. Will you and this young man lay him in the back seat of my car and then ride with me? I'll take him right away."

The two men did as they were told. Stanley had lost weight in the years since he came home from Vietnam and seemed a frail shadow of the robust frame of his youth. Making a chair of their arms, they lifted him to a sitting position and placed him in the back of the Doctor's big sedan. Pale and weak, Stanley stretched out on the seat and closed his eyes.

Doctor Daly had already started the car as Daddy Bug and Junior shut the rear door and slid in the front seat on the passenger side. Daddy Bug waved at Vanessa as they sped off. She stood forlorn and weeping and lifted her hand slightly in acknowledgment.

Glancing in the back seat as they rode, Daddy Bug could not help noticing how old Stanley looked. His face was deeply lined and his hair, moist from sweating, was like white lamb's wool clinging to his head. He was breathing faintly and his frail chest rose with each exhalation.

The Doctor interrupted his thoughts by saying, "Daddy Bug, I'll have to find out what kind of medicine he's taking. When we get to the hospital, call Miss Vanessa and have her read what's on the bottles. You write it down and get it to me fast. I can't give him anything until I know what he's taking."

"I'll have Junior do that, Doc. I want to stay with Stanley." Then to Junior, "Hear that, boy? Make sure you get it right."

Junior shook his head in compliance and stared straight ahead. Daddy Bug did the same, watching as Doctor Daly slid around the curves of Stop Gap road as it snaked down the mountain into Lake Chastain. He had driven since he was ten years old, sometimes at high speed, but he couldn't mask his trepidation of an early demise at the hands of the free-wheeling Doctor.

"Hey Doc, what were you before you became a Doctor - a race car driver?" he asked half jokingly.

"Time is of the essence. I've got the car under control. Don't you worry," Doctor Daly reassured him.

Within minutes the Doctor braked to a stop in front of the emergency entrance and raced inside with his bag. Two attendants immediately emerged from the same entrance with a gurney and bundled Stanley onto it, strapping him down while in motion.

Daddy Bug and Junior followed as the attendants wheeled Stanley into an examining room already inhabited by Doctor Daly. The Doctor was waiting with his stethoscope.

"Go call about that medicine, young man," the Doctor ordered. Junior left to find a phone.

The Doctor listened again to Stanley's heart and looked into Stanley's eyes. Daddy Bug thought they appeared dilated and dazed.

"Stanley, listen to me. How much of your medicine did you take today? And when did you take it last?"

"I don't remember, Doc. I woke up around four o'clock with a nightmare. I think I got up and took some then. Then, I took some more this morning because I felt awful nervous and jittery."

"Then what did you do?"

"Then, I thought I'd go out and do a little rabbit hunting and next thing you know, Junior's blowing in my mouth."

"He's taken an overdose of whatever he's taking," Doctor Daly looked at Daddy Bug. "We're going to have to pump him. Why don't you go and check him in at the station. Tell them I'm keeping him overnight."

As Daddy Bug turned to go, the Doctor said, "Stanley, what did you take the pills with?"

Stanley opened his eyes and smiled, "I just took them with a bit of the recipe, Doc. No harm to that is there"

Daddy Bug shut the door before he heard the answer. He knew the answer already and so did Stanley. That was like pouring gasoline on the fire. He wondered if Stanley was tired of living and was trying to check out.

Junior was at the pay phone talking and writing on a piece of paper. Daddy Bug stood next to him as he finished writing the names of the medicines and the dosage.

"Let me talk to Vanessa before you hang up, son." Daddy Bug took the receiver from his hand and said into the phone, "Honey, the Doc is going to pump his stomach. He had a close call, I think. Took too many of his pills with the whiskey. He knows better. I don't know what to think."

"Do you want me to call Mark or Sue Halbert to come and bring me there? I want to talk to Stanley. Will he be all right?" Vanessa's voice sounded desperate and excited to Daddy Bug

"No, tell Mark that Junior and I need a ride home from the hospital. You stay there. I've got to check Stanley in and then when the Doc gets done, I'll talk to him. Don't worry, honey. He can't do anything while he's in here. I'll be home soon.

Vanessa hung up the phone and sat at the kitchen table. She was disturbed at the latest news of Stanley and suspected that he did indeed want to end his life. She had the same feelings; those feelings of isolation and loneliness; those feelings of helplessness. Did one really have control over one's happiness and sorrow? It seemed to her that all was pre-ordained by a higher power.

Pulling herself from her reverie, she walked to the phone and called Sheriff Mark Halbert. He answered on the first ring.

"Mark Halbert here."

"Mark, it's Vanessa. Daddy Bug called from the hospital in Lake Chastain. He and Junior need a ride home from the hospital."

"Why is he at the hospital, Vanessa?"

"Stanley got sick and they had to take him there in Doc Daly's car. He's staying overnight for some tests and they need a ride home. I managed to get the pickup to the house, but I don't drive much. It makes me too nervous."

"Are you all right, Vanessa? Should I send Sue over?"

"I'm doing fine. Daddy Bug says he'll be ready to go when you get there."

"I'm sending Sue over to sit with you, Vanessa. I'll pick up Daddy Bug and Junior, and we'll be there shortly."

Vanessa hung up the phone and sat back down at the kitchen table to wait. Stanley was her brother and her only close blood relative. Her mother and father had been killed in an automobile accident nine months ago.

She had been able to take the stress and pain of that incident because she had leaned on Daddy Bug and Stanley. They had made it easy for her to realize that God wanted to call her parents home. They would have wanted to go together. They were a team and neither could have gone on without the other. Stop Gap road was icy and they couldn't slow down on that last turn. It was a drop off of the cliff of one hundred feet that did it. The car exploded. It was instant and merciful. She accepted that.

Now, she was faced with the prospect that Stanley could not live with his nightmares, his fears, his medicine, and the death of his parents. Daddy Bug had basically expressed the same worries.

Once before, she thought she had lost Stanley. Then, he was back from Vietnam and they again shared the same closeness they had growing up. He was in peril again by his own hand. The Viet Cong were still draining his brain through the nightmares. What could she do?

Vanessa sat hunched at the table and the knock of Sue Halbert sounded on the kitchen door. Sue did not wait for an answer, rather she sprang into the kitchen and hugged Vanessa around the neck.

"Honey, Sue is here to take care of you. Mark told me what happened. Let's have us some ice tea and wait for the guys to come home."

Vanessa let the tears flood her face. "Sue, what more can happen to us? I just don't know."

"Never you mind. You'll be all right. Now have some of

this ice tea. You still have Daddy Bug and he knows how to make everything alright."

"Sue, I could take my parents going to heaven. I can and have taken a lot, but I worry that I can't take Stanley leaving too. He's the last man of my family. My blood line. Why would he want to kill himself when he got through that horror in Vietnam?"

"Vanessa, we can't question these things. Who knows why anything happens? Just never you mind right, now. Drink this tea and we'll face anything that comes up together."

Vanessa sipped her tea as Sue bustled around the kitchen. She had started supper before the phone call from the hospital. With her tea gone she realized that she should help Sue. At least she needed to try and carry on with the normal activities.

As she wiped the kitchen counter, she heard Mark's cruiser pull into the driveway. Then she heard voices as the three men headed for the kitchen door. She wondered what the news would be. Would it be good or bad?

Mark Halbert, Junior and Daddy Bug came dragging through the door. It was obvious that they were tired

"How is Stanley?" Sue Halbert said as she ran to meet them.

"Sue, maybe I'd better take Vanessa back to our room to talk to her," Daddy Bug said. "Junior, go get your parents and bring them here. And Sue, Mark will fill you in on everything."

He took her hand and pulled her to him. "Honey, come on back with me. I've got some bad news for you."

# 24

The loss of Stanley took its toll on Vanessa. The details of his death were never explained to her. The sudden fibrillation of his heart, the defibrillator that did no good - she was spared all clinical information. The electric current seemed to evaporate into thin air. Stanley was not a conductor; maybe it was his choice not to be.

Stanley's funeral was held on a hot summer day. It threatened to rain. The clouds in the sky peaked in an ice cream sundae mirage. He was laid to rest as a veteran and a hero of his country. No twenty-one gun salute heralded his entrance to heaven, but the local American Legion (of which he was a card-carrying member) honored him with an American flag, folded properly, and presented to his grieving sister, Vanessa Henderson Garland.

Vanessa temporarily reverted to her former lifeless self. Daddy Bug, in his turn, felt he had lost a good and faithful friend. For weeks they wandered around the grounds, hand in hand. He with his innermost thoughts to comfort him and she with an aching emptiness that dominated her every waking minute. They said little, but were there mentally for each other. They did not make love, but his hand would search for hers as they watched the small television he had purchased for their bedroom.

Jimmie and Lydia Anne were frequent supper guests, as were Sue and Mark Halbert, each couple taking turns bringing the food. The household atmosphere was quiet and pensive.

Junior took over the operation of the business, temporarily. It was the least he could do for his Daddy Bug and Aunt Vanessa. He already knew the schedule and all of the distributors.

The only thing he missed was the company of Mona Lisa Skruggs. He rarely had a moment to call his own and he talked on the telephone with her late at night when he had finished the last of his work. She would cry and complain that he was neglecting her, but she understood the pressure he was under at the moment.

Junior knew that he was the man of the family for the time being. It was a great burden for a young man barely nineteen years old. All of a sudden, the men in his family had become the children and he was left to make sure that his family survived this tragedy.

He took it in stride and assumed a new demeanor. His walk became heavier. He did not swagger - he treaded with the balls of his feet to the ground, as if he were keeping his footing on a ship rolling on the gigantic waves of the sea.

Jimmie Haywood, Jr. was a man.

He managed Daddy Bug's business. He took care of his Daddy and Momma. He kept Mona Lisa happy on the rare occasions that he had the chance to see her. For months, he held the business and family together while everyone else was grieving for Stanley Henderson.

Finally, he could take no more. One evening, he went to Daddy Bug and sat w h him on his front porch. The November mists were rising over Cather Mountain. The full moon struggled to shine through and cast an eerie white shadow upon the lawn.

He spoke to himself aloud, "Well, I guess it's time to get back to normal now. Its been a few months since Stanley died. I'm gonna need some help if we're going to keep on."

Daddy Bug looked at the clean profile of his nephew. He realized that Junior had been carrying the load for a long time. The older man knew that he wasn't old, but he felt old. So many things had happened. He was also aware that it was time to take back the reigns. His nephew was telling him as much.

He took a sip out of a glass of his own white whiskey and said, "I hear you, son. It's time for me to come out of my trance and give you back your life. Let me give it a short try tomorrow. I'll meet you at the stills in the morning at six o'clock. We'll make the change over in the next few days."

Junior grabbed the jug sitting on the porch and touched it to Daddy Bug's glass, took a swig and said, "Here's to me growing to be a man and you getting back to being a man. Tell my Aunt Vanessa that I'll always be there for her and I'll always be there for you too."

"I pray to the Lord that it'll always be that way. That's the way it's supposed to be. Thanks, son, for your strength during this time, but it's time to get on with life. You were there when I needed you,"

Daddy Bug drained his glass, got up from his chair and hugged his nephew for the first time in his life. It was a rare moment for both. Hugs between the mountain men were unheard of. But it felt good for both of them. It signified a bond. Naturally, it would never be transformed into conversation, this bond. But, they both were aware of it.

Daddy Bug turned and went into the house and Junior crossed the lawn to return to his home. He had grown up next door to Daddy Bug and his parents remained close. He had a sense of security with them all. Somehow, however, he felt a deeper sense of brotherhood with Daddy Bug than with his own Momma and Daddy, Lydia Anne and Jimmie, Sr. He could not explain it to himself. He just did.

When he got in the house, his parents called to him from the front room. He answered, politely as he had been brought up to do, and went to his room.

His first thought was to call Mona Lisa. She was getting a little impatient with his "family duties." He dialed her number from his bedside telephone.

"Hi, honey, I just got in. How about you and me going to a movie tomorrow night?"

Her voice was far from warm. "I think I've got plans for tomorrow night. Call me tomorrow and I'll let you know for sure."

"Mona Lisa, I was busy tonight. I'm sorry. I had things to straighten out. I'll have more time now. I talked to Daddy Bug, tonight. We'll get everything worked out tomorrow. Alright?"

Her voice was like dry ice clinging to his ears. "Well, I should hope you would get things straightened out. I'm beginning to feel like you don't care if I exist or not. Besides, I have something to tell you, but I'm not going to tell you over the phone."

"What is it, honey? You know you can tell me anything."

"Pick me up at six tomorrow night. I'll tell you then."

"Tell me now. What's the matter. You sound so distant."

"Well, it has to do with you and me. Now, go to sleep. You need your rest. Good night!" Her hang-up clattered in his ear.

He wandered around his room, picking up his dirty underwear and socks scattered under his bed. What could Mona Lisa be talking about? She certainly was being mysterious these last couple of weeks. Finally, knowing that sleep would not come to him, he went into the front room to have a short visit with his parents who were enjoying a late night talk show on television.

They looked up at him when he sauntered into the room. He knew they were surprised to see him. It was rare that he got to spend any time with them since he started dating Mona Lisa Skruggs, and even more rare since the death of Stanley Henderson and his heavy work load. His interests and his life seemed to be moving farther and farther away.

"Hi Momma and Daddy. What keeps you up so late?"

"We just couldn't sleep and decided to watch a little television," Jimmie offered. "Want to sit a spell with us?"

Junior sprawled in the lone easy chair in the room. "I thought it might be nice for us to spend some time. It's been so long since we've had a chance to talk."

Lydia Anne adjusted her glasses, "Well, I hardly think it's been us that have been busy. She exploited the hurt in her voice.

"Well, Momma, I'm sorry, but I'm not going to let you play the martyr in this family. I've been keeping mighty busy trying to keep things going. I've had to grow up real fast since Stanley died. I've done my best and I just wanted to talk a little to you tonight."

"I'm sorry son. I didn't mean to sound like a 'martyr' as you call it. I guess we've all been through a lot. What did you want to talk about?"

"I wanted to talk about Mona Lisa and me. I've been neglecting her a lot lately and she's never been here for supper. She's been at Daddy Bug's and Aunt Vanessa's when you were out of town, but she hasn't really gotten to know you. I've been to her house for supper and

I've gone to her church. So, I'd like to have her here for supper real soon."

Jimmie, Sr. shook himself out of his pre-sleep fog. "When would you like to have her over, Junior? We'll make it real nice for you and her."

"My twentieth birthday is coming up on November 22. That's two days before Thanksgiving so it's all right if we celebrate it on Thanksgiving. I'd like to have a combined birthday and Thanksgiving dinner - not a supper - and invite Mona Lisa and her parents to our house. I've never had a chance to celebrate my birthday if the 22nd falls on Thanksgiving, so this year I'd like to do just that. We can have Daddy Bug and Aunt Vanessa, and Mark and Sue Halbert, too. Juggie and Tessa will be home from college and we can have a great time with everybody here. I may as well tell you, I'm thinking of marrying Mona Lisa and it's time we all got to know each other."

"That's a real nice thought, son. We'll try to make it real good for Mona Lisa and her parents. Can we do anything special? Do they like any special kind of food? We could go squirrel or rabbit hunting." Jimmie was more than eager to please.

"How about that we just have a regular turkey dinner, with dressing and some cranberry sauce and some vegetables? How about let's just be a normal family at a normal Thanksgiving dinner?"

Junior saw the hurt look in Lydia Anne's eyes as she glanced at her husband. "I never knew we were not normal, Junior. We've always tried to be normal. Sometimes we had squirrel and rabbit because there wasn't any turkey to hunt. Sometimes God puts his hand in things. He doesn't want us to have turkey, so he doesn't provide any. Then we make do with what he does provide and we don't complain."

"What I mean Momma, is that we can get our turkey from the Piggly Wiggly in town. We can thaw it out. Maybe God is providing a freezer at the Piggly Wiggly so that we don't have to shoot a turkey. Maybe God is giving Piggly Wiggly a turkey for us to buy."

"Well, I never thought of it like that. I guess we can do all of that. I want you to come with us to the store and pick out the whole dinner. We'll make sure that everything is just perfect for your birthday and Thanksgiving celebration. It will be nice to get to know Mona Lisa and her parents. Who knows, we may all be related some day."

"Momma, whether we're all related some day or not. I just want to get back to having Thanksgiving and my birthday on the normal days. President Kennedy died twenty years ago. I respected what you told me about him. I had no choice. You respected him - I admire that. We've just got to get back to normal and Mona Lisa is my ticket into that normal world."

Junior knew he had hit a nerve when his father took his mother's hand and pulled her to her feet. Without looking at his son, he addressed his wife. "Come on, Lydia Anne. Let's go to bed and let our son figure out how we had him, if we're so abnormal."

# 25

The arrangements for Junior's birthday and Thanksgiving dinner threw the two households into pandemonium. An attitude of "so much to do, so little time" prevailed. Junior woke up more excited than he had ever been.

Daddy Bug nodded solemnly when Junior told him of the plans. He realized that his father and uncle were not excited about the prospect of sitting down with Mona Lisa Skruggs and her parents. But, the dinner was supposed to be, by unspoken agreement, a family affair. He hoped that they would cooperate because it was for him and he had done his best to keep everything together since Stanley's death.

November 22 dawned and so did Jimmie Haywood, Jr.'s twentieth birthday. Everyone wished him a happy birthday, but wisely did not mention in front of him that it was the anniversary of President Kennedy's assassination. The family sat down to a breakfast of pancakes and bacon. Lydia Anne put two candles in Junior's stack of pancakes and they sang happy birthday to him.

After Lydia Anne cleaned up the dishes, the three Haywoods drove to the Piggly Wiggly in Lake Chastain. Junior wheeled the shopping cart around the store, stopping here and there to study the merchandise on display. Finally, he picked a twenty-three pound frozen turkey; the biggest in the frozen meat case. Then, he selected cranberry sauces (jellied and whole berry), raw carrots, celery, two each of frozen apple, pecan and pumpkin pies, ice cream, frozen peas, frozen beans, instant mashed potatoes and boxed stuffing mix.

Putting his selections on the checkout counter, he grinned at his parents, "Now, Momma won't have to start cooking at four o'clock in the morning. Just thaw this bird and throw it in the oven around eight in the morning. Then everything else will only take about an hour before we sit down at the table."

The young girl at the checkout counter looked at him with a love-sick expression and smiled. "You sure are considerate of your Momma, Junior." She had been a sophomore in high school when Junior was a senior.

"She's the only one I've got. Got to make sure she doesn't work too hard." He flashed his white teeth at her in his best imitation of Robert Redford.

Looking as if she were going to faint, she gushed, "The whole bill comes to sixty-seven dollars and thirty two cents."

Jimmie stepped forward, wallet in hand, but Junior stopped him. "I'm paying for this myself, Daddy. I saved most of my money from this summer. This will be my treat."

"There's no need for that son. Keep your money. I can afford to pay for this."

Junior threw four twenties on the counter. "Nope, I said it's mine."

Without further argument, the elder man put his wallet back in his pocket. Stepping back, he took Lydia Anne by the hand and whispered, "That boy is all grown up. He's not a little kid anymore." Junior could just make out what he said and picked up his change with a smile on his face.

They trooped to the car loaded with the bags of groceries. On the way home, Junior sat in the back seat and whistled. He was satisfied now the Thanksgiving dinner that his momma would cook would be just like any other American Thanksgiving dinner.

It wasn't that his momma wasn't a good cook, or that her food tasted any different than any other good mother's would. It was just that past Thanksgiving and Christmas dinners were far from traditional. Sometimes, she even cooked fish for those special days. They usually had whatever they could hunt or catch, along with some home canned vegetables, things from the root cellar, and peach cobbler for dessert.

Junior had seen pictures on television and in the movies that showed him how they were different from the rest of the world. That's how he knew what to buy today at the Piggly Wiggly. He was sure that Mona Lisa Skruggs would be impressed when they sat down at Thanksgiving dinner.

It didn't make him ashamed to be different, but it made him curious about how the rest of the world lived. He wanted to find out more about those people.. The people who lived in the big cities.

He also talked to Juggie and Tessa who were off at college. They said Lake Chastain was a great place but slightly behind the times. And "Doctor" Precious Halbert told him the people of Lake Chastain were sheltered, old fashioned and eccentric.

Well, Jimmie Haywood, Jr. was not going to be considered sheltered, old fashioned and eccentric. He was going to be up to date.

He loved all of the people of Lake Chastain and he wouldn't want them to change. Lake Chastain had always been his home and he would always live here, but he didn't have to be "slightly behind the times."

As the car turned in to his parent's driveway, his mind suddenly snapped to his present surroundings and he heard his mother say, "Junior, if you'll help me find a space for all this frozen food, I'll sure appreciate it."

"Sure, Momma. Daddy Bug said we can use his freezer if we need to."

The full reality of everyday life took precedence over daydreaming. Scrambling out of the car, he took the frozen groceries (which he had bagged separate) from the trunk and headed next door to Aunt Vanessa and Daddy Bug's house. The couple sat on the front porch and watched as he approached with the bags.

"What a sight for sore eyes that boy is." Daddy Bug smoked his pipe and rocked back and forth.

"He sure has turned into a handsome man," Vanessa smiled. "Today is his birthday, but we're not to celebrate it until Thanksgiving. That's the way he wants it."

"As fine a boy as he is, I don't see what he sees in that Mona Lisa Skruggs. She looks like she's been rode hard and put up wet," Daddy Bug said.

Vanessa looked shocked. "Why, honey, that's an awful thing to say about such a young girl."

"Young in years ain't always young in mind. I believe she's got some experience along certain lines. I've been talking to a few more people in town."

"Well, don't say anything to Junior You might hurt his feelings. Lydia Anne told me he said he might marry Mona Lisa some day. Now, hush before he hears you."

Junior came up the steps two at a time. He smiled at his aunt and uncle and said, "I've got the makings of a great Thanksgiving dinner and Momma won't even have to work that hard to make it. Do you mind if I put these frozen things in the freezer, Daddy Bug?"

"Just go right in and help yourself. Move things around if you need to make them fit." Daddy Bug jumped up to open the door for him.

"Yes sir. Thank you. I'll just do that."

He watched while Junior carried his bags through the door and back to the pantry room. Junior returned to the front porch empty handed..

"Aunt Vanessa, you should take a look at what I got. I even got a frozen turkey. We're going to have such a feast for Thanksgiving and my birthday. Mona Lisa and her parents will really be impressed, I know."

Daddy Bug rocked in his chair and smoked his pipe. Vanessa smiled at Junior and said, "I'm sure they will be impressed, and I'm sure we will be too."

"If what we have isn't good enough for the Skruggs, then I'll be danged. Did you see where they live? We're in high cotton on our worst days around here compared to them," Daddy Bug said as he winked at Vanessa.

"The Skruggs' can't help that they don't have enough money for nice houses like we live in. The only money he gets is from the collection plate, and that house is furnished to them by the church. It doesn't have a real rich congregation," Junior protested.

"Well, soap doesn't cost that much and there are two healthy females over there. That place looks like a pig sty. I've seen it."

Vanessa, ever the peacemaker, jumped in. "Never you mind, Daddy Bug. Junior doesn't want to hear all of this." Then, "Now, Junior, why don't you go over to your house and see if you can help your Momma and Daddy get the big folding table set up on the Florida porch. There will be too many people for us to eat in the kitchen."

"Sure thing, Aunt Vanessa. That should work out just great. Then I have to go see Mona Lisa. See you later." He turned and waved as he crossed the yard to his house.

Vanessa got up to go in the house. As she opened the door, she heard Daddy Bug curse. He had never done that in front of her. He must be boiling inside, she thought.

She left the front door open to get the warm November air. It smelled so good to her. Passing the hall mirror, she glanced into it. She saw the gray streaks in her hair. Her complexion was still creamy and her skin unlined except for the few wrinkles around her eyes and her mouth. Her neck showed signs of becoming a "turkey neck." She thought that she had weathered her difficult life pretty good. Her face was a puzzle, even to her. It wasn't old and it wasn't young.

She had outlived her entire family and she was the only Henderson left on the mountain. That wasn't to say there were not other Henderson's in North Alabama. She was the only one of her very own Henderson blood line left.

Still, she realized that wasn't true. She had passed her blood to Juggie and Tessa. Even though their given names were Garland, they still carried her blood. She would not be wiped from the face of the earth when she died. She, or at least her essence, would still exist in the next generation, and the next.

Daddy Bug came up behind her as she gazed in the mirror. "What in the dickens are you staring at, woman?"

"I'm looking in the future, Daddy Bug. I'm looking at you and me and Juggie and Tessa and Lydia and Jimmie, Sr. and Junior. I'm wondering what we're all here to do. I'm wondering where Stanley and Momma and Poppa are."

Daddy Bug gently put his arms around her waist and clenched her close to him. "Honey, you're amazing when you want to be. Don't ever lose your sweetness and your goodness. You're way above me in the way you think and that's why I still love you after all these years. Somehow, you always put a kind, gentle face on the troubles of the world."

Vanessa turned to Daddy Bug. Her face glowed with the pureness of her innermost being, and her eyes were moist as she took his face in her hands.

"Don't ever forget what we have. Don't ever forget that Junior is in your hands. He looks up to you and admires you. Jimmie, Sr. and Lydia Anne are his parents, but you are his idol. I can see it. The tough thing about being an idol is that you are on a pedestal. When you are on a pedestal, you can be knocked off. Just watch what happens to him."

"Why, honey, nothing is ever going to happen to my relationship with Junior. We're kin. We're close as can be. Nobody or nothing will ever come between us. You can bet on it."

"I won't bet on anything. I'm too attuned to what can happen when you least expect it."

Daddy Bug hugged her and went to see his stills. Vanessa hoped nothing would ever come between the King of Cather Mountain and his nephew.

# 26

The sun rose brightly on the Thanksgiving morning of Jimmie Haywood, Jr.'s twentieth year. It looked like it might be an unseasonably warm day after a cool night. The mountain was shrouded in a mist that looked like billowy clouds sitting directly on the surface.

Junior awakened early and jumped from the warmth of his bed. His thoughts were racing about the excitement of the day.

The activities were already underway for his birthday party and Thanksgiving. The prior evening he personally thawed and trussed the turkey in preparation for baking today. Even while his daddy teased him about doing "woman's" work, he hummed Happy Birthday to himself. Nothing could spoil this special day.

After his shower, he dressed hurriedly in some of his nicer clothes while listening to the noises coming from the kitchen. He smelled the turkey roasting in the oven and heard the murmur of his daddy's voice in conversation with his mother and Daddy Bug. Good, that would mean Aunt Vanessa was already here, helping his mother.

Mona Lisa had told him on the telephone the previous evening that she and her parents would arrive around eleven o'clock. Her daddy planned to have a nine o'clock Thanksgiving service, so the parishioners could "start this special day in prayer" and that would be the earliest they could get there. "After all, Daddy's calling is the more important than socializing," she explained.

Then, she dropped the bomb on him. "Junior, I couldn't tell you last night, but I have to tell you now. Momma and Daddy are starting to stare at me."

"What are you talking about?"

"I'm pregnant and I'm starting to show. I'm going to have to tell Momma and Daddy soon. What are we going to do." The words tumbled out in a torrent of whining blame. "I'm so excited. Aren't you going to say anything?"

"I'm sorry, Mona Lisa. I'm excited about it too. Let's just get by ourselves tomorrow and discuss it. I'll have to think about it overnight."

He had hung up and gone to work on the turkey. It was good to have something to occupy his time. He guessed he wouldn't be able to sleep. He thought long and hard about the situation and then went to bed. He was asleep in minutes. Now, as he finished preparing himself for the day, he thought about who else was going to be there.

Mark and Sue Halbert intended to come over around ten o'clock. Juggie and Tessa were driving in together and would get there around the same time. Everything would be just perfect for this was to be Junior's day.

The only mar on the day was that Precious Halbert could not make it. It seemed that she was on call duty as a resident in the Birmingham hospital. She said she would try to get someone to cover for her, but it was not hopeful. Everyone wanted to be home for Thanksgiving and she got the short straw. Oh well, he would make it up later to Precious.

He went to the kitchen and greeted his parents and aunt and uncle, giving each of them a hug. Grabbing a glass of orange juice and a slice of toast, he wandered onto the front porch.

The sheer beauty of the panorama of the mountains had delighted him when he was a child and he still sustained a feeling of awe. He sat on the rocking chair and looked out over the valley. Finishing his toast and juice, he decided to wander down to the stills and check around. He ambled slowly, noticing how the leaves on the trees were turning the vivid reds, yellows and browns that created the beautiful spectacle that was his favorite season and favorite place - Autumn in North Alabama .

His happiness remained as he made his way along the narrow path to the place where he and Daddy Bug worked the family business. Suddenly, he heard a moan from the right. It seemed to be coming from deep in the thicket.

Junior made his way to the back of the deep brush. He saw a lock of black hair and hurried to its source. "Help, I can't get up. I've been raped."

"Precious, what are you doing here? I thought you had to stay at the hospital. I thought you were in your last year of residency."

"Junior, I was coming home for Thanksgiving. I was going to surprise my folks. Someone finally volunteered to take over my place. My car was on the blink so I hitchhiked home and took a ride from a stranger. He was big and he was strong. Much too strong for me. I told him I wanted out at Stop Gap Road. He stopped before we got there and dragged me in here. I don't want to tell you all the details. Just help me get to your folk's place. Momma told me you're all having Thanksgiving together. I wanted to share it with you."

"Precious, let me go and get your daddy. They're supposed to come over to our house at ten. They should be there about now. If not, I can drive daddy's car over to your house and get Mark.

"Let's don't make a big deal about this. I don't want to spoil the day. Just help me out of here. We'll get the guy who did this later."

"You're a mess, Precious. We need to get you cleaned up. Let's go over to your house and you can take a shower. I'll bring Daddy's pickup down to the Stop Gap entrance. We'll go over, you get cleaned up, and then I'll say I found you walking along the road to home."

"Sounds like a good plan to me. I've been stupid my whole life. Trusting men because they look honest. They all want one thing, it seems like to me - except you, Junior. You're the one who has always been a true blue person. You're the one who has always been honest."

Junior hugged Precious and retreated to the path he had traveled for years. What could he say to his folks and his aunt and uncle? Precious was right, it wouldn't do to bring up this situation at Thanksgiving. It would just get everyone upset and ruin the day. But, at this moment, Precious needed him. He had always been supportive of Precious and he wouldn't stop now or ever. He hurried back to his house and ran into the kitchen occupied by his closest relatives. "Daddy, I need to take the pickup to the store. Most of them close at noon. I forgot something real important for the dinner. Is it O.K.?"

Jimmie took a sip of his coffee and looked at his only son in surprise. "Sure, son, it's O.K. But I think we'll have enough food for an army the way it is. What did you forget?"

"Something real important. I wanted to get some vanilla low-fat yogurt for the pies. It's a favorite of Mona Lisa's. I think the Cozy Corner Market is open until eleven. Then, they close down for Thanksgiving. Just want everything to be perfect for a perfect day."

"Go ahead, son. We'll be here to welcome everybody. How could we say no to you on your day?"

Junior sailed through the room and escaped to the driveway where Jimmie's pickup stood in a prominent location. Gunning the motor, he skidded to the entrance to the driveway where Stop Gap Road intersected. By the road side, Precious stood with her battered suit case and her bruised face.

"Hop in. No one suspected a thing. Let's get you cleaned up and after all of this is over, I promise you we'll get the guy who did this. Do you remember what he drove - or what he looked like?"

"I remember everything, Junior. I'm a Doctor now. It's my job to remember." Precious opened the door to the pickup and daintily settled into the seat beside Junior. She was bruised about her upper arms and a cut in her mouth oozed blood which she was trying to cover with a tissue.

"Junior," she said. "I've known you since you were a baby. I'll never forget what a man you have been today. Just help me get all of this covered up so I don't upset momma and Mark or Daddy Bug and Vanessa. You and me will take care of this in our own way. I've got his license number and I know what he looks and smells like. He won't get away, but we've got more important things to do right now. And besides, you're a man now. Your twentieth birthday was on Tuesday and Momma said we're gonna celebrate it today."

"Precious, that's the farthest thing from my mind right now. Here, we are at your house. It looks like your Momma and Mark are already at our house. I'll wait here. Run in and get cleaned up. Then, we have to go and get the vanilla yogurt ice cream. That was my excuse to borrow the pickup."

"What's the hurry to get back? I thought you had everything covered."

"Mona Lisa and her parents are set to arrive around eleven o'clock. I need to be there as if nothing is wrong. Besides, I would hate to hear Mark if he found out what happened to you."

Precious grabbed her suit case and stalked to the recently painted mansion. Using her key, she disappeared. Junior had to wait for only ten minutes. Amazingly, she looked refreshed and alert when she emerged in a clean pair of jeans with a poncho thrown casually over her shoulders. She still carried her suitcase. Junior observed that all of her bruises were covered with something. She looked like she had come out of a Holiday Inn after a restful night.

"Let's go, Junior. We don't want to be late for your twentieth birthday. You're a fine man. I'm real proud of you. You'll be someone someday." Precious seemed calmed and confident once more, as she had when he had observed her as he was growing up.

The short distance to the Cozy Corner was consumed as Junior pressed his foot to the gas pedal. He was in and out with a gallon of frozen yogurt ice cream in no time and within ten minutes was gliding his daddy's pickup to its allotted parking space in front of his house.

He escorted Precious into the parlor where all of the guests were assembled. Mona Lisa, her parents, Sue and Mark, Daddy Bug and Vanessa, Jimmie and Lydia Sue, Juggie and Tessa all looked when the door opened and Junior guided Precious into the room.

"Look who I found walking along Stop Gap. She's sure a sight for sore eyes. It's our Precious. She got someone to stand in for her at the hospital after all," Junior announced.

Mark and Sue Halbert jumped to their feet. "Precious," Mark said. "We're so pleased you could make it. You told us yesterday you couldn't."

Junior ducked to the back of the house to put the yogurt ice cream in the freezer, carefully avoiding Mona Lisa's surprised look. She followed him and was at his side within seconds.

"What happened to you Junior? I was real upset when you weren't here. We got here a little early and I thought you'd be here."

"I'll tell you about it later, Mona Lisa. I just had to go and get that yogurt you like for dessert. Everything is on schedule. How are you feeling?"

"Well, it's like I told you before. I can't wait much longer to tell Momma and Daddy. They're beginning to suspect something. I can't hide it much longer."

"Let's wait and tell everybody after we have the dinner. I'm sure they'll be as happy as we are. And, while we're at it let's set a date for the wedding. I'm plumb ecstatic that we're going to be starting a new family and Daddy Bug will probably pull out the jug for a toast when we tell them all the good news."

"Well, what is this all about Precious? I thought she couldn't get off work. What happened that she could?"

"She had a bit of trouble, but she made it home for this dinner. That was important to her. She just wanted to be here. Remember, she has been part of our family for a long time. Even though she's not blood kin, we consider her part of the family, just the same as Mark and Sue."

"What happened to her, Junior? She looks like she's been through three wars and lost all of them. I can tell she's tried to cover it up. Us women know each other."

"She got someone to take her shift for Thanksgiving day. Her car was laid up so she hitchhiked home and some guy hogtied her and raped her. Then he dumped her out by the Stop Gap entrance to our property. I found her when I was checking the stills. She doesn't want Mark or Sue to know anything about it. She's a big girl. She's a Doctor, now. She said she'll take care of it and I can help her. She doesn't want to upset the day. Can we just forget it for now and get on with it?"

"Whatever you say, Junior. Are we going to announce our engagement today?"

"Let me take the lead on this. Let's see what the mood of everyone is. I'm thinking this might be the right time for us to do it."

"I hope so. It's getting real hard to conceal that I'm pregnant."

"The best thing you can do right now is to go out and ask my momma what you can do to help with this dinner. I know that Aunt Vanessa and my momma have been working on this for a long time to make sure everything will go just right."

"But, what can I do? I haven't had any cooking lessons and I never have ever cooked a whole meal?"

"Just go out there and act like you know what you're doing. Set the table. Put on a smile. Get in the swing of things. It really ain't so hard. Us men don't expect a lot out of our women. Just put on a good meal and be pleasant. We'll do all the rest. We take care of our women."

"Junior, you're asking a lot of me. I'm use to taking care of myself. Momma has always been a reader and a recluse and Daddy has always had his calling. I've just kind of made my own way with nobody to guide me."

"Well, you've got me now. I'll always take care of you and our child. So get on in there and get to be part of this family." Junior smacked her bottom and hugged her neck, while kissing her full on her cherry-blossom lips.

Mona Lisa made her way into the parlor. She looked at the full regalia of ADULTS. How could she enter this family unit that she couldn't fully understand. Yet, she was forced into their world by the child she carried within her. She had to cross the threshold of their environment. She knew she was one of them. Her body told her so.

For six weeks she had battled the nausea of morning sickness. Running to the bathroom, holding a towel to her mouth, she had stifled the gagging green bile that came from her stomach. The crackers that she kept on her night stand helped, but the dizzying dry heaves and the retching fullness of her stomach each morning prevented the faint feeling from completely leaving her throughout the day.

She entered the room with a smile and a composed demeanor. "Lydia Anne, is there anything I can do to help you?"

Lydia Anne, as well as everyone in the room, had a surprised look on their face. It amused Mona Lisa to shock them.

"Why yes, you can set the table out on the porch if you want to. I think everything is about ready. How nice of you to ask."

Mona Lisa looked at Lydia Anne, her future mother-in-law and bowed her head. "Well, the least I can do is set the table. You're so nice to have my folks and everyone else to Junior's special dinner."

She took control of Junior and the room with that statement. Somehow, she would let them know that Mona Lisa Skruggs had grown up and had something to tell them.

Her parents looked at her in amazement. By her manner, she commanded the respect of Daddy Bug, Vanessa, Sue, Mark, Precious, Tessa, Juggie, and most of all - Jimmie and Lydia Anne. It was obvious that they were surprised, as everyone was. What was different about Mona Lisa Skruggs on this Thanksgiving day?

After Mona Lisa had set the table on the porch and helped Vanessa and Lydia Anne set the turkey with all the trimmings on the table, she oversaw the seating of each of the adults. She knew she was in charge from that moment on. After all, she carried the newest Garland-Haywood-Skruggs birthright within her. It was her body and her choice. Finally, Junior Haywood was hers. It wasn't a hard fight. They were there for the picking.

When everyone was seated, the prayer of thanksgiving given, and Daddy Bug had carved and served the turkey, all of the family took their glasses of the family recipe and toasted Junior on his birthday. The pies, the special birthday cake that Lydia Anne had baked and the vanilla yogurt and another "Happy Birthday to You" song would come later.

Everyone in the family knew this was a special day. They were all happy that day; family, best friends and close acquaintances could be together on this Thanksgiving day. The mood was light and cheerful. Everyone ate so much of Junior's special meal, that they couldn't move. Junior opened the token birthday gifts that were piled on the small table at the side.

They all sat back from the table, stretched and groaned about their fullness, while Junior stood and tapped on his glass of white lightening with his fork.

"I want to thank everybody for being here. Also, I want everyone to raise a glass for a toast on what I am about to say."

Everyone lifted a glass of water or whiskey, according to his or her choice.

Junior continued, "I want y'all to know that you are all my family and I want to be able to share any good news I have with you first. So here it is. Mona Lisa and I are getting married and we want to announce that there is a good possibility of there being a Jimmie Haywood the third. For that reason, we're going to be married before Christmas."

"So, here's to you Mona Lisa and to our child and to my wonderful family. It's the best Thanksgiving and most of all, it's the best birthday, I've ever had."

Junior touched the water glass of the beaming Mona Lisa with his and sipped as he looked around the table. It seemed there was an absolute vacuum in the room. No one drank a toast with him. No one said anything when the two looked into each other's eyes and Junior placed an engagement ring upon Mona Lisa's finger. For once, everyone was shocked into silence

Suddenly, as if a volcano had erupted, the room was filled with astonished congratulations and excitement. Lydia Anne jumped to her feet and hugged the newly engaged couple.

Reverend and Mrs. Skruggs examined the ring. Mark, Sue and Precious Halbert offered pats on the back and best wishes. Juggie and Tessa crowded around.

Daddy Bug sat in his chair and stared in shock at his nephew. What had happened to all his teaching?

Junior was engulfed in the good wishes of everyone. Mona Lisa Skruggs beamed at her new husband to be.

Precious Halbert sat back on her chair and watched the excitement. She imagined that no one would be interested in the fact that she was just raped by a stranger. Besides, she didn't want to spoil Junior's day. Consequently, she filed the incident in the back of her mind, beside her childhood memories of her half-brother, Archie Thurmon. She knew she would tell Junior to forget about it as she hoped she could. Why bother Mark and Momma about it. They would never catch the guy anyway. Some things were best forgotten.

# 27

It was a huge wedding that united Jimmie Hayward, Jr. and Mona Lisa Skruggs. Naturally, since Reverend and Mrs. Skrugs were virtually indigent (or so they claimed), Daddy Bug, Vanessa, Lydia Anne and Jimmie, Sr. paid for the entire affair. Reverend and Mrs. Skruggs supplied the wedding cake. The Reverend Mr. Skruggs officiated at the ceremony at the Presbyterian Church. He would accept no offering. After all, this was his daughter getting married.

Junior's parents provided the reception at their home, as well as ali the food and drink. When the newlyweds left on their honeymoon, they offered all of their friends jars of the family recipe and took enough with them to insure that Daddy Bug would have to work long and hard to replenish the stock for his distributors.

Mrs. Skruggs made it known that she was not amused that liquor was served at the reception and declined to take even the first sip. Her husband, the Reverend, managed to slip behind the house with Daddy Bug more than a few times to take a quick slug from the jar conveniently left on a bench by the latter for just such occasions.

This was the start of the union that would give Daddy Bug his most horrible moments. It was the the beginning of a rift in their family.

As soon as the couple returned from their honeymoon, the Reverend and Mrs. Skruggs insisted that the couple move into Mona Lisa's room. From that angle they could direct the misguided couple to their heavenly countenance and conciliation with the most holy Lord for their sins.

Daddy Bug did not disagree at the time because he felt that he had been betrayed in the most desperate of ways. Never before had such an immense decision been made without a trace of discussion with him.

The entire act of betrothal, marriage and expectant parenthood was done without his express permission. Most of the aforementioned betrothal and expectant parenthood was done without his knowledge. He was beside himself and for the first time in his life, he felt impotent about controlling his life and the activities of those around him. So, he did nothing but observe and try to be pleasant for Vanessa's sake.

Yet, he saw that Junior was changing. He was trying to become the ultimate married man and potential father to the offspring that was developing inside his wife. Junior's demeanor became defensive and authoritative when Daddy Bug asked him why he did not show up for a ride to the distributors.

Junior had other responsibilities, he told Daddy Bug. He could not be on constant call for the family business. After all, he was now a family man and he had to make sure that he took care of his family first.

When May came, Mona Lisa was in full bloom with her pregnancy. Junior told Daddy Bug that she had forbidden him to travel more than one hour away from her. He lethargically performed his duties at the stills for two or three hours a day and then rushed home to see Mona Lisa. His actions were not lost on Daddy Bug. He was not amused, but he did his best to be patient.

Ultimately, he did not show up at Daddy Bug's business at all for awhile. There was no word from him for three days. Daddy Bug made a vow to himself that he would not interfere, complain, or push Junior while he was going through the newness of his role as husband and father-to-be. He had been through it himself and was determined to put no pressure on the nephew he loved as his own son. He worked, along with Jimmie, Sr. at his occupation and said little about the situation.

Daddy bug knew that Jimmie had not contacted his son, either. It was an unwritten law of the mountain that you didn't interfere with a man or his family when they wanted to be alone. They contacted you in time of need. You didn't nose around in their business.

Junior arrived at his father's house at five o'clock in the morning with a two day shadow on his face and a sheepish grin splitting his jaws in two.

"Mona Lisa had the baby at three forty-five. It's a boy. He's got my hair and Mona Lisa's eyes and he's got perfect fingers and toes!"

Jimmie, Sr. tucked his pajama top into his overalls and plugged the coffee pot into the outlet. "Son, we've been a little worried about you, but we knew you would handle everything right and let us know if you needed us. It's great news that you're a daddy now, but I think I'm too young to be a grandpa." Jimmie hugged Junior with genuine affection.

"Daddy, we're going to call him Abraham after Mona Lisa's father. I hope you don't mind. Mona Lisa has always wanted to have a son named Abraham. She loves her Daddy and since she went through all this pain in the last two days, I decided that she at least deserved to name our son what she wanted."

"I realize you have to go along with Mona Lisa on the first name. What did you choose for his middle name?"

"Well, I naturally gave him two middle names. His full name is Abraham Jimmie Billy Haywood. I realize it all doesn't go so good together, but I wanted to honor both you and Daddy Bug at the same time. Kinda' like those Kings of England have all those names. If they can do it, we can do it. We'll just call him Abe for short. Like Abraham Lincoln was called Abe."

"Well, I'm right pleased and I know your Momma will be. That will be quite a name to live up to. Now, you better get on back to your wife and son. I'll make sure your mother and your aunt and uncle know about all the details. We'll see you later in the day and when you decide it's time for us to see the little guy, just let us know."

Junior left his parents house with a happy feeling in his heart. He would carry on the family name. Finally, he had proved to his family what he already knew - he was a man.

He had left Mona Lisa and her parents carrying the bliss of a lifetime with him. What a wonder it was having a son. It was a miracle he would never forget. The mid-wife allowed him to witness the birth. He recreated the scene in his mind as he drove back to his in-laws' house.

The baby arrived early. Mona Lisa was sweating and screaming. Just watching gave him nausea in his stomach that threatened to put him away. Finally, there he was. Abe was nineteen inches long and weighed nine pounds. He looked like he was three months old. No wrinkles like he had heard they had. Just a beautiful newborn baby boy. The product of his and Mona Lisa's love.

She fell asleep almost immediately, so fatigued was she by the four-hour labor. His in-laws called Doc Daly to weigh and measure the baby and sign his birth certificate. Doc Daly pronounced the baby "fit as all get out," and left only fifteen minutes after he had arrived.

When Junior pulled into the driveway of his in-laws' small, ramshackle house, he noticed the silence surrounding the breaking dawn. A few birds had awakened early and were heralding the other feathered creatures with hesitant, chirping sounds.

He made a vow to himself and God that someday he would give his son everything that had been given to him. A nice home, a loving family, and support and guidance would be Abe's heritage. After all, he couldn't have any less than his Daddy had when he was growing up. He was a Haywood and an Unger. Both names to be proud of. Junior forgot, for the moment, that Abe was also half Skruggs.

He crawled from his pickup and made his way toward the front door, and noticed Mona Lisa's parents sitting on the front porch with the family dog. Each of them held a cup in hand and looked at him intently.

"Hello, Son," said the Reverend Mr. Skruggs. "I take it you told all of your family about our grandson. Mona Lisa and Abraham are asleep and I suggest you get some too. We've got a lot of things to talk about tomorrow - or I should say later on today."

"Thanks, Papa Skruggs. I could sure use some shuteye. I dare say, it's been a long night."

"Junior, it's going to be an even longer life. There's a new life in this world. We all have an interest in him. We want to make sure he gets the best that this world has to offer. So, go in and get some rest so you'll be ready to get up and provide the best. You can grab some sleep in the parlor. Mother Skruggs made up a bed for you on the sofa."

"This is the best night of my life. I can't wait for the rest."

Junior went into the house and proceeded to undress in the parlor. Just as he laid his head on the pillow, he heard a whimper from Abe and a low cry from Mona Lisa in the small bedroom they called their own.

He pulled on his pants and hurried in to see what was the matter. The baby lay next to Mona Lisa jabbing the air with his tiny fists. Mona Lisa lay sobbing with her arm over her eyes.

"What's the matter, honey? Can I get you something?" Junior sat on the edge of the bed.

"I don't know what's going to happen to us," she said. "We can't live in this shack forever with my folks. You just have to get us something better. I can't bring up Abraham in the same kind of poverty I've been through."

Junior stroked her hand and patted his son on the head. "Mona Lisa, I won't let us live here forever. You're crying because you've been through a lot. Let's take one day at a time and we'll work through this. Daddy Bug will help me out, I know. He helped my daddy and momma to have a nice life and I'm sure he'll help us. After all, he's trained me in the business and he'll give it to me and Daddy when he goes. In the meantime, I'll just see if we can build our own little house on some of his land. He's got at least ten acres on Cather Mountain and I'm sure he won't mind. In fact, I'll bet he'll be so glad to have us there that he'll help us build it."

"Junior, I don't want to live near them, or on Cather Mountain. I want us to have a nice house in Lake Chastain. You know, like the Mayor and his wife. I want us to have a house overlooking the lake. I want our son to be admired and respected in this town."

"Honey, just go on to sleep. Abe is counting sheep and you should be too. We'll have to discuss all of this tomorrow. We can't decide anything right now."

"Well, all I know is, I want more for us and our son than Daddy Bug can ever give us. Don't forget, our son came from both of us - not just your side."

Junior kissed his wife and ambled to the parlor. He knew Mona Lisa's wants were only the beginning of his new found manhood. When he lay his head on the pillow, his escape from that knowledge was instant sleep.

# 28

Baby Abe was the apple of his daddy's eye, which wasn't surprising. Mona Lisa tolerated him during the day and let her mother and father fawn over him and baby him. When Junior returned from Daddy Bug's after his work was finished for the day, she corralled herself in their room, literally divorcing herself from the rest of the house.

Junior and Abe spent the rest of each day together, bonding and doing all the things that father and son did together. When Abe grew older, he recognized Junior's call to him when he came in the house. He would coo and jabber and show all the signs of excitement that warmed Junior's heart.

Eventually, Mona Lisa tired of the job of being a mother and turned the care of her son over to the Reverend and Mrs. Skruggs and Junior. She told Junior the department store wanted her to model for them when they had their monthly luncheon fashion show. This was her big chance. No longer did she care if Abe was teething or crawling. She was sure that she would soon be modeling in the fashion houses of New York and Paris. Junior listened with patience, sure that she didn't mean the part about caring what Abe was doing.

Mona Lisa realized that she had at last achieved what she had always wanted. Her husband adored her and would do anything for her. She had given him a son and as repayment, she could do what she wanted to do.

In the meanwhile, the communication with Daddy Bug, Vanessa, Lydia Anne and Jimmie, Sr. became less and less frequent for her. She certainly didn't need them anymore. She had bagged Junior.

He went along with her ambition. He was aware that Mona Lisa had suffered from neglect when she was a child and he wanted to encourage her in her dreams of success. He fed and diapered Abe when he got home. He took him for long walks in the evening. He felt he was in paradise, so happy was he with his son.

Junior started taking Abe to visit his relatives on his own. On Saturdays, he would put him in his car seat and drive him for a visit and supper. Daddy Bug had already fashioned a wagon for Abe and painted it red. The entire gang of Ungers and Haywoods would troop down the turnoff to Stop Gap Road and amble along for as much as a mile before starting back to the homestead with the precious bundle who was screaming with delight in the body of the wagon. The only one missing was Mona Lisa.

She complained that if she went along, she would be missing her "beauty sleep" and she needed the time to prepare for her modeling assignments. Junior stifled his true feelings and defended his wife when his family questioned her actions. She was trying to find herself. She had missed the best years of her life by having a baby so soon.

Daddy Bug silently questioned the role of a mother who showed no interest in her responsibilities with Abe, but didn't say anything. He was having the best time of his life with his great-nephew. Abe was soon calling him Daddy Bug and tugging at his hand for their walks on Stop Gap Road.

Along the way, Abe picked up rocks and twigs for his collection which Daddy Bug was helping him to assemble. He had a box full of treasures he had collected. He even stored them under the sink at Daddy Bug's house.

Daddy Bug was aware that Abe's mother did not want the things, as she called them, in her house. That was alright with him. Daddy Bug was satisfied to be the boy's confidant; his uncle that shared his dreams with him. Abe told him that Momma was the pretty lady that left the house on some afternoons and came home tired at night. Daddy Bug saw less and less of her as she withdrew into her own world and what she called her career.

Junior used to apologize to him for Mona Lisa being gone so much. Now, he seemed relieved that Aunt Vanessa, Daddy Bug, Grandma Lydia and Grandpa Jimmie were available to play with Abe all the time. And so was Daddy Bug. He didn't miss Mona Lisa at all.

One such day, Junior brought Abe to the Haywood house for supper. Seated at the picnic table under the trees on the side lawn, Mark and Sue Halbert joined Junior's parents, Daddy Bug and Vanessa. They all shouted greetings as Junior and Abe approached.

"Go in the house and get the high chair for Abe, Junior,"

Lydia Anne said. "Supper will be on the table in about five minutes. We'll eat out here tonight."

As Abe ran to sit on Grandpa Jimmie's lap, Junior went in the house to get the high chair Daddy Bug had made. In seconds he joined the others at the picnic table.

"I'm sure glad to see y'all," he spoke to Mark and Sue. "How does Precious like practicing in Atlanta?" Precious had finished her internship and had been fortunate enough to get established with a prestigious group of doctors in Buckhead.

"She likes it just fine, Junior," Mark said. "We just don't get to see her enough. When she gets any time off she goes off to fancy places with her fancy friends."

"That's a shame, Mark. It seems like you put everything you've got in your kids and then they go off and forget you're even alive sometimes. Look at Juggie and Tessa. The only time we hear from them is when they need something or around the holidays. I guess they just get too busy with their own life. Now, you take Junior here. I don't think we'll have to worry about him. He's not one to forget his family ties, are you, Junior?" Normally, a quiet man, this was one of the longest string of sentences anyone had ever heard from Daddy Bug.

"You sure don't, Daddy Bug. It's especially important to me now that we have little Abe."

When the ladies, followed by Abe, went into the house to get the food, Mark spoke. "Not to change the subject or anything, but I wanted to talk to you boys about a little matter that I'm thinking about. I'm thinking of retiring as Sheriff. I'm just getting too damn old to hustle after the no-goods in this county anymore. Beside that I'm getting too weak to hold my gun steady."

"Why, Mark, Lake Chastain wouldn't be the same without you. You know all the business of everyone in the County. You know who all the people are who are into that drug business that's getting so bad. I doubt a new man could step into your shoes," Jimmie said.

"Well, I'm headed for the wrong side of sixty. It's time to hang it up. But, I've got a proposition. I'd like to see Junior here run for Sheriff. I'd back him and everybody else would too, if I told them to."

The statement took everyone by surprise, particularly Junior.

"Mark, I've never even thought about running for Sheriff. I wouldn't know the first thing about it."

"Never you mind, son. We'll talk after supper. Here come the women with the food. We'll take Abe for a walk after supper and I'll explain my ..."

"Daddy Bug and I will go with you while the women clean up," Jimmie interrupted. No plans would be made about Junior's future without him being present.

After supper, the men excused themselves and took a walk to the stills. As usual, Daddy Bug poured the mist for everyone present into plastic glasses he kept in the shed for just such a purpose.

"Now Mark," he said as they settled into sitting positions around the clearing. "Just what is all this about Junior running for Sheriff of Dixon County?"

"Daddy Bug, I've been thinking a lot about the situation. I've got to quit. I can't take it no more. We need a man in that office that will see that things go right here. I've been watching Junior and I'm impressed with what I see."

"But Mark," Junior interjected, "I don't know anything about running for office."

"Never you mind. You're old enough to run, and I'll guide you every step of the way. You've become a responsible husband and father. Your daddy and Daddy Bug will help you, too. You can win, Son. I know you can. What do you think about the idea, Daddy Bug and Jimmie?"

Jimmie seemed excited about the prospects for his son. He had never dreamed that Junior would have the opportunity to become the Sheriff of the County. The position held a certain amount of respect and prestige. Jimmie, himself, would never have aspired to it, but he could see that his son was a strong, brave, and handsome man that might appeal to the voters.

"I, for one, would be for it if Junior wanted to try for it. He'd have my backing," said the proud father.

Daddy Bug took a sip of the white whiskey and leaned back against the shed. "Let's let Junior decide. If he wants to, I'll back him all the way."

"Well, the election"s coming up in November and we only have a few months to get this thing going. He'll have to make up his mind pretty soon." Mark said. "I've got a few markers to call in, if he decides to run. I'll have to have time to get to my contacts. Plus, we'll have to get a few campaign contributions from some influential people. Hell, we'll take anybody's money. The town fathers will just about go along with what I say."

Junior looked dazed. Jimmie was aware that everything might be going too fast for him. Here they were, three men were talking about his future and he hadn't done more than listen.

"Let me talk to Mona Lisa about this. I'll make up my mind within a few days and we'll take it from there," Junior said.

"Don't take too long, Son. If you decide to do this, we've got a lot of work to do. Fred Jennings is already campaigning pretty hard for the Republicans and he doesn't have any opposition in the primary. Everybody thinks I'll run again so there's nobody running against me in the primary in June. We could pull off a real good thing if you jump in with me backing you. Fresh blood and all that." The Sheriff grinned at his own cleverness. "Get tough son. If you want to run with the big dogs, you've got to learn how to piss in the tall grass."

Junior picked himself up from the damp earth and stretched both of his muscular arms toward the full moon.

He glanced at Daddy Bug who stared at him intently in the pale shadowy light.

"Daddy Bug, I need to get Abe home to his own bed. Why don't we talk about this on Saturday, next? By that time, I can get a lot of things straight in my head."

"Don't let anybody force you into anything, son. Talk it over with yourself. See how you feel and what it would do for you and your family. Whatever you decide, we're all with you." Daddy Bug rose with the other two men.

They strolled back to the house in silence. Four grown men heading for the fate dealt to them by the mountain, their heritage and their lifestyles. None of them believed in predestination, but predestination was not a fickle mistress to be seduced by these mountain men.

# 29

So, thought Junior as he excitedly drove his young son home. He was to be a political entity in his home State of Alabama. It was practically guaranteed by Mark Halbert, and he was backed up by one of the most influential men in North Alabama - his Daddy Bug - his Uncle Daddy Bug.

Junior talked to Mona Lisa when he returned home. He told her about this opportunity that had been handed to him on a "silver platter." He mentioned that Mark Halbert was stepping down and that Mark wanted Junior, himself, to take up the torch and continue the law enforcement in Dixon County.

He sat with her at the table in her parent's house after he had tucked Abe in his crib. His manner was somber and mature. He explained the astonishing offer and his ambivalence about his feelings until he talked to her.

"But, Sugar," she said. "How could it possibly be of an interest to us for you to be the Sheriff of Dixon County in this day and age? Sheriffs don't really have any influence anymore, do they?"

"They have more than you think," he said. "It could be the road to becoming the Mayor of Lake Chastain, the Attorney General, a Congressman or even the Governor of the State of Alabama. Who knows what it could lead to? It's a start. I'm only twenty-two years old, almost twenty-three, and I've got the most powerful Sheriff and the most powerful men in Dixon County behind me, namely Mark Halbert and Daddy Bug."

"Well, Junior," she said as she lounged in her bathrobe at the table, "let me tell you one thing. You can do this if you want to, but I refuse to allow Daddy Bug to direct our life anymore. I'll appear with you on the campaign and I'll be sweet and wonderful so you can get elected Sheriff of Dixon County, but don't expect me to kiss up to Daddy Bug. He didn't have my respect in the past and he won't have my respect in the future. I've just heard too much about what he does to keep control of everybody. Being like I am, I'll keep control of myself and that's that."

"I guess that's all I can ask from you is that you back me and our own family. Help me and it can only get us ahead in life. We've got nothing to lose. I'll be the one to deal with Daddy Bug and Mark Halbert. You just be my pretty little wife and take care of our son and I'll take care of all the rest."

"Does that mean that we could have our house on the lake where Abe could grow up with his head raised above the white trash of this town?"

"Honey, it would mean that it's the beginning of something great for us. It all depends on how much you support me. You'd have to keep yourself up a little better. You've been letting yourself go since Abe was born, that is except when you go on your modeling assignments. Maybe you could put on a little makeup when we go out. Do up your hair in curls. What do you think? Do you think it would be worth it?"

"I guess I always knew you were going to be somebody. Maybe that's why I put up with that uncle of yours. He thinks he's God's gift to humanity. I never could stand him, but I know you love him. Did your daddy and momma go along with this thing? Were they even in on it?" She was filled with questions.

"Daddy was in on the whole conversation and he completely backs it. Momma will go along with what Daddy thinks. Remember, Momma is Daddy Bug's sister. He has taken care of her since she was a little girl. She trusts him completely in every decision."

"Well, it just seems like when it comes right down to it, Daddy Bug makes every decision for everybody in this family, including us. I want you to run for Sheriff if it will be good for us and Abe, but not just if it will please Daddy Bug. After all, we are a family ourselves, now. In case, you never realized it, you and me and Abe are a family separate from your momma and daddy and Daddy Bug."

"That's one thing I don't want you to dwell on. Daddy Bug has been a big influence on me and he practically taught me everything I know about responsibility. It's because of him that I'm the man I am right now. Mark said I was grown up and responsible and I think I owe most of that to Daddy Bug. He took it upon himself in these past few years to make sure I knew how to take care of myself and my family. And, that family was you for a while and now Abe. He would never take anything from me for it, but he helped me know people."

"Well the only thing I can say is, I don't care about anything but us and our family. By that, I mean you and me and Abe. So anything you do now has to be totally dedicated to the three of us. If you can do that, then I'll do whatever it takes to get you elected. Just tell me what I need to do."

"I knew I could count on you, babe. Mark told me tonight that I have to go and register and get qualified. He's holding a press conference within the next week and announcing his backing for me in the primary. He said he would be calling in his markers. I guess that means that some people owe him favors."

"What about Sue? What does she say about him retiring? Surely, she has something to say about it."

"Sue leaves everything to Mark. She's a smart girl. You could take some lessons. The only thing she says anything about is what they have for supper."

"What you want in a wife is a little old know-nothing that you can boss around, Junior. You got the wrong person, if that's what you want. What I want is a partnership that's going to raise a fine, intelligent son, namely Abe. I will not put up with anything less. Take it or leave it."

"What are you talking about, girl? All I wanted to do is try to make a life for us. Now, I've got an opportunity to get us ahead. What's going on with this conversation?"

"What I'm saying, Junior, is that you go to that press conference with Mark. Push your chest out and hold your chin up. Look like the man you are. But, let Daddy Bug and Mark know that you're your own man and that you won't be a pawn for anyone. I know you can do it."

Junior looked down at the table and then looked at his Mona Lisa. So far, he had abided by her wishes and had done all right. Yes, Daddy Bug had warned him about being true to his blood. He had not compromised his family, thus far. However, something in Mona Lisa's demeanor threw a red flag into his reasoning. It was a threatening flag that flew in the face of everything he had ever learned in his upbringing. It made him sit up straight at the table and look directly into Mona Lisa's captivating eyes.

"I'll never be a pawn for anyone, Mona Lisa, but I'll never go against my kin, least of all, Daddy Bug or my own

Daddy. Don't forget that a man can't go against his blood. Don't ever ask me to do it. Don't ever ask me to choose."

"I'm not asking you to choose, Junior, but don't ask me to choose between Daddy Bug and Abe either."

"What do you mean by that, Mona Lisa? I'd never ask you to choose between Daddy Bug and Abe. It's no contest."

"What I mean, sweetheart, is that if Daddy Bug gets in our face too much while you're becoming a big-time Sheriff, I'll take Abe away from you and you'll never see him again."

"You do that, girl, and you'll not only have Daddy Bug to contend with, you'll have me, and I won't be easy on you. Now, I've just about heard all I need to from you. Get on to bed."

"It'll be a cold day in hell when you can tell me what to do in my own parents' house. You can sleep on the couch tonight."

And so ended the day that was supposed to be the beginning of the rest of Jimmie Haywood Jr.'s happy life. He didn't get to sleep until nearly daybreak. When the sun came over the crest of the mountain, he looked out the window, rolled over to face the back of the couch and slept. His final thought before drifting off was that he had made up his mind that he was going to be the best Sheriff Dixon County ever had.

# 30

The political climate was gearing up in Dixon County, Alabama. Lake Chastain was rapidly becoming a hotbed of activity, with practically every candidate for every office maintaining a campaign headquarters for the coming primary.

Aside from the headline news that Sheriff Mark Halbert was stepping down and endorsing a new, young candidate, the buzz was about the controversy of Lake Chastain becoming the only "wet" city in Dixon County. Most counties in Alabama were dry. But, Lake Chastain was fast becoming a popular tourist attraction and not a few of the tourists were complaining that they needed to stay in a town where they could wet their whistle without worrying about the law.

The recent actions of the Alabama legislature had made a law that individual towns within a County could sell alcoholic beverages, even if the County was dry. This was the boon that movers and shakers of Lake Chastain had been waiting for. It was a way to keep their tourist trade happy, but keep the county dry as it was intended to be. The referendum was to be put on the ballot for the citizens of Lake Chastain. Should they have open liquor sales or should they stay dry like the rest of Dixon County?

Daddy Bug didn't live inside the city limits of Lake Chastain, but he knew their actions would have a great impact on his operations. Some of his best customers lived there. He was against the State of Alabama Beverage Commission taking those customers away.

If this referendum got on the ballot in the Fall, the good people of Lake Chastain could walk into any ABC store or retail liquor store and stock up on legal stuff. They would pay a lot more for it because of the taxes, but they wouldn't have to worry about having it in their car or homes. They could openly pour a drink for the Mayor or any other guest in their home.

Daddy Bug went to Mark Talbert about the problem. Mark was sympathetic and tried to assure him his customers would be loyal to him. The impact would be on his distributors who were supplying other North Alabama areas. The same referendum was going on the ballot in other counties and cities in the State. Mark would talk to as many people as he could to get them to vote against the local referendum.

Daddy Bug worried that this was the beginning of the end. He was becoming a dinosaur to the enlightenment of the younger, more progressive people moving to or transferring into the state.

Things were changing in other ways, too. Many of the younger people had taken jobs with big firms in Atlanta and Birmingham. If they moved back to the North Alabama area, they wanted the same privileges they had grown accustomed to in the huge cities.

Those privileges included having cocktail parties with liquor being poured from proper bottles, with proper labels to both men and women. Women were now considered almost on an equal with men, when it came to having a cocktail. They could serve what they wanted to and drink what they desired. At least many of the people of Lake Chastain and other progressive communities thought they could. The public sentiment was running strongly for the referendum.

Daddy Bug spoke to Vanessa about his worries as he paced the bedroom floor. He considered that this might be his final swan song.

"Honey, they may well take the food out of our mouth if this thing passes in all these cities. We won't have Mark to back us up. I don't know how to fight it anymore."

"Daddy Bug, stop your worrying. Junior will take over as Sheriff. We won't have to worry about as much expense. The house is paid for and we can go on as we were."

"There's also Lydia Anne and Jimmie, Sr. to worry about. What if we get shut down? How are we going to go on?"

"Their house is paid for like ours. We've got all this acreage to grow things. We can make do. I know you've got something set aside. Juggie and Tessa are doing fine in Atlanta with their jobs. We don't have anybody else to support."

He continued as if he hadn't heard her. "I just don't know what to do. Maybe I can sell off some of this land to the developers. I hate to have a bunch of close, nosey neighbors, but if push comes to shove, I might have to."

He went on, "August Seaman asked me about buying some of my land when I met him in town the other day. He wants to build one of those fancy subdivisions and sell high-priced houses to all those rich Yankees moving to this area to retire.

"Actually, his Daddy before him had been trying to buy some of the land when all those rocket scientists started to move into the area years ago. My Pa told me he just laughed at him. He told Pa that those people wanted their homes built in the mountains and would pay a pretty penny. Pa said that people in hell wanted ice water, too, and no snooty scientists would live on his mountain."

"Honey, let's don't worry now about selling our land. We may not ever have to. Between us and Lydia Anne and Jimmie, we'll all get along just fine. It would break my heart for you to go and sell any of our land just now. Besides, maybe the referendum won't pass and we'll just go on like before."

Vanessa knew Daddy Bug was lost in his own thoughts when he got up abruptly and headed for the back door. He would be headed down to his stills. That's where he always went when he got worried.

She sat at the table and drank her ice tea. Whatever happened at the election, she wanted him to know that things would be all right. Things had to be all right.

Sue told her that the support for Junior was at an all time high and kept her up to date on the campaign. He had won the run-off easily. His opponent for the November election was a Vietnam Veteran with a limp who campaigned half-heartedly.

Handsome, friendly and outgoing, Junior Haywood, was taking the County by storm. His political message was that he, as Sheriff, would bust all the illegal stills in Dixon County and work with the State boys to rid Dixon County of bootleggers and runners. He knew this would appeal to all the tea-totallers in the County, plus all the people who wanted the ABC and retail liquor stores in Lake Chastain. He couldn't lose. His campaign was jam up and jelly tight to win. He had forgotten to mention that none of those promises applied to Daddy Bug's stills.

Junior bragged to everyone that Mona Lisa had gotten real good at holding political lunches for his female supporters at the local cafe. The cafe was donating the lunches free, as a show of support.

Sometimes, Junior would make a personal appearance at these lunches. The women would shout and clap as if he were a famous country singer. They couldn't get enough of his handsome face, his beautiful white teeth and his strong physique.

Sue, Mark and Lydia Anne would sit with Mona Lisa at these appearances and quiet her fears that someone was going to take Junior away from her and Abe. Junior did his best to make her confident. He told her how beautiful she was and to take pride in his popularity. "You can bask in the limelight right along with me."

Now, with less than a month to go in the election, Junior out-polled his opponent by two to one. He was a shoo-in for Dixon County Sheriff.

As Vanessa finished her tea and started to clear the table, she thought back to the day of his birth nearly twenty-three years ago. So much had happened to all of them since then. Her parents and brother were dead. Juggie and Tessa were grown and living on their own; neither had married. Precious Halbert was a Doctor who had also never married. Benji traveled the country as a television evangelist with his bleached blonde wife.

They rarely heard from Benji. They had never even met his wife. Juggy and Tessa got home only on Christmas and Thanksgiving. They usually rode with Precious from Atlanta.

Vanessa remembered, too, her episode with alcohol and her mental illness. Her cure was instantaneous when she saw her brother safely home from Vietnam. Now, she knew that it had been a major depression and was not so ashamed of it. She had been a good wife and mother since that time.

Vanessa felt a heaviness in her chest. It had been a long hard day of canning vegetables, and she was worried about Daddy Bug's change in attitude. He was getting more and more passive about life. That simply wasn't his style. As long as she had known him, he had been the king of his family and the mountain.

She was tired. Maybe she would go sit in the cooling evening air and rock a bit.

Daddy Bug's appearance at the back door brought her from her thoughts. "Why Daddy Bug, what's the matter with you? You're all red in the face. Are you sick?"

"No, I'm not sick." he said, "I just tore down two of the stills. I'll only need just one now. I kept the one Pa and I had. I'll sell the other two."

Vanessa was shocked, but managed to say in a calm voice, "If you think that's for the best, I'm the last one to complain. Maybe we can do a little traveling now. Maybe, we can go to Atlanta and see the kids. I've never been there."

"Woman, I don't ever intend to go to Atlanta and I'm not getting out of the business. I'll make enough for the customers I keep."

"What about your distributors?"

"I've already told them earlier today by phone. Two of them want to buy the other stills. They said there is no way their separate areas will ever go wet. So, I'm putting them in their own business. The rest will have to do something else."

"Well, we'll know soon enough whether Lake Chastain is going wet and we'll know soon enough whether Junior will be Sheriff. Let's go out and sit on the porch and not worry about it."

You go and sit on the porch if you want, honey. I've got to load up those stills and get them to Pinky and Alan. It's almost dark and I want to get back by midnight."

"Are you going by yourself?"

"No, I talked to Mark this morning. The outgoing Sheriff of Dixon County is going to do one last mission of mercy for the good people. He's going to personally help me deliver these two stills and rid the County of two more blights upon society."

# 31

Daddy Bug and Mark rumbled along in the pickup. Mark stared silently through the windshield and Daddy Bug was thinking about everything that had happened during the twenty-eight years since his Pa died.

He loved his way of life, and he knew it was coming to an end. The whole thing was coming unraveled at the seams. He formerly had three stills in operation. As of tonight, he had one.

Full circle. He had started with only one and now he was delivering his other two to his distributors. It was fair. He would end up with what his Daddy did. They really didn't need more than that. He could take care of his family with one still. Back to the basics, he thought.

"Well, Mark, we've been through a lot together, haven't we?" Daddy Bug spoke to the older man who had been his friend for all of those years.

"Don't think we won't go through a lot more. Maybe we can get in a little more fishing and hunting together now."

"I sure hope so. Sure does make me sad to get rid of these two stills, but I can use the money. Besides, I got to thinking that with the business sure to go downhill, maybe I could take Vanessa for a few little trips. She's never had a vacation during our whole marriage. It's high time she got some pleasure out of life."

We're two lucky men, Daddy Bug. Sue is just about the greatest wife I could have ever gotten and your Vanessa is a sainted angel."

"I knew she was for me the minute I met her in high school. All the other guys were dating those high-falutin' cheerleaders, but Vanessa was the one for me. She was sweet and shy and real. Plus, she was a real beauty, too."

"Yeah, I know what you mean. I felt the same way when I saw Sue sitting on that stool in the restaurant. I had to go and introduce myself. Course you and I both know she was still married to that old hog-face Thurmon. Best thing I ever did was blow him away when he was holding your brother Benji hostage."

"It took Benji a long time to get over that, but he turned out all right. He doesn't like to come back here though. I wonder if it's connected to when that happened to him?"

"Could be. They say sometimes you keep those kind of terrors someplace in your head and try to forget them, but they affect you in different ways. Anyway, you tell Benji hello for me if you see him."

"He's a preacher now. Travels all over. Goes on the television. That's the only place I see him."

The conversation lulled as the two men drove through the winding roads of the North Alabama mountains. The moon, although a mere crescent, cast an strange light on the trees that surrounded the road. They drove with the windows down and occasionally spotted an owl darting from the branches to snatch up some small prey that scurried about.

The lights of the pickup shone on racoons and possums running from the road or lying dead at the side.

Their first destination was the northeast corner of Alabama, the territory run by Pinky Gleason. They had to go through several small towns and counties to get there. He wasn't afraid of being stopped in Dixon County because he was the Sheriff. However, he urged Daddy Bug to take side streets when passing through towns and to watch his speed at all times.

He knew first hand about the abundance of speed traps in some towns and counties. He knew because he had some in Dixon County. His deputies knew just where to park and observe the out of state and out of county license plates. Out of state were the best, because the drivers usually wanted to pay their ticket immediately. When the deputies had failed to issue their quota of tickets toward the end of the month, Mark gave them the go ahead to issue tickets to other Alabamans.

Since it was the last week in October, Mark knew that extra forces would be out all over these counties. He didn't want to take a chance on getting caught. Any deputy would check under the tarp and see what they were carrying.

A statewide alert had been sent from the drug boys in Montgomery that there were thousands of marijuana plants being grown and sold in the North Alabama mountains. They advised that the plants were probably transported to buyers at night. Mark knew any deputy worth his badge would be delighted to discover the dismantled stills in the back of the pickup. His status as Sheriff of Dixon County wouldn't help him here.

Mark's other worry was the helicopter surveillance. He often heard them flying over the area day and night. If they should spot a lone pickup traveling these back roads, they could radio a car to stop it. Or, they could simply spotlight the car and order it to pull over with their loudspeaker while they landed for the search.

Hesitantly, he broached the subject with Daddy Bug. "You figure we'll get these things delivered without a pull- over?"

"Mark, don't you worry about a thing," Daddy Bug assured him. I've been running whisky for so long, I know most of the law up here."

"What about the State Boys? I don't want to run into any of them. They're out in full force looking for marijuana growers trying to transport their product."

"I don't either. Think I ought to leave both of these things at Pinky's and carry the other one to Alan Cotter during the day tomorrow?"

"How far is it to Pinky's from here?"

"We've only got a few miles to go. He's right near the Georgia border. Maybe a fifteen minute drive from here."

Mark breathed a sigh of relief. He sure didn't want to spend his retirement in the Federal pen.

"That's great. Maybe we should just unload everything there, then. No sense taking crazy chances."

Daddy Bug glanced at the still handsome profile of Sheriff Mark Halbert. "Do I detect a bit of caution in the fearless Sheriff of Dixon County?"

Mark laughed at the question. "I don't look good in prison clothes. Besides, I'd lose my retirement after all these years. Then, Sue might leave me for someone else."

"She'd never leave you because of money. Old man Thurmon left her a bunch of money, didn't he?" Daddy Bug felt at ease asking such a personal question of his old friend..

"I was just kidding. Yes, she inherited the house, car and old Thurmon had a stash of money in the First National that she didn't even know about. He cried poor mouth to her all the time. Wouldn't even paint the house."

Daddy Bug turned off the state road onto a small gravel road that ran through a grove of trees. Although it could not be seen from the road, Pinky Gleason's house stood on a small rise about a quarter mile back. It was a modest brick ranch, neatly maintained, with a separate garage and work shop.

Pinky always told Daddy Bug it didn't pay to look too rich or too poor. If you looked like one or the other, it always drew attention. Daddy Bug, who had been at the house many times, couldn't agree more. It was precisely this policy by which he maintained his own house, and Lydia Anne and Jimmie's house.

The pickup turned in the driveway and Pinky stepped from the side door to meet them. "Hi, y'all. See that you made it O.K."

The two men stepped from the truck and shook hands in greeting. "This here is Sheriff Mark Halbert, Pinky. He's a good friend of mine."

Pinky shook hands with Mark, but he had a puzzled look on his face. "Good to meet you, Sheriff. How is it you came all the way up here with Daddy Bug?"

"I'm along just for company and to help you unload these stills, Pinky. What are friends for if they can't help out once in a while?"

"Well, I'll be darned. You said a mouthful, Sheriff. Let's unload it in the garage. Then I can lock the doors for the night."

"Pinky," said Daddy Bug, "I need to leave both of them with you for the night. I'll come back tomorrow for the other one to carry to Alan Cotter. The Sheriff here thinks it's too risky tonight. Thinks a lot of State boys are out checking vehicles for marijuana."

"That'll be just fine with me. I'll be here tomorrow. Just give a call before you come."

The men proceeded to unload the two stills into the garage. When they finished, they said their goodbyes and drove back to the state road, satisfied that they would get safely home without being stopped.

They settled in for the long drive home, chatting about the upcoming election and other things that concerned them. Daddy Bug still could not believe that his life was changing so much. He knew that he would have to change his way of doing things. He had taken for granted the fact that he would have to work hard all of his life. Now, both he and his friend would have some time on their hands.

Suddenly, interrupting their conversation, a flashing light appeared in the rearview mirror and a siren blared its impatience. The cruiser was speeding rapidly to the rear of the pickup.

"Holy shit, he wants us," Mark said. "Wonder what he's trying to get us on."

"I wasn't speeding or anything. I better pull over. Thank God we unloaded those stills."

Bug pulled to the side of the road with the cruiser right behind him. Both men got out of the car as the deputy got out of his.

"What seems to be the problem, Deputy?" Mark spoke first.

The deputy stepped up to Mark. "Are you Sheriff Mark Halbert?"

"Yes, I am. What can I do for you?"

"I got a call from dispatch about a half hour ago. Your wife's name is Sue isn't it?"

"It sure is. Is something the matter?" Mark's voice had a sense of urgency.

"Well, she said to call home right away. She had to tell you something. She wouldn't say what it was. Just told central approximately where you would be and what kind of vehicle you would be in. I've been cruising the area since then."

"Where's the nearest phone from here?"

"There's one right up ahead at the gas station. Just follow me."

The deputy got in his car and pulled ahead of the men on the road. Daddy Bug and Mark got in the truck and sped after him.

"Wonder what's going on. Sue knows not to ever call me when I'm helping you. This kind of worries me. Hope nothing's wrong with her," Mark said.

Within minutes the men followed the cruiser to the public telephone booth. Mark jumped out of the car and made a credit card call home.

Daddy Bug thanked the deputy and got back in the pickup. He could see the concern on Mark's face as he spoke into the receiver. Finally, he hung up the receiver and got back in the truck.

"What's going on?" said Daddy Bug.

Mark put his hand on the younger man's shoulder. "I don't know how to tell you this, old friend. Vanessa had a heart attack. She was gone instantly. There was nothing they could do. Sue was there when it happened."

Daddy Bug put his head on the steering wheel and cried. Vanessa was his life and she was dead. He could not take her on vacation now. It was too late.

# 32

He attended the funeral in a daze. Almost oblivious to the crowd and the fact that Juggie and Tessa supported him, he stood and watched as they lowered the casket into the grave near the tombstones of his mother and father. He watched the crowd depart and leave him standing beside the grave with Juggie, Tessa and Precious.

Tears rolled down his cheeks as he turned to walk back to Precious' car. Soon he would face the emptiness of a house without Vanessa. Juggie, Tessa and Precious were to leave the next day for Atlanta. Then, he would be all alone. He didn't think he could survive.

Tessa took his arm and helped him back to the car. He staggered trying to get in the back seat. "Pa, watch your head. Just sit back and relax. We'll be home in no time."

Juggie drove as Precious sat on the passenger side of the front seat. Neither spoke. Occasionally, one of them sobbed..

Suddenly Daddy Bug spoke in a slow, sad voice, "I'm just glad it was fast and she didn't have to suffer. But, I don't know what I'll do without her.

Tessa held his hand and said, "We'll come home a lot more often. You have Mark and Sue, and Jimmie and Lydia Anne. Did you know Junior offered to move in with you? Then, you'd have Mona Lisa and Abe to keep you company, too."

"It won't bring her back. Nothing can bring her back."

"Pa, I know this is so painful for you right now. Just take it one day at a time. We'll call you every day," Tessa was crying now as she put her head on her father's shoulder and hugged his neck.

When they arrived at Daddy Bug's home they saw that neighbors had come to share their bereavement. There were about twenty cars of various makes and models parked along the long access road to Daddy Bug's house.

Inside, Lydia Anne and Sue arranged all the food the neighbors brought, setting it on the big kitchen table. A jar of the recipe sat in plain sight along with paper cups and a pitcher of iced tea. Lydia Anne didn't care what anybody thought. They could drink it or not.

She poured a cup of it and brought it to Daddy Bug who immediately went to his bedroom. "Here, you go, brother. Have a few sips of this. It'll make you feel better."

She sat down beside him on the bed and put the cup in his trembling hand. He was shaking all over, so intense was his grief. He took the cup and drank from it.

"Thank you Lydia Anne. This will just make me numb but right now that's better than this feeling I have. I feel like a part of me is gone forever."

"We all loved Vanessa, too. We know we can't feel the loss that you do, but we'll miss her."

"Thank all the folks out there for bringing the food. I hope they understand, but I don't feel like socializing right now. I think I'll just stay back here and try to get a little rest."

"I'll do that for you, Daddy Bug. Don't you worry about a thing. Just rest for now. I'll fix you a plate after they all go."

"Lydia Anne, tell Junior and Mona Lisa that I would like for them to move in with me. It would be nice to have little Abe around."

"They said to just give them the word. I think they'll stay over tonight so you won't be alone," Lydia said as she stood by the door.

"That's good. I'd like that," Daddy Bug said and laid his head on the pillow. He was asleep before the door closed.

He awoke with a start. It was starting to get dark in the room. He could hear the quiet conversation in the parlor. Junior was talking to Abe in his special father's way. Abe was laughing and talking. Daddy Bug loved to listen to his great-nephew. He was the picture of Junior and indeed, reminded Daddy Bug of all the pleasure he had in helping to raise Junior. Then, he remembered where he had been that day and his thoughts again returned to Vanessa.

He arose and splashed water in his face, glancing in the mirror as he did so. Wrinkles appeared upon his face that were not there three days prior. At forty-four years of age, he looked like an old man.

When he went into the parlor, only Junior, Mona Lisa and Abe were there.

"Where did everybody go?" he said by way of greeting.

"They all left after only an hour," Junior said. "Momma and Daddy said to call them if you need them. We'll be staying with you for a while if that's okay."

Daddy Bug sat next to Junior on the couch and took Abe onto his lap. "I'm grateful for the company, son. It will be the best thing in the world for me now."

Mona Lisa arose and lifted Abe off of his lamp. "Daddy Bug, I have to put Abe to bed now. It's getting late." Then to Abe, she said, "Say goodnight to Daddy Bug, punkin."

"Night night, Daddy Bug," Abe said in his sweet young voice. "I love you."

"I love you, too." Daddy Bug said, his eyes suddenly moist.

Mona Lisa and Abe left the room and Junior turned and grasped the older man on the shoulder. His gesture seemed to comfort Daddy Bug.

"Daddy Bug, I realize this may not be the right time to bring this up, but it could help to fill some time in the coming days. Would you mind taking care of Abe when Mona Lisa and I have to go campaigning? The election is less than a week away, and we have to hit it hard. Momma and Daddy have to go help Grandpa finish the house they're building, so we'd sure appreciate it."

"Give me a day to get some things done and I'll be glad to take care of Abe. I've got to go up to see a couple of my distributors and take care of some unfinished business. As a matter of fact, you can go with me tomorrow if you're not busy."

"Where do you have to go, Daddy Bug?"

"I have to go up to Pinky's place and get one of the stills I left with him and take it over to Alan Cotter's. I'm only keeping one for myself."

"Why is that. No one is sure the referendum will pass in Lake Chastain."

"Well, my heart's not in the operation now anyway with Vanessa gone. I'm just keeping one to supply a few of my old faithful customers who'll keep coming to me even if the town goes wet."

"I'll go with you tomorrow, Daddy Bug. But, after that I'll have to stay away from anything to do with the business. I'm going to be Sheriff and I don't want anybody to think I'm double-dealing."

"That's fine with me, Junior. Just forget all about it. I won't be demanding that you help me with the business. Just make sure that no ABC boys come around here. I've had enough heartbreaks for now. I sure don't want to end up behind bars at this late date."

"You can count on me, Daddy Bug. My lips will be sealed on anything about you or the business after I'm Sheriff. If Mark didn't see anything wrong with it, I guess I have to go along with it. I just can't take part in it."

"In case you don't know it, Junior. The business is what raised you and made you what you are today. Remember, it was also your daddy's business."

"I realize that Daddy Bug. That's why I said I'll keep the secret. Nobody will hear it from me."

When Mona Lisa entered the room, both the men shifted the conversation to something else. They were keenly aware that she hated the business, but put up with it for Junior's sake.

"Did you get Abe put down?" Junior asked.

"Yes, and don't make any noise. I don't want to have to get up with him. I'm going to bed as soon as I get a glass of milk."

Daddy Bug looked at Junior and winked. He was used to Mona Lisa's curt manner around him and it usually amused him. Junior winked back.

"Sure thing, honey," he said. "Daddy Bug and I were just having a discussion about the election. He's taking care of Abe when we have to go out and campaign."

"Well, that's right nice of you, Daddy Bug," she said. "Just make sure nothing happens to him. He's a handful sometimes."

"I'll watch him with my life, Mona Lisa. Nothing will happen to him while he's under my care."

"Well, just make sure of it," she said flouncing out of the room and slamming the door to the bedroom.

The two men rose to say their goodnights and Daddy Bug realized that Mona Lisa had never expressed her sorrow that Vanessa was dead. He also realized that she had not cried, and in fact, had remained aloof about the whole matter.

In the days following, the fact that Mona Lisa cared nothing about him made itself apparent. She and Junior went to different clubs and meetings to campaign strenuously. She would write instructions for Abe's care in her rounded handwriting. The handwriting of a child, he thought disdainfully.

*Put Abe down at eight. Make sure he gets his bath and juice before he goes to bed. Don't let him watch too much television.* She ordered him on paper. Neither a please, nor a thank you, was given written or verbally.

When they arrived home, she immediately checked to see that Abe was still alive and had not come to a bad end by the negligence of Daddy Bug. While Junior was appreciative and told him so, Mona Lisa simply acted as if he owed it to them to make sure that they could be at all their appearances.

The day of the election, they all arose early. Daddy Bug was still in his nightshirt when Junior and Mona Lisa left to vote. They wanted to be early at the polls so the television cameras could record their entrance and broadcast it the rest of the day. One last showing on the air couldn't hurt. With Junior's smile, it was bound to get them a few more votes from the late comers.

"Make sure Abe has his special breakfast and turn on the TV for him so he can see Momma and Daddy," she said.

Daddy Bug stood at the door with Abe in his arms. He said nothing, but simply looked at her while Abe waved goodbye.

"Goodbye, Daddy Bug. See you soon. We'll be back in time for you to vote," Junior called from the driveway.

Daddy Bug waved and turned to go inside. He put Abe in the high chair at the table and fixed a soft boiled egg and toast for each of them. He flicked on the small portable television he had purchased for Vanessa for Christmas.

Settling into his own chair, he watched the seven o'clock news while they ate. The turnout was heavy in Lake Chastain. The announcer told the world that Junior Haywood was a heavy favorite for Dixon County Sheriff and the referendum to make Lake Chastain "wet" was going to pass.

Abe talked to the television, pointing and asking who those people were. Daddy Bug largely ignored him until he recognized Junior and Mona Lisa talking to the camera.

"Momma and Daddy are on the television," Abe shouted.

"They sure are, son. You're looking at Momma and your Daddy, who will be the next Sheriff of Dixon County. I'm not sure I like the notion, but he'll win."

Daddy Bug was right. At the end of the night, with 98% of the boxes reporting, Junior Haywood was the Sheriff, and the town of Lake Chastain was officially wet.

He had not even bothered to vote. Feigning illness, he took to his room for the rest of the day when Junior and Mona Lisa returned. Junior didn't need his vote to win and neither did the referendum that took away two-thirds of his livelihood.

# 33

His life changed radically with the inclusion of three people in his everyday life. Even though he was related to them, he found himself increasingly disturbed at the loss of his privacy. He still ached with loneliness for the serenity he enjoyed with Vanessa.

He felt empty inside in spite of the constant activity surrounding him. His ears rang with their frequent demands as he tried to focus on the here and now.

"Daddy Bug, can you do this? Daddy Bug can you fix this?"

Whether the questions came from little Abe, Mona Lisa or Junior, they seemed an intrusion upon his grief. After several months, he felt he could take no more of them on a daily basis.

He particularly resented Mona Lisa who had taken over the house, rearranging furniture, changing the window dressings and virtually eliminating any trace of Vanessa from the house. Daddy Bug put his foot down when she started to pack up Vanessa's clothing and personal articles from his bedroom.

Junior was busy with his new job as Sheriff. He was gone when Daddy Bug got up in the morning and usually came home long after Daddy Bug went to bed. He would lie there and listen to them argue about Junior's long hours and hear Mona Lisa whine about being stuck with "that old man and a little kid." At those times, he wanted to get up and order them out of house.

When Spring arrived, he decided the time had come to talk to them. Although he loved Junior and little Abe, he was frustrated with Mona Lisa and her nagging and complaining about everything and everybody. One rare evening when Junior got home earlier than usual, Abe was asleep and he broached the subject as they sat on the front porch.

"Junior, I think it's time you two thought about your own place. I appreciate you staying with me during a real rough time, but you make a good living now and all young couples should have a place of their own."

Mona Lisa started, "Don't try to kid us, Daddy Bug. You just don't want us here. I told Junior the other night how you didn't even answer me anymore when I talk to you."

"Mona Lisa, that's no way to talk to Daddy Bug," Junior said. Then to Daddy Bug, "Sir, have we been acting out of line? I'm right sorry if we have been. I guess I've been putting in so many hours being Sheriff, I've been neglecting the home front."

"I have to be honest with you, son. When a body gets older like me, it's hard to have so much commotion around all the time. It's nothing against you or Abe. Besides, I think Mona Lisa might be happier if she didn't have to put up with me."

"Well, Daddy Bug, give us a few days to find a place, and we'll get out of your hair. Sure hope there are no hard feelings. You know I love you as if you were my own daddy," Junior said.

Mona Lisa said nothing. She jumped up, ran into the house and slammed the door. The men listened to her as she talked on the phone. Junior looked down at his feet as her voice drifted out to them.

"I've never been so mortified in my life, Momma. He actually told us we have to get out of his house. After I've worked my fingers to the bone for him." After a pause to listen, she continued, "I don't want to move home with you. In one thing he's right, it really would be nice to have our own place where we can do what we want to. I'll talk to you tomorrow, Momma."

They heard her hang up the phone and the television go on in her bedroom. Junior look at Daddy Bug, who had a hurt look upon his face.

"I'm truly sorry, Daddy Bug. I know Mona Lisa can be hard to live with, but she's my wife and then there's Abe. I'll do my best to try to talk to her."

"Son, you don't have to apologize for the actions of another. Let them take their own medicine. I love you and Abe, but I can't abide by someone who has a mouth that won't quit and someone who doesn't show me some respect. I've kept quiet for a long time, but I can't put up with her treatment anymore. I've tried my best to be good to her and give her every benefit of the doubt."

"I'm sorry we didn't talk before this. Let's don't hold any hard feelings."

"There are no hard feelings against anyone on my part. It breaks my heart that this happened. I'll try to help you find a nice place tomorrow."

"That's a good idea. I've been putting in a lot of extra hours, so I don't feel bad about taking a little time. If there's not an emergency let's leave around eight in the morning and try to find something in Lake Chastain."

The cool night air crept into Daddy Bug's bones and he noticed a pain in his back when he rose to go in the house. He knew he was developing arthritis like his daddy had. All the men in the Garland family developed it sooner or later.

He turned to clasp Junior's shoulder and said, "I'll be ready to go in the morning. You better go on in with Mona Lisa. I don't think she's too happy with either one of us."

The two men retired to their respective bedrooms, and Daddy Bug noticed the lights were on in his. He entered the room, closed the door and sat on the bed to take off his shoes. It was then he noticed the cardboard box in the corner.

He walked over and looked inside. Packed haphazardly inside were all the toys and stuffed animals he had given to Abe. She knew how to hurt someone. He considered the box an omen of things to come.

He put the box in the closet and finished undressing. He climbed into bed and lay watching the moon through the window. He wasn't sure when he went to sleep, but when he woke he noticed the sun was just beginning to come up.

Glancing at his watch, he saw it was almost six o'clock. His head felt heavy and his back still ached. After he showered and shaved, he felt a little better. Some good hot coffee and toast would improve things even more.

When he went to the kitchen, Junior, Mona Lisa and Abe were already there sitting around the table. He was determined not to create any tension about the box of toys.

Setting his face in a pleasant expression, he said, "Good morning, everybody. Looks like a beautiful day out there."

"Good morning, Daddy Bug," Junior and Abe chorused.

"Mornin' Daddy Bug," Mona Lisa muttered. Clearly, she would not be a happy camper for a while.

Junior said, "Mona Lisa, Daddy Bug and I are going out and find us a place. We'll find something in Lake Chastain you'll like. Of course, I promise you'll be able to see it before we make a final decision."

"We shouldn't be too long," Daddy Bug said. "I got to thinking about those new condominiums along the lake. Then there are some smaller houses right in town. If you need some help with the down payment, I've got a little set by that I can loan you."

The first semblance of pleasantness crept onto Mona Lisa's face. "Well, I guess that would be all right. What do you think, Junior?"

"We've got to find a place first. Then we can talk about all that. How about we get started after you have your coffee." He talked to the older man.

"I'll take it with me. You can drive." He turned and waved good-bye to Abe as they went out the door. He waited until Junior was near the pickup, then, he turned back and said to Mona Lisa, "I think you better empty that box back out. You can't return something that wasn't yours to begin with. And, I don't want to hear anymore about it."

Junior and Daddy Bug drove to the site of the new condominiums. Several had been completed and the realtor was just arriving to open the model.

"Good morning, Daddy Bug, Junior," she said. "Are you here so bright and early to buy a condominium?"

"We might be here to do just that." Junior smiled his disarming smile at her. "Can we take a look at what you got?"

She unlocked the model and stepped inside, followed by the two men. "Just go ahead and look around. I'll be right in here at my desk if you have any questions."

Junior went quickly up the stairs and saw the opulent furnishings of the two bedrooms. One was slightly larger than the other and each had its own bath. Perfect, he thought. He noticed the luxurious tub in the corner of the larger bathroom and the king size bedroom suite in the master. He then went downstairs where he saw Daddy Bug checking out the circuit breaker in the small laundry room.

The kitchen was small but ultra-modern with a cooking island and all the most modern appliances. The walls were covered with beautiful wallpaper and the window treatment was elaborate. A small breakfast nook overlooked a patio which was enclosed with wooden fencing.

The combination living-dining room had a huge stone fireplace with a window on each side overlooking Lake Chastain. It was luxuriously furnished with a sectional sofa, end and coffee tables.

The realtor's desk stood on the raised dining area. She was seated there smiling and watching the excitement grow on his face when he hurried once more around the room.

"Well, Junior, do you like what you see? Seems like our new Sheriff would fit right in this kind of place."

"I sure do. What would it take to buy this place? How much is it?"

"I can let you have it for $60,000."

"Wow, I can't come up with that much, right now. I guess I'll just have to look around for something else."

Just at that moment, Daddy Bug came into the room. He had heard Junior's exchange with the realtor.

"Junior, if you like this and if you think Mona Lisa would like it, I can go to the bank with you. Let them work out the payments and see if you can afford them."

"I know Mona Lisa would love this. Can I buy it with all the curtains and everything that's in it?"

"I'd have to raise the price a little bit and get my desk out of here. I'll check with the builder and see how much," she said.

Daddy Bug looked at the realtor and said, "Write something up that we can take over to the bank. I'll trust it'll be something fair if Junior here is expected to sign it."

The realtor took out a contract and began filling it out with her typewriter. She called the builder on the phone to get the final price.

"He said you can have everything in here including the refrigerator-freezer for an extra $5,000.00. That will bring the total to an even $65,000.00."

After Daddy Bug and Junior read and signed the "done deal" contract, they drove to the bank. When they left after an hour, Junior was the proud owner of his own condominium. In his excitement, Daddy Bug knew he forgot he promised Mona Lisa she could see it before they bought anything. Daddy Bug did not see fit to remind him of the promise.

When they drove in the driveway of Daddy Bug's house, Lydia Anne was sitting on the front porch playing with Abe. Mona Lisa was nowhere to be seen.

"Momma," Junior said. "Where's Mona Lisa?"

"She had to go to town to get some boxes. She said you two were moving today if you had to end up in a tent. She seemed real upset. What happened?"

"Nothing much happened. Daddy Bug thought we might be happier in our own place. That's where we've been. I bought us one of those new condominiums by Lake Chastain, Momma. It's a real beaut. I even bought all the furniture in it since we didn't have any."

"You bought a place before Mona Lisa could even see it? You know your wife. She'll pitch a fit."

"Momma, if she doesn't like this place, she wouldn't like anything. It's a place we've both dreamed about. It even has one of those huge tubs with spray jets in the master bathroom."

Daddy Bug said little as he held Abe, but was bemused at Junior's enthusiasm. It made him happy just to watch Junior's happiness.

At that time, Mona Lisa drove up in Lydia Anne's car. The car was filled with cardboard boxes. Junior went over and opened the door for her.

"It's a good thing you got those boxes, honey, I bought us a condo this morning. It's beautiful with beautiful furniture. And I think you'll love it because it's on the lake."

"You bought a condo without letting me look at it first? You promised I could see it before you made a final decision. What's going on in your head Junior Haywood?"

"Well, honey, I just wanted to surprise you. I know you'll love it. Come with me now and I'll show it to you."

"I don't want to see it. I'm taking Abe and going to my momma's, so get out of my way. Abe and I will be out of here in ten minutes." She shoved past him.

Junior grabbed her arm and spun her around to face him. He saw tears in her eyes. He grabbed her shoulders and shook her.

"Now you listen to me. I've about had enough of that mouth of yours and so has everybody else. You're going to get in the pickup and I'm going to take you to see the condo. Then we're going to pack, and you and me and Abe are going to move into it as a family. Do you understand me?"

She looked at him with defiance and then down at the ground. He had never spoken to her before in this manner.

"I at least have to go in and put on some lipstick if I'm going to see our new home." She smiled weakly at him and headed for the house.

Daddy Bug and Lydia Anne watched the whole scene in amazement. Mona Lisa strode past them and Daddy Bug thought that at last Junior showed some backbone. The little filly was finally broken. It wasn't the first time he was wrong and it wouldn't be the last.

# 34

Life returned to normal for Daddy Bug soon after Mona Lisa, Junior and little Abe moved to their new condominium. Mark and Sue Halbert, along with Lydia, Jimmie and Daddy Bug helped them move. One trip and an hour later the young people were unpacked and serving sandwiches and iced tea to their helpers in their new house.

It turned out that Mona Lisa loved the house and acted as if she had personally designed it. She even seemed gracious to Daddy Bug when he helped set up Abe's youth bed in what she termed "the nursery."

Even though his own house was quiet, Daddy Bug relished the feeling of having his own space. At his request, Lydia Anne and Jimmie came over and helped restore the house to reflect Vanessa's tastes. Jimmie and Daddy Bug moved the furniture back to its original position and Lydia Anne rehung the former curtains. Luckily, Daddy Bug had insisted the curtains be stored in the cedar chest. It looked like home again.

His memories of Vanessa were still keen, but the dull ache of his grief was slowly subsiding. Although it was only in his subconscience, the notion that life was slowly returning to normal, had planted its seed.

He took most of his evening meals with Jimmie and Lydia Anne, or Mark and Sue Halbert. However, when he had finished his work with the family business in the morning, he would drive into town, sit in Tommy's, the local cafe, and eat a sandwich or a bowl of soup. While there, he would talk with several other widowers who congregated around a booth in the back.

This became a regular part of his routine. It abated the loneliness and gave him something to look forward to. After all, they had all lost their wives and that gave them something in common. On the weekends, some of them would get together for fishing or hunting.

Irene Moore, the waitress at Tommy's, was good-natured and jovial with the group. She teased them and they teased her back. Each of them knew that this was in no way to be considered flirting. She was a married women with grown children whose husband hadn't held a job for years.

Most of the men knew about her situation and sympathized with it, although they never let her have reason to believe they felt sorry for her. Daddy Bug also knew her husband. His name was Kenny. He was one of Daddy Bug's customers when he had some money. Many times, when Irene either wouldn't, or couldn't, give him any money, he came to Daddy Bug and ask him to put it on credit.

Daddy Bug gave him credit before he scaled down his operation to one still. Now, he had to tell Kenny no. Cash on the barrelhead. No more credit. Can't afford it.

Kenny didn't like it and told Irene that if she didn't give him more money, he was going to report her good buddy from Tommy's Cafe to the state boys.

Irene adored Daddy Bug. Of all the men who got together at Tommy's, he treated her with the most respect. She didn't want to be responsible for Daddy Bug getting busted, so she started giving Kenny more and more of her hard-earned money. After a year, she fell behind in her payments on her car and the finance man threatened repossession.

Something had to give. She told Kenny he had to quit spending and get a job. He would get no more money from her. Kenny hit her in the eye and knocked her to the floor. Jerking her by her hair, he hit her again and kicked her in the back and left with the money in her billfold.

After a sleepless night she went to work, covering her blackened eye as best she could, with makeup artfully applied. Her back ached, but she managed to walk pertly through the door. It wouldn't do to let the people of Lake Chastain know she was married to a wife-beater. After all, enough people thought he was useless and sorry.

He hadn't come home last night. She wondered where he was.

She saw Daddy Bug sitting in the booth when she came in. He was there an hour earlier than usual. She spoke to him in her casual, happy tone.

"Well, hi there good-lookin'. What brings you out so early?"

"Can you set a spell with me, Irene? There's nobody else here. I need to talk to you about a few things."

Irene checked that the six o'clock girl had done the set-ups and made more fresh coffee. That girl was a treasure, she thought.

She sat across from him. "Sure can, sugar. What's on your mind?"

"Irene, I got a call from Junior last night. One of the deputies picked up Kenny last night. He was drunk as a skunk. Got some whisky from the ABC store and was weaving all over the road in his car."

"Oh my God. Is he in jail?"

"Junior is holding him for bail. He's still sleeping it off this morning. I checked."

"I don't know what I'm to do. I don't have any money for bail. He took the last of my cash last night."

"It looks to me that wasn't all he did last night. Did he hit you?"

"You've got good eyes, Daddy Bug. He beat the hell out of me. He got mad because I wouldn't give him any more money."

"I'm sorry about that, Irene. Why don't you go down and take a warrant against him. That would keep him in jail for awhile. But, I've got another problem. Before, he passed out, he kept yelling at the deputy that he was going to turn me in to the state boys for bootlegging."

"I know. He told me that same thing. He said he would if I didn't give him more money. I just got to the point where I couldn't even make my car payment. They were threatening to take it away. I told him no more and that's when he beat me up and left."

"Irene, he may wake up sober and wiser, but I can't take the chance. Somehow, you've got to shut him up. I've got a little money you can have. Dole it out to him a little at a time until I can figure out what to do."

"I can't take your money, Daddy Bug. That's not right."

He shoved an envelope across to her. "There's enough in there for his bail and for you. Tell you what I want you to do. Go over to the County jail and threaten to take a warrant on him for assault and battery. Then when nobody's around, tell him you won't take the warrant if he keeps his mouth shut about me. Tell him you'll start to give him as much as you can on a regular basis."

"I'll never forget you for this Daddy Bug. I'll pay you back every cent, I promise."

"You can take your time about that, Irene. You're a kind, nice lady and you've had more than your share from that guy."

"I can't really divorce him," she said. "I'd probably end up paying him alimony. I just know he'll beat me up again the first time I refuse him anything. What's a body to do?"

"If he beats you up again, let me know right away and I'll have Junior come out and arrest him. We have the new law which says you don't have to take a warrant against him. Any officer can take one on him if he comes to your house and sees any signs of violence. That way, you're in the clear and so am I. Junior can just say he had a call about some ruckus at your house and came to investigate."

"How can I get hold of you if he's standing right there?"

"There's enough money in that envelope to get a portable telephone. Buy one and hide it in a room he doesn't go into. My phone number is written on a piece of paper inside the bag. Keep it next to the phone."

Just then, workers on break from the chicken processing plant started to come in by the numbers. Irene had to jump to her feet to help the other waitress. Daddy Bug saw his widower cronies come in at the same time. He got up and winked at Irene.

"Remember, Irene, you've got to start taking care of number one. You only go round once in this life. It's not a dress rehearsal."

She grabbed his hand and gave him a kiss on the cheek in front of everyone. Then she hugged him. He stood with his arms at his side, his face growing even redder that it normally was.

One of the men who slid into the booth quipped, to the amusement of everyone, "Looks like Daddy Bug has himself either a girlfriend or a big fan."

Daddy Bug quickly sat down and covered the sides of his face with his hands. He knew everyone was looking at him and smiling. The proud man from the mountain was embarrassed. He wasn't used to being the center of attention, and, in fact, preferred his privacy and the attention of no one.

After finishing lunch with his friends, he did some errands and got some supplies before starting his drive back home. He drove and thought about Irene and her gesture of affection. It had been almost two years since Vanessa had passed away and no woman had kissed him on the cheek or hugged him, except his sister. He missed the closeness he had shared with Vanessa.

But, Irene was married. He was not the kind of man to take another man's wife. Yet, Kenny was a worthless piece of shit in Daddy Bug's estimation. Any man that would hit a woman fell in that category - especially any man that would hit a nice woman like Irene Moore.

He walked across the yard to see what Jimmie and Lydia Anne were doing. He needed someone to talk to and they were always there with open arms and minds.

He walked in the door without knocking as was their usual custom all these years.

"Anybody home?" he called to the silent house.

Sensing something wrong, he went through the house to the kitchen and out onto the back porch. He looked down the slope in the direction of the still. Wisps of smoke were curling up from the trees that surrounded the area.

Grabbing Jimmie's shotgun from the corner behind the back door, he rushed down the arbored path. His breath came in gasps by the time he reached the area. Lydia Anne and Jimmie Haywood, Sr. lay face down on a bed of burning sticks and twigs. Each had been shot once in the back of the head, their hands tied behind their back.

Daddy Bug jerked them from the burning debris and knelt beside their bodies, tears streaming down his face. His best friend and his sister were gone.

He screamed to the forest, "Who could have done this?"

He was like a wild animal. He beat the trees with the shotgun. He lay on the ground and beat it with his fists. He was inconsolable.

Finally, he was spent and got to his feet. He went to his own house, dialed the County Sheriff's department and asked to speak to Junior. How could he tell him about his parents?

"Junior Haywood here." The young man's voice sounded in the older man's ear.

"Junior, it's Daddy Bug. Son, you better get out here right now."

"What's the matter, Daddy Bug. I'm up to my ears in alligators down here."

"Junior, it's your Momma and Daddy. Someone's murdered them. I don't know why. I just found them. Get on home."

"Holy Jesus, Daddy Bug. That just can't be right. Who would want to do such a thing? I'll be right there."

Daddy Bug waited in the parlor for the Sheriff's cruiser to drive up. He thought about any enemies they might have. He knew that whoever did this had a gripe against him. Everybody loved Jimmie and Lydia Anne. But, who could hate him so much they'd kill his sister and brother-in-law out of spite?

Within a few minutes, Junior and his deputy in the cruiser and an ambulance skidded to a stop in front of the house. Daddy Bug ran out and led them to the scene. Junior wept at the sight of his dead parents. The ambulance took them away to the County morgue. The deputy attended to the investigation.

Junior and Daddy Bug sat in the parlor and looked at each other. Neither knew what to say. The silence united them in a shared condolence for their loss.

Daddy Bug finally spoke first. "Son, where did Kenny Moore go when he got out of jail today?"

"Irene paid his bail and then they went back to the restaurant to pick up her check before she took him home. At least that's what Irene told me she was going to do."

"I think we'd better find out where Kenny Moore is right now. I know it's hard to think about looking for him at this time, but I'm a little worried about Irene, his wife, too. I'll tell you about it on the way."

The two men hopped into the pickup and drove toward Lake Chastain. Junior spoke first as they rounded the curves of Stop Gap road at break-neck speed.

"Do you think Kenny Moore had anything to do with what happened to Momma and Daddy?"

"I'm not sure, but Irene told me he was threatening to turn me in to the state boys when she wouldn't give him any money and I wouldn't give him any credit."

Junior looked at Daddy Bug with dismay. "Why would he come up here and kill Momma and Daddy. I heard Irene tell him she would give him some money and she also paid his bail."

"All I know is my intuition tells me he went on a rampage against me. Lydia Anne and Jimmie were just in the wrong place at the wrong time. As you know, they often walked down there just for exercise. They may have surprised Kenny down there''"

"That still doesn't explain why he would be mad at you. At least not mad enough to kill people. He told me last night he was going to turn you in. Luckily, I was the only one that heard his drunken babble. By this morning, he was tame as a kitten."

Daddy Bug turned the pickup into a parking slot in front of Tommy's Cafe. He jumped out and rushed into the place as fast as his arthritis would let him. Junior followed close behind.

"Tommy," Daddy Bug said to the owner, "where's Irene right now?"

Tommy grinned at Daddy Bug, "Seems like you two just can't stay away from each other. You just have to see each other all the time."

"I'm not joking around. This is serious stuff, Tommy. She may be in danger."

Tommy knew Daddy Bug meant business. "She and Kenny stopped by here to get her paycheck. Then, she was going to take him home and come back to work. I guess she decided she would stay home."

Junior said abruptly, "What was Kenny like when she was in here?"

Tommy hesitated, then said, "You know it's the funniest thing. He was pretty cheerful until we teased him about Irene giving Daddy Bug a kiss on the cheek and a hug in front of everybody. Then he got real quiet and told Irene they had to go."

Junior looked at Daddy Bug. Without a word, they rushed out the door and got in the pickup. Daddy Bug turned north toward Simpson Shores. Irene had told him in one their many conversations she lived in the first mobile home on the right as you drove through the entrance.

"Junior, I don't want you to get the wrong impression, but I loaned Irene the money to bail Kenny out of jail. Kenny beat her up because she wouldn't give him any more money. Poor lady was getting set to lose her car."

"It just doesn't make any sense for him to kill my parents over something like that."

"Well, I don't think he came out to the house just to kill them. If Irene told him I gave her money, then he heard that teasing at Tommy's Cafe, he could have snapped. He's got a mean, hair-trigger temper from what I understand. You know, maybe he thought Irene and I were courting and snapped."

"Well, were you courting her, Daddy Bug?"

Daddy Bug didn't answer while he maneuvered the car to a parking space next to Irene's mobile home. He switched off the ignition and turned to face his nephew.

"No, Junior, I wasn't seeing Irene because she was married. But if she wasn't married, I'd court her. I loved your Aunt Vanessa, but she's been gone a long time and a man gets lonely. Now, let's go in and see her."

They knocked on the door of the trailer and waited. No sound came from within. Junior, by now an astute officer of the law, noticed there was no other car parked nearby. He again pounded on the door.

"I think we better go in, Daddy Bug. With everything you told me, her life could be in danger."

Junior tried the door and it was locked. Taking his 38 pistol from its holster, he shot the door lever off.

Still holding his pistol, he edged into a darkened living room. Daddy Bug followed, reaching for the light switch by the door. Light flooded the room and they saw that every piece of furniture was overturned. Inching slowly and carefully along, the men made their way down the narrow hall to the bedrooms in the back.

They checked the bathroom and the first bedroom, turning on lights as they went. Finally, they reached the second bedroom. The door was closed. Junior tried it and found it locked. He stepped back and kicked it in.

Dim light was filtering through the slats of the closed venetian blinds and the men could make out a form on the bed. Junior flicked the light switch and bathed the room in light.

Irene lay on the bed holding her hands to her purple, bruised face. She raised her head slowly and looked at the Sheriff and his Uncle.

"He called me a whore. I tried to call you and warn you, but you didn't answer your phone."

# 35

Junior and Daddy Bug drove to the Dixon County Court House where Junior instructed the dispatcher to put out an APB on Kenny Moore. He described Irene's car and its license number. The deputy had already written up the report on the deaths. As instructed, he sent an ambulance to Irene's trailer house.

Next, they drove to the County morgue to identify Junior's momma and daddy and sign the release of the bodies to the Harbor Funeral Home.

There would be no autopsy, except to retrieve the bullets from the corpse's heads. It was obvious how they died. They met their death brutally and quickly, murdered by a deranged person. Then, that deranged person set the bodies on fire.

Kenny Moore was at large, but would be found quickly unless he could get out of Alabama before they caught him. That was foremost in the minds of all of the law enforcement men in North Alabama. The highway patrol, Lake Chastain police department, and all the County Sheriff's departments had been alerted to watch for him.

Experiencing the fatigue that comes only with extreme sadness and bereavement, the two men drove to Junior's condominium. They came through the door as Mona Lisa, dressed in her finest, was preparing to leave. She had a babysitter installed on the couch to watch Abe.

"Where are you going?" Junior said, when she met him at the door.

"I've got to go to Huntsville. The Lee Department store is having a fashion show and tea at four o'clock and I'm going to model in it. You and Daddy Bug can make yourselves a sandwich. Dolly will watch Abe when he gets up from his nap."

"Please don't go today. Something awful happened. Momma and Daddy were murdered today. Somebody killed them and tried to burn their bodies." He took her in his arms and the tears rolled down his cheeks.

"Oh, my God. Who could have done it?" She hugged him and patted his back.

"We think it was Kenny Moore."

He sat on the chair in the living room and held his bowed head in his hands. "Daddy Bug thinks Kenny had a gripe against him. He thinks Kenny went out to do some damage to his operation or to confront him and Momma and Daddy surprised him."

Mona Lisa looked at Daddy Bug who was still standing by the front door. Her face was alive with rage. She stood with her hand on her husband's bent shoulder and faced him with all her pent up fury.

"Every bad thing that happens in this family, happens because of you, Daddy Bug," she shouted. "Why don't you just go home and leave us in peace? I don't want you around my house or my family. I've had about enough of you and the evil that surrounds you."

"In case you don't remember, Lydia Anne was my sister and Jimmie was my best friend." Daddy Bug spoke softly with a slow, mournful voice.

His head was bent and his shoulders slumped when he turned and walked out the door. He walked slowly toward his pickup and got in. Junior did not follow him.

He drove home and went into his house. The rooms shouted their emptiness at him. He wandered aimlessly through the house and finally settled on the back deck. The sun was just painting its deep scarlet hues upon the horizon. He got up and noticed the ache in his entire body.

The arthritis was starting to affect his legs and arms now, as well as his back. He went into the pantry and got his daddy's old jug. Filling it with the recipe, he took it back to the lounge chair on the deck, and took a swig from time to time. He watched the sun go down and the moon come up over Lake Chastain.

He had begun to use his daddy's jug after Vanessa died. It gave him a feeling of continuity with the past. He was sure that his own son, Juggie, would never do the same thing. Both Juggie and Tessa were ensconced in the Metropolitan Atlanta society as professionals of note. Benji, that television preacher brother of his never ever called, let alone visit, him.

He was truly alone, except for Mark and Sue Halbert and Junior. Now, he wasn't even sure of Junior. Daddy Bug knew Mona Lisa blamed him for Lydia Anne and Jimmy's death.

Junior had not defended him after her outburst. Maybe he was too crushed by their deaths to realize that Mona Lisa had, in effect, ordered Daddy Bug out of their life. Maybe he had given up on Daddy Bug.

After what seemed hours, Daddy Bug rose from the lounge chair and went into the parlor. He flicked on the television set and started to watch the six o'clock news. He saw the usual graphics and then the newscaster started to tell the lead story of the day. Kenny Moore's picture flashed upon the screen. He was picked up at the Georgia border by the Alabama Highway Patrol on suspicion of the murders of a Dixon County couple, Jimmie and Lydia Anne Haywood. The Haywoods were found in the woods in back of their house, the newscaster explained.

Daddy Bug leaned forward with interest. The last thing he wanted was to have his name on television. The reporters would come snooping around and possibly discover his small operation in the woods. His name was not mentioned.

He was happy that they caught Kenny Moore and Irene would be safe. He went to the telephone and called Junior's house.

"Hello," said Mona Lisa.

"Mona Lisa, is Junior there?" Daddy Bug tried to be casual as he spoke.

"No he's not. He's down at the County jail. Besides, I thought I told you not to bother us any more."

The receiver went dead in his hand. He dialed the County Jail and asked to speak to Junior.

"Junior Haywood, here."

"Junior, I saw on the television where they got Kenny Moore. I hope you can keep him in this time."

"Daddy Bug, are you all right? You sound funny."

"Well, Mona Lisa just hung up on me and I feel real bad about it. I'm still thinking about the way I found your Momma and Daddy, too."

"I'm thinking of it too and it really makes me sad. I think we can get the Judge to set a pretty high bail for Kenny - or completely deny bail. He had a gun in the car when they stopped him. It's the same gun that killed my parents according to the lab, and his are the only fingerprints on it.

"Daddy Bug, I have to tell you something else. Kenny is yelling his head off about your operation. It seems he told the officers with the Alabama Highway Patrol that you were a bootlegger and had a still in your back woods."

"I'm not worried about it. Just tell the officers that you used to live right next to me and you never saw anything like that. They'll take your word over some pile of shit like Kenny Moore."

"I'll do my best, Daddy Bug. Tomorrow, I have to get all the funeral arrangements done for Momma and Daddy. Can you meet me at the funeral home around ten in the morning?"

"What about Mona Lisa?"

"Never mind her. I'd rather have you there and besides, she said she has to be in Huntsville for an appointment."

"I'll meet you there tomorrow, son."

He hung up the phone and proceeded to fix a sandwich for his supper. Looking out the window, he could see Jimmie and Lydia Anne's darkened house.

He stood by the counter and ate his sandwich, not wanting to settle in for a night of television. His mind was racing with the events of the day. Suddenly, he remembered the sight of Irene Moore's bruised and broken face. He reached for the telephone book and after looking up her number, dialed the phone.

A muffled voice answered. "Hello."

"Hello, Irene. This is Daddy Bug. Are you all right?"

"I'm making it. Don't mind how I'm talking. My mouth hurts pretty bad," she slurred.

"That's alright. Did you hear the news about Kenny?"

"I just saw it on the news. I'm awful sorry about your sister and her husband. I know you were close to them. If Kenny did it, I hope they fry him."

"I do too. I called you because I'm feeling awfully bad tonight and I also wanted to see how you were."

"Thanks for calling the ambulance for me. They took me to the medical center and treated me. Then they brought me home. I've got some pills for the pain, so it's not so bad."

"Irene, they're going to put Kenny away for a long time.

They've got enough evidence on him to maybe even get the death sentence for him. You'll be safe now."

"I'm just sorry, it had to take the deaths of someone close to you to do it, Daddy Bug. I'm filing for divorce against Kenny tomorrow."

"I guess this will be a bond between us from now on. After this is all over, do you mind if we keep a little company together?"

"I'd be right proud if that should happen. The only time I've been happy in the past few years has been when I'm joking with all the people at the restaurant. And I think you know, you're my favorite."

Daddy Bug blushed into the receiver. He felt like a teenager.

"Why, Irene, how you go on."

"Daddy Bug, I mean it. You are one of kindest, nicest men I've ever met. Kenny made my life hell and you always made it nice."

Daddy Bug squirmed and said, "I have to meet Junior to make arrangements Jimmy's and Lydia Anne's funeral tomorrow and then there's the funeral itself. I'll check and see how you are on Saturday. Maybe I'll stop by."

"I'd like that, Daddy Bug. Come for supper. Let's give the neighbors something to talk about."

He hung up the phone and sat at the kitchen table with his jug. He hoped Vanessa would understand that a man got lonely after a while.

# 36

Daddy Bug barely made it through Lydia Anne's and Jimmie's funeral. He felt he would faint when he stood by the grave sides. Mona Lisa sat with Abe separated from him by Junior. He vowed that the only funeral he would go to in the future was his own.

It was a crowded affair since the County Sheriff's parents were the victims. It appeared that everyone who voted for him in the election attended, along with the Haywood's family and friends.

Mark and Sue Halbert drove Daddy Bug to the funeral and took him home with them afterward. They consoled him as they always did for every grief he had experienced. He even stayed with them for a couple days.

On Saturday, he phoned Irene Moore from their place and told her he would come over around four o'clock if that was all right with her. Sue and Mark winked at each other. They looked happy that Irene was there to divert his attention from his grief.

When the time approached, Mark drove him to his own house where he bathed and shaved. He patted on a little of his Bay Rum aftershave for the first time in ten years. Then he put on the new pants and shirt he bought for the funeral. Looking in the mirror, he thought he looked pretty good. He combed his thinning hair a second time and put on a tie.

Next, he drove to Edith's flower shop. Inside, he selected a crystal bud vase and a single long stemmed red rose. Edith teased him a little bit, but he was sure she wouldn't gossip about his purchase. He was well aware that when you owned a flower shop, it was very likely you would be privy to a lot of secrets. If you told those secrets, you'd be out of business in no time.

His pickup truck approached the entrance to the trailer park, and Daddy Bug could feel nervous perspiration ring the armholes of his shirt. His hands gripped the wheel in a white-knuckled hold.

Suddenly, he was there. He sat for a moment and worked up his courage. Carrying the vase with the rose, he walked to the trailer and rapped on the door. Irene answered immediately.

"Come on in, you sweet thing." She smiled and opened the door wide to allow him to pass.

"I brought you something to cheer you up." He handed her the bud vase when he came through the door.

"Why, that's the nicest thing anybody's ever done for me. It's beautiful!"

She kissed him once more on the cheek and went to fill the vase with water. Daddy Bug's face burned crimson again. He sat down on a chair in the living room.

He had gotten a look at her face before she turned away. She still had some bruises, but the swelling had gone down and her speech was normal.

She re-entered the room with two glasses. "I made us some lemonade. I thought we'd sit a spell outside on the porch before we ate."

Daddy Bug looked at her and relaxed a bit. She was about as natural as anyone could be. It was as if he'd known her for years. They settled into the lawn chairs on the porch with their lemonade and she spoke first.

"I filed for divorce against Kenny yesterday. They said the Complaint for Divorce would be served against him today at the jail. I expected him to call me ranting and raving, but I haven't heard a thing."

"Well, don't worry. You'll hear something from him. He's not the kind to shut up about something that aggravates him and I imagine this will aggravate him plenty."

"I don't relish talking to him at all. Maybe, I just won't answer the phone."

"You can't go around avoiding phone calls, Irene. If he calls, just tell him you won't abide any yelling or swearing. If he still does it, hang up on him. He can't do anything to you while he's in there and they're holding him without bail until his trial."

"Speaking of that, how are you doing since the funeral? I've been worried about you."

Daddy Bug drained his glass. "I've been making it, but it sure is hard. Seems like everybody I care about is gone in one way or another. Everybody except Mark and Sue Halbert, and now you. I don't even get to talk to Junior and Abe now. Junior told me Mona Lisa threatened to divorce him if he has anything to do with me. He asked me if we could cool it until he can talk some sense into her. It gets to be too much for a body to handle."

Irene stood up and took his hand. "Let's go in and eat. I made you some pot roast and potatoes. Plus, I made some key lime pie for desert. Hope you like it. It's my Momma's recipe to get to a man through his stomach."

They went in the trailer and Irene served the pot roast on her best dishes. She had a tablecloth on the small table and placed a candle in the middle.

They ate with relish and small-talked through the dinner. He complimented her and declared the supper, "one of the finest he had ever eaten."

While they sipped freshly brewed coffee, the phone in Irene's trailer rang. She looked at Daddy Bug with alarm.

"Go ahead and answer it, Irene. He can't hurt you," he said.

She answered hesitantly, "Hello."

Mark Halbert was at the other end of the line. "Irene, tell Daddy Bug to get home right now. I need to call him there. Something important has come up."

"You can talk to him now if you want to. He's right here."

"Tell him, I'll talk to him at his house." He hung up abruptly.

Irene put the phone on the hook and turned to Daddy Bug. He was looking at her with a question in his eyes.

"Daddy Bug," she said. "That was Mark Halbert. He said to get on home right away. Something important's come up. I don't know why he didn't want to talk to you on the phone here, but he said to get on home and he'll call you at home."

Daddy Bug was on his feet and walking toward the door. Mark Halbert would not steer him wrong. Something was terribly wrong.

"Irene, I better go right away. That was a great supper and I thank you." He took both of her hands and kissed her cheek. He ran toward the pickup and gunned the car through the arched entrance to the trailer park.

His mind raced on the way home. Mark wouldn't think of interrupting his supper date unless it was mighty important. He sped up Stop Gap Road and turned into his gravel driveway. He ran in the house and heard the phone ringing. Breathless, he pick up the receiver.

"Daddy Bug, here."

"It's Mark, Daddy Bug. You better make some preparations. One of my buddies from Montgomery just called me and told me they had two people inform them about your operation. They said they had no choice but to do a bust on your still. They even said they were going to get Junior to lead it, since he's the County Sheriff and knows where it is."

"Did your contact say who the informers were?"

"They said one was an anonymous woman. Sounded young. The other one was Kenny Moore, who called collect. Both called them direct. I feel like something's going down tonight. You better get on it. I'm here if you need me, but I can't come around and help."

"The anonymous woman was probably that bitch, Mona Lisa. No other woman hates me as much as she does. I'm not surprised about Kenny. He's hated me for a long time."

"They told me they wouldn't have believed Kenny, but when they heard from the woman, they couldn't ignore it anymore. It might make the papers that they were ignoring their job and it wouldn't look good for them."

"Did they tell you when they plan to do it?"

"They said the full moon is out tonight. They usually try to make a midnight bust for the surprise effect."

"Thanks Mark. I'll have to sit and think what to do."

Daddy Bug hung up on the phone. He felt beaten. He hadn't been able to sleep at night for a long time in anticipation of this moment. He had a premonition that Mona Lisa might be his Waterloo. He sensed it when he first laid eyes on her. It was her call that made the State boys bend to their duty.

So this was what it had come to. He got his Daddy's jug and went to set on the lounge chair on the back deck. He watched the sun go down and the moon come up. He sipped the recipe and thought back over the years of his life.

He thought about his youth. He thought about his family. He thought about what he had won and lost and where he was at the moment. He thought about Vanessa, Juggie, Tessa, and now Irene.

What could he do. He had always tried to be a good man and do the best for his family and friends. He had done what his father taught him. He had made some mistakes and now they were trying to take everything away from him. His Daddy's still was all he had left of the past.

"I'd rather blow it up myself that let them destroy it."

With his arthritis reminding him of his years, he got the dynamite and twine. He made sure he had matches. Grabbing his shotgun, he made his way to the still. He attached the dynamite to the frame and lit the match. It was then that he heard the voice of his nephew, the Sheriff of Dixon County.

"I wouldn't do that if I were you, Daddy Bug. Put out that match and step away from the still."

Startled, Daddy Bug looked at the clear, handsome face of his nephew and the serious faces of two ABC agents. All three men had drawn guns. The match continued to flame between his two fingers. He touched the flame to the wick of the first stick of dynamite. It began to ignite and fizzle. Quickly, he lit the other dynamite stick, dropping the match and jumping into the nearby bushes in nearly simultaneous movements.

He scrambled to his feet when he heard first shots, and then, the explosion that destroyed his daddy's still. If he could make it to his pickup, he knew he could hide out at Mark's house until he decided what to do.

The betrayal of his nephew brought to him a penetrating realization that there were no absolutes in the world. In his wildest imagination, he had given no thought to the possibility that Junior would betray him in this manner. If the situation were reversed, he would have refused to accompany the agents rather than fail to uphold the sacredness of the bloodline he shared with Junior.

All of these thoughts, and the anger he felt, rode with him as he ran back to the house. The stiffness in his body hampered him, but he rushed to the pickup and got in. Roaring away from the house, he saw one of the agents round the corner and raise his gun to fire at the pickup. At that moment, Junior came up behind the agent and knocked the gun from his hand.

Daddy Bug slammed his truck to a halt at the Stop Gap Road turnoff and watched the agent leap for the gun. He stooped in a crouching position and pointed it at Junior. Junior raised his hands above his head and stood still while the agent approached him.

Daddy Bug turned the pickup around and went back to the scene. He couldn't let Junior take the punishment by himself.

He got out of the truck and walked slowly toward the two men with his hands raised. The show was over.

"This man is my nephew," he said to the agent. "He just didn't want you to shoot me. Take me if you want me, but don't blame a man for wanting to keep you from shooting his own uncle."

"Get over here next to the Sheriff, old man. We'll wait until my partner gets here and then we'll tell you what's going to happen."

Daddy Bug moved next to Junior. Junior looked at him with compassion.

"Daddy Bug, I had to come with them. They knew you had the still up here. I was just hoping we wouldn't see you. Don't you see, I had no choice but to help them bust the operation. As Sheriff, it was my duty to guide them up here."

"Never you mind, Son. I know that bastard, Kenny Moore, told them about it and when Mona Lisa called them too, they had to believe Kenny."

"I can't believe Mona Lisa called them. Who told you she did?"

Daddy Bug smiled ruefully. "I have my sources. But, it's really a no-brainer. Don't you know that this was her way to finally have her revenge on me and break our ties off completely? She knew that you'd be forced to come with the agents when they came to destroy me and that would be the straw that broke the camel's back."

"You two shut your mouths for a minute," said the agent. His partner limped around the corner of the house.

The two agents walked a short distance away from Junior and Daddy Bug and began to quietly discuss the situation. They knew that in a way, they had botched their operation.

Everything they did depended upon an element of surprise. Someone had gotten to Daddy Bug with the word of what was in progress. They would appear unprofessional and inept if word got out that Daddy Bug beat them to the still and exploded it practically right in their face and then got away. If he hadn't come back to aid the Sheriff, he would have been out of Alabama before they could get him. It was even worse that the County Sheriff was Daddy Bug's nephew and they didn't know it. It would make them both look like damned fools, they decided.

Finally, they returned to stand in front of Daddy Bug and Junior, who stood with their hands in the air.

"Tell you what we're going to do," the first agent said. "Since you blew up your own operation, you saved us the trouble. I'm pretty sure we can't get anyone to testify you sold any of your liquor to them, so we can't get you for that. We're letting you go on the condition that you keep all of this quiet."

"What about my nephew? What will happen to Junior? Daddy Bug threw his arm across Junior's shoulder as they waited for an answer. The two agents looked at each other and grinned.

"I can't take any offense about a man trying to stop his uncle from being killed. Nobody got hurt. If we'd known you were his uncle, we wouldn't have had him come up here with us."

The two men turned without another word and walked toward Stop Gap Road. They would file a report stating that the tips they received about a still on Cather Mountain were in error. It didn't exist. At least, they rationalized as they got in their car, it didn't exist anymore.

Junior and Daddy Bug went in the house and pulled out the jug. They sat at the kitchen table and Daddy Bug poured each of them a hefty drink of the mist. Junior spoke first after taking a big gulp. "Daddy Bug, if it's true that Mona Lisa turned you in to the state boys, I'll make sure she never does anything like that again. I'll make her understand that neither she, nor anyone, will get in between us."

"Son, you'll do what you have to do. I knew tonight that no matter what you said or did, I couldn't hate my own sister's child. No matter what you do, you'll always be part of my family and to me, it's cast in concrete that I honor that. I'm not that good with words, but you know what I mean."

"I sure do, and I honor that, too." Then, Junior changed the subject. "What are you going to do now, Daddy Bug? You don't have the business anymore."

"I'm going to enjoy my life and what's left of my family. I want to take Abe fishing and if you ever get some time, Junior, I want you to go along, too. Then, of course, Mark and Sue Halbert are a great solace to me.

"What's this I hear about you and Irene Moore?"

"She's a sweet lady who's getting a divorce. When it's final, I plan to court her. Until then, we'll just be friends and I'll help her as much as I can. She's had a hard life, and she deserves better."

"Well, it looks like she took your mind off of your loneliness for Aunt Vanessa. She must be quite a woman."

"There will never be another Vanessa. I loved her when I married her and I loved her until the day she died. No one will ever take her place. That doesn't mean that Irene can't occupy another position in my life."

"What do you think the people in Lake Shasta will think if you marry Irene?"

Daddy Bug took a sip of his liquor and gazed into the now empty glass as if pondering the idea. He was silent for a full minute.

"They'll think I'm about the smartest mountain man they ever knew."

He winked at his nephew and laughed. He was no longer big and mean, but he was finally happy. He was resigned to living his life with the hand he was dealt.

Daddy Bug surmised that he had learned the hard way that some relationships are fated to last, while others disappear mysteriously and completely, into the past.